SHADESMOOR

SHADESMOOR

Jason Foss

This first world edition published in Great Britain 1995 by
SEVERN HOUSE PUBLISHERS LTD of
9–15 High Street, Sutton, Surrey SM1 1DF.
First published in the USA 1995 by
SEVERN HOUSE PUBLISHERS INC of
595 Madison Avenue, New York, NY 10022.

British Library Cataloguing in Publication Data
Foss, Jason
  Shadesmoor
  I. Title
  823.914 [F]

  ISBN 0-7278-4784-8

Typeset by Hewer Text Composition Services, Edinburgh.
Printed and bound in Great Britain by
Hartnolls Ltd, Bodmin, Cornwall.

For Helen

Prologue

"Traitor!" Tyrone said.

"Traitor!" Vikki repeated, with extra conviction.

Jeffrey Flint looked across the narrow table in the cabin of his houseboat. These were his friends. Tyrone, his research student had the square-jawed, cropped blonde-headed look of a Nazi submarine commander, with politics to match. Vikki was Flint's sometime lover, dark, cute and diminutive. He had only just met the pretty American undergraduate named Mary-Ann who blinked at him from behind Tyrone's elbow.

"Say 'Traitor'," he urged her, "everyone else has."

"Traitor", she giggled.

His news had been kept back until the three dinner guests were deep into their Chinese chicken with cashew nuts. Flint had hoped for a more warming reaction.

"Congratulate me," he appealed.

Tyrone was smartly dressed in a light plum shirt and variegated jungle tie. A wayward beansprout joined the foliage, as he tried to manoeuvre chopsticks at the same time as expressing protests.

"You can't leave, you're supposed to be my supervisor."

"You've finished," Flint said, "I'm not going until July, by that time your thesis will be on my desk and you'll be out in the big, bad world."

1

"What about me?" Vikki had an uncompromising East End accent and an expression to match.

"You're off doing tabloid television half the time. You won't miss me."

"But Yorkshire?" Tyrone sneered.

"It's not the end of the universe. The Romans civilised the Brigantes, remember? It's not all dark satanic mills."

"But you're throwing yourself into a black hole. Who's ever heard of the University of North Yorkshire?"

"It used to be North Yorkshire Polytechnic . . ."

"A poly!"

"Not any more."

"So they stuck a new sign at the gate. A poly is a poly no matter what they call it. This is death to your career, Doc. Why are you doing it?"

"Yes, why?" Vikki asked, grabbing at the Liebfraumilch bottle and overfilling her tumbler.

Flint jabbed a chopstick at his student. "Money," he said, then switched the point towards Vikki. "Power," he said. "You wouldn't pass it up, either of you. Lecturer II, another five grand a year and only one body between me and the professor's chair."

Tyrone continued to attack. "You always said you never wanted to be a professor."

"You used to say 'all power corrupts'," Vikki added. "You're selling out, Jeff." She leaned across to Tyrone. "Can't you just see Professor Flint one day in one of those silly little flat hats and a batman cape?"

"I think it's great," young Mary-Ann suddenly intervened, then doubted herself.

"Glad someone does." Flint raised his own tumbler. "A toast to selfish success."

2

"You haven't got the job yet," Vikki retorted.

"I've been invited to apply for the post, the interview's next week: it's mine on a plate."

"There's a catch," she said. "I bet there's a catch."

Flint was drinking his own health, and gave himself a few moments before responding. He decided he would have to do something about Vikki's taste in wine.

"Tyrone, did you ever meet Tom Aitken? Big bloke, hunky, doesn't suffer fools."

"Didn't he speak at the last Field Archaeology Conference? He's a bit pushy."

"That's him, the Action Man of northern archaeology. Well Tom wanted this 'ere job that I'm going to make my own."

"What stopped him?" Vikki asked.

"Three weeks ago, someone cracked him over the back of the head with a Palaeolithic hand-axe."

Vikki had wide, very dark brown eyes to complement her short spiky hair. Her pupils dilated to swamp all colour from her irises'.

"I knew there'd be a catch."

Chapter One

Theakston's Old Peculiar was on sale at the staff bar of the University of North Yorkshire. As the rich, black, fruity liquid touched Flint's lips, he knew there was a bonus in moving north. Half a pint only, just enough to steady the nerves and raise the pulse. He felt unnatural in the new charcoal-grey suit and subdued floral tie. His straw-blonde beard had been trimmed close to his cheeks and his hair now hovered above the collar. A last-minute switch of glasses saw him in executive gold rather than radical red. Uncomfortable and apprehensive, he needed all the reassurance he could buy.

"So the job is as good as mine?" he asked, once his mouth had savoured its treat.

Opposite him in a low green chair slouched a short, spreading academic, dark haired and a little unkempt. Although some two or three years Flint's senior, Keith Barnes was making little headway into the archaeological establishment. He had briefly held a research place at Central College, where Flint and everyone else had known him simply as Barney.

"It's yours," Barney said. "Betty likes to think she's still an *enfant terrible*, so anyone left of Trotsky is okay by her."

Flint had always found it hard to think of Professor Betty Vine as anything but a mouse-like

4

schoolmarm, but knew she struck like a ferret when aroused.

"Wasn't she at the Sorbonne in '68?"

"So the legend reads. It must have been about the same time they built this dump."

Another sip, then a glance around at the ambience of the split-level bar. Its suspended ceiling had given Flint the urge to mind his head as he had walked in. The pine panelled walls were a mistake and the modern art was not as modern as it had once been. In compensation, the bar manager made up for the late '60 layout by lavishing care on his ales and time might come when Flint needed a handy sanctuary.

"I'm a little surprised you didn't want this post." Only a little, but Flint had to be polite with the man who would be his junior. "Did you go for it?"

"No, no, my papers don't include sufficient reference to dead French sociologists . . . and I don't dig."

"You should – it enhances your street cred."

"It's a nasty, messy business only to be undertaken by undergraduates and consenting adults."

"Okay, so you're out of the running, but doesn't Betty fancy anyone else?"

"She wanted Tom Aitken."

"Why? He wasn't one of us desk-bound academics, he was a true, red-blooded field archaeologist. I can't recall him ever writing a challenging, cerebral paper, certainly not from a Marxist perspective."

"He dug, she wanted a digger."

"But I'm told he was impossible to work with."

"Now that's not entirely correct old bean; he was a man you either loved or hated. You either applauded his methods, or he got right up your nose."

"Where did you lie in the love/hate stakes?"

5

Barney took a deep quaff of his beer and wiped away a little froth from his thick, rubbery lips. "We were at Newcastle together. I hate to speak ill of the dead, but he was an arrogant shit. I think Megan would have resigned if he had been appointed."

"Doctor Megan Preece?"

"That's the woman, *Power and Gender in Mediaeval Wales*: you must know the book, its a classic piece of feminist bra-busting nonsense. She's Reader in Medieval Archaeology and definitely your type. She was also Tom Aitken's type, incidentally."

Flint had always found Barney unsubtle, or perhaps he was only blunt with his confidences.

"He was a bit of a lad, wasn't he? Was she one of his old flames?"

"Discarded bit of fluff." Barney raised a thick black eyebrow. "Tom was hardly a lad either, he must be my age . . ."

"Thirty-eight." Research was never wasted.

"Yes, well. He should have grown out of it."

Flint knew that Barney was a determined bachelor. He leaned in over his beer. "I had an uncomfortable thought riding up in the train this morning. Could there be any connection between the bizarre way Tom Aitken met his end and the choice of me as favourite to replace him?"

Barney nodded, long and slow, with obvious amusement.

"Whodunnit, Barney?"

When Barney grinned, his face looked as if someone had begun to inflate a pink dinghy.

"Oh, we were all suspects. Things became quite exciting for a day or two, they took statements from the entire department. 'Where were you on the night of the fifteenth?' and all that rigmarole."

6

"And did you have a good alibi?"

"Yes – I was at the early medieval pot conference in Carlisle. The police even rang the organiser to check I was not committing perjury. Still, we were all able to breathe freely, for the police arrested a felon only a day or two after the foul deed was discovered. You must have read the story in the papers? The accused claims he was set up by international art thieves: 'it's a plot, a capitalist plot.'"

Flint remembered something he'd read in the *Guardian* about a massive theme park development at the edge of the North Yorkshire Moors. "Does any of this have anything to do with Shadesmoor?"

"Oh we do recruit bright boys, right on the nail! Do you see why we need you? We want someone who won't get bashed on the head with a hand-axe when he upsets the wrong people."

"Is that likely?" Flint was after a cushy academic sinecure, not violent adventure.

"No, no, forget it, only jesting old bean."

Flint took a deep gulp of the beer. Oh Barney what a liar you are, was the message which accompanied the alcohol to his brain. Archaeology is a small world, so Barney must know that Flint's investigations had found him looking beyond the realms of academia into murkier provinces of death and disappearance. Vikki's flamboyant reporting had done much to promote Flint as some kind of archaeological Sam Spade – or at least, "Sam Trowel".

The golden hands of the minimalist clock ticked round another minute and Flint made a determined effort not to leave his beer standing.

Barney began to play at interviews. "So, Doctor Flint, what do you think of Competitive Tendering?"

"It stinks. I mean, you discover a site which could

be of national importance, then you ask half a dozen excavation units to fight for the contract to excavate it. Who wins? The best? No, the cheapest, and archaeology suffers."

"So, does Developer Funding raise your hackles too?"

"That and all the other horrors which crawled out of the 1980s. Seriously, Barney, developers don't care about archaeology, they just want it out of the way. I'd admit it sounds like a sparkling idea to force them to pay for the excavation of their sites, but then we're back to the pursuit of the lowest tender."

"Ah, don't repeat all that for Betty, will you, because your job description requires you to split yourself fifty-fifty between lecturing and running the college excavation unit."

Standard practice, thought Flint. "And I assume the unit tenders for external work?"

"It will – it has to. We need the money."

"Does the unit just employ students or have you any permanent staff?"

"Betty is talking of two excavation assistants on six-month contracts."

"You can't ask people to work six-month contracts!"

"Yes you can – they like it, or they're on the dole. The nation has no shortage of unemployed archaeology graduates. I think you're in for a shock, Jeffrey. This is not cushy old Central College London; working here means adapting. Come the revolution, you can change things the way you want them to be, until then . . ." Barney had dull brown eyes set in milky-blue, which rolled noticeably as he sought his watch. "Time for the interrogation chamber," he announced. "Best of British, and don't worry about Betty. She'll love you."

The architecture of the Polytechnic was low-rise, late 1960s, brutal and modernist. Its saving grace was light, which flooded into every office and seminar room through floor-length glass windows. The panel of two men and two women who interviewed Dr Jeffrey Flint were thus bathed in brilliant yellow sunshine.

"It was a glorious ideal, Doctor Flint," Professor Betty Vine declaimed as the interview began. "Demolish an airbase and build a centre of learning; swords into ploughshares."

Betty Vine crouched over her desk, passing a pencil from hand to hand, bushy grey eyebrows tending to frown, her jaws asking urgent questions. Flint blazed his way through the responses, which were hardly challenged, creating an illusion that the procedure was a mere formality. Towards the end of the interview came the rub: the excavation unit – and Flint had come ready-armed with a strategy for leading it in the field.

". . . so you already have ideas about the archaeological unit? It needs to return a profit – I know this sounds strange, but we live in strange times. Do you knowt about the Shadesmoor development?"

"A little," Flint said, hoping his little would be adequate. "Shadesmoor Castle is being turned into some sort of medieval theme park. Where does the university stand on that? Hasn't there been a lot of opposition?"

Professor Betty looked at one of her august and almost silent colleagues. "The history of the project is long and tortured. We were initially appalled, but the

9

planning process has been followed to its conclusion, and the conclusion is that there shall be a theme park. I'm told that this is the only direction the heritage industry can take."

The professor explained that once planning permission had been given, events would snowball. Statute would demand that archaeologists investigate the site to identify areas of historical importance or archaeological deposits which could be damaged by the development. The developer would be informed and he might adjust his plans to miss the most sensitive areas. If not, these areas would have to be excavated before development could proceed. Flint knew all this, but nodded politely.

"It will be a big project, lasting several years and the millionaire big shot person . . ." Betty fished for a name, "Mr Grimston – is talking about spending amounts of money which the average excavation unit could never expect to see."

For all his idealism, Flint knew there was a time to be a radical anti-materialist and a time to be pragmatic. He feigned enthusiasm. "We need that project for our unit," he said, trusting this was the required answer.

His familiarity caused four smiles along the interview panel. "I don't think we have any more questions, do we?" The Professor prompted grumbles of assent. "Could you wait outside, Jeffrey, for a few minutes?"

Corners of Flint's London office had not seen daylight for years. Books migrated towards packing cases, whilst box files stood in expectant heaps. As he squatted on the floor, the song he hummed was a tuneless piece of trash he'd caught on late night radio – "*Daisy*

Chainsaw" or some such talent. Flint rolled his poster of the Portland Vase and slipped an elastic band over the end. A knock was followed by Tyrone poking his blow-dried blonde fringe around the office door.

"Hi, Tyrone, wander in, step over the mess."

Kitted out in slacks, suspended by crimson stock-broker braces, Tyrone was hardly the typical research student. He manoeuvred around a pile of green box files, then stuck both hands into his pockets. "Hey, Doc you're taking this seriously."

"Northern lights a-calling me . . ."

"You got the job?"

"Sure did." Flint beamed, expecting opposition. "Thesis done?"

Tyrone grinned. "I'm taking it to the binders this afternoon."

Flint had already glanced through Tyrone's monster Ph.D. thesis, enticingly titled, *De-Romanisation in fourth and fifth century Britian*. At some 100,000 words of typescript (plus plates), it would take up half a supermarket box on its own.

"Doctor Tyrone Drake?" Flint mulled over the idea, feigning pain. "How will the world react to that? There's still the viva, perhaps we will manage to stop you at the oral examination."

"There's no stopping me now!" Tyrone asserted, with just a little uncertainty. "When will it be?"

"Autumn sometime, give me a chance to have the brute weighed."

"You'll return to do the examination?"

"Of course, and so will you."

"What do you mean?"

"You're unemployed, Tyrone. You're one of the three million, a burden on society, a social parasite . . ."

11

"Oi, not yet!" The Thatcherite was offended. "I'm going to set up my consultancy. I'm calling it 'Diggers Unlimited'."

Flint indicated a space on the floor. "Sit!"

His student seldom responded on command, and would normally argue every toss.

"Sit!" Flint repeated.

With obvious reluctance, Tyrone slid down beside the filing cabinet and Flint began to lecture, with parentary finger raised in warning.

"Problem: no one will consult a consultant with no experience."

"I have . . ."

"You've served a total of nine months in the field on twelve digs, with six weeks as stand-in supervisor. I've read your CV, it's rubbish. You've spent too many holidays swanning around Europe with your chums and their Sloaney girlfriends."

Tyrone goldfished an objection.

"Solution: get yourself some real experience, out in the dirt."

Usually super-confident, Tyrone let his expression slip as the point sank home.

"Problem: I have to run an archaeological field unit on a shoestring budget. I have to meet developers, cost projects, prepare estimates and make commercial tenders. That's not what I came into archaeology to do."

"Solution?" Tyrone asked, although he had no need to ask.

"Wanna job kid?"

"In the frozen north?"

"Buy yourself a flat cap and ferret, so you can blend in. I'll teach you to drink John Smith's Bitter and pronounce 'eeh, bah gum'. Life's good up north, there's plenty of space and the natives are friendly."

Tyrone's eyes wandered up and down the pile of box files by his side. "I'll have to think about it."

"Think quick, the biggest project this side of the Millennium is about to take off right on our doorstep."

"Shadesmoor Castle?" Tyrone asked instantly.

"Right. I'm not officially in post until August, but the deadline for tenders is June 30th. That gives you what, four weeks to draw up a costing for Phase I: that's the preliminary assessment campaign."

Tyrone's lips worked around the words "four weeks".

"If our bid succeeds, we have to recruit a team of diggers and be ready to start work by the start of August."

"But I'm knackered. I've been working flat out to get my thesis finished. I promised myself a summer off."

"All work and no play makes Jack a Ph.D. North Yorkshire can be quite balmy in August. Just think, camping on the moors, rural pubs, pretty student volunteers. Phase I is only supposed to last two months. You can relax in the autumn."

Tyrone thought about this and heaved a heavy sigh for effect. "If this is just an assessment, when would the main excavation start?"

"New Year? Whenever, it's going to be a biggie, plenty of funding and no end of research material, it's a gift." He emphasised his own Yorkshire accent. "One day, lad, all this could be yours."

Flint reached up to his desk and pulled down a thick brown A4 envelope. "This is the spec. Read and inwardly digest. All the big units are tendering for this one; all the cowboys and all the sharks."

Tyrone took a peek into the envelope as Flint passed it to him. Suddenly, his face brightened. "We'll just have to be the biggest shark in the sea."

Chapter Two

June wore on; only lines of dust filled the shelves and the desk, for once, was almost clear. Archaeologists are seldom in a hurry: a week counts for nothing when centuries have to be considered. Since Flint had decided to move back north, he had found himself swept away by an avalanche of triviality; so many irritating tasks to complete before he could turn his back on London and rediscover fresh air.

One of the last files to be packed was a new one, with the letters TA written on the spine in bold black letters. Vikki had brought a dozen press clippings about the murdered man and a dozen more (of decreasing length) in which a convicted Leeds house breaker made appearances in court charged with the crime. He'd managed to photocopy a few articles by the dead man and dropped these into the file, together with his obituary culled from a local archaeological newsletter.

Aitken had been killed "in the early hours" of April 16th. An intruder had surprised him in his study (or *vice-versa*) and had struck him from behind with a "stone age axe" Aitken had kept as a paperweight. His body had been discovered three days later when a neighbour came searching the garden for a lost rabbit and found the French windows of Aitken's study swinging open.

Flint closed the file with a snap, the noise conjuring the image of a skull cracking under the impact of a crude stone tool. It wouldn't happen to him – would it? He could just imagine journalist Vikki composing the ironic headline "FLINT SLAIN BY FLINT".

A knock at the door prompted him to dodge behind the desk and pretend interest in a list of figures that Tyrone had left for his attention. The student knocked again and Flint called him in. Tyrone's face carried a thrilled beam, his work obviously pleased him.

"What do you think Doc?"

"It's all very, very . . ." his eyes were lost amongst the numbers, his mind still undecided how to treat them. Flint played for time. "So have you broken the news to Mary Anne yet?"

"Who?" Tyrone asked.

"The woman who's been sharing your bed for the past term."

"Oh, she'll understand." Tyrone quickly changed the subject back onto his own ground. "These are the units we're up against." He poked another list under Flint's nose. "I rang the local firm that hires out portable toilets – they've done quotes for most of them. We can undercut these three units, everyone says they're too expensive. I don't know about Northern Field Unit . . ."

"Four blokes and a Honda van – forget them, they're not up to it."

"What about First Archaeological Services?"

"They were Tom Aitken's field unit. Heresay has it that they might have won the contract, but without Aitken, they're just falling apart: forget the opposition. How's our equipment?"

"Your poly has got zilch. My dad's giving us

16

a dumper and I've scrounged some trowels. The Middlesboro and Tees unit folded up last month, so I've put a bid in for all their stuff: wheelbarrows, spades, drawing boards, staffs – they even had an EDM."

"I hate gadgets. Do we need an EDM? Isn't a good old fashioned tape measure and dumpy adequate for surveying?"

Tyrone overrode the technophobia. "Electronic Distance Measurement is state of the art. It's like an old-fashioned dumpy, with a laser to produce three-dimensional survey data. If we get a laptop computer we can input all the EDM data in the field. Think of the money it will save."

"And cost."

"It's a snip."

"Mobile phone?" Flint raised his eyebrows at another item. "Jeep?"

"Shadesmoor is miles from anywhere, we'll need transport."

"Okay, let's move on to staff costs – I don't believe these figures."

Tyrone came around to Flint's side and leaned over the desk, taking up a pen as pointer. "Okay, first, we use your poly students and pay £40 per week."

"What? Are you planning to re-introduce serfdom?"

"We won't get circuit diggers for less than £160."

"I should hope not! Why are these two salaries negative?"

"We recruit two American students, then charge them for meals, accommodation and instruction. They get course credits back home."

It was an old trick, but one Flint had never had the cheek to try. "Are you selling the pottery?"

17

"No."

That's one slender source of relief. I hate this Tyrone, I really hate it. You can't ask people to work for a handful of beans, it's immoral. The way I see things, the Shadesmoor Group has a huge budget, let's milk it, let's give the diggers decent pay and let's inject some money into the profession!"

"And lose the contract? I'm using sales tactics here, Doc. Think of this as a loss leader. We stick in the lowest tender for Phase I, win the contract, do the evaluation. Then, when it comes to Phase II, we're in a strong bargaining position with the developer. That's the time to work in a good profit margin."

Profit margin. Flint closed his eyes, aware of a painful truth. The profession was changing and he had to move with the times or become as redundant as knights in armour. After a few moments spent reconciling this academic blasphemy he muttered, "Do it."

The following day they were driving north, taking the M1, then the A1, the Great North Road. Tyrone had asked to see the site and Flint wanted to meet Bob Grimston; the brains and the money behind the Shadesmoor scheme. The castle itself belonged to a lady named Eleanor Balleron, but she seemed to remain in the background in the more controversial newspaper cuttings.

Tyrone owned an ageing Triumph Spitfire, painted green and brown camouflage, with RAF roundels on the doors and the letters TYR-1 now somewhat chipped on the wings. Although professing to be a car lover, Tyrone mistreated his vehicle cruelly. Gears crashed as he threw TYR-1 around another Yorkshire bend.

"I'm going to need a four by four up here," he shouted.

"Not on my budget," Flint said, watching the hills roll by.

"In the winter, on these lanes. I fancy a jeep."

"Suzuki?"

"No, Willy's. You can get genuine reconditioned jeeps for a couple of grand. I'm going to do one up, with a big star on the bonnet. I'll research all the badges and markings to make it look authentic. Best of all, I could put a mounting up here," he waved an arm above his shoulder.

"What for?"

"A fifty cal. machine gun."

"The police will love you."

Tyrone simply grinned. "Have you asked the police about the Aitken case?"

"No, but Vikki found out which solicitor is defending the guy accused of killing him. He claims he was framed. One of Vikki's dodgy friends said there's a rumour that it was some sort of contract killing."

"Wow!" Tyrone pulled the Spitfire into a turn that would have done Douglas Bader proud. "Are there any leads?"

Flint waited for his inner ear to settle down once more.

"I'm not looking for leads, just avoiding tragic coincidences. First, I've just been appointed to a post that Aitken wanted. Second, I'm running a field unit on his patch and competing against his old unit for a contract. Call me paranoid, but I think we should just watch our backs, that's all."

Arable farms had given way to stock farms, with cattle on lowland and sheep upon the exposed slopes. Shadesmoor loomed above them, a collage of greens,

19

burnt yellows and browns, overlaid with a tracing of drystone walls. The Spitfire ground around bends, winding its way onto The Top, as locals called the moors. Walls became less common, man-made structures being limited to stretches of fences intended as improvised sheep-shelters to trap snowdrifts. The horizon seemed distant and the sky close, the parched heather shimmering amidst a June drought which was becoming routine. Several miles of sheep, moor, and sheep slipped effortlessly by.

All of a sudden, the road dipped downwards and to the left. Shadesmoor Castle rose into sight, standing on a spur at the far side of the valley, pink, gaunt and magnificent. Below it lay a different world, a snake of green working its way into a cleft in the dusky moors. A river glittered past a sandstone hamlet, with its prominent manor and parkland. Woods filled the depths of the valley and the many coombs which led off it.

"*The Last Valley*," Flint said aloud. "Ever see it?"

"No."

"Omar Sharif and Michael Caine – much underrated."

"Wasn't it Sean Connery?"

"No, you're thinking of *The Man who would be King*."

Burton-by-Shadesmoor was little more than a shop and ten houses: there was no church and no pub, which set Flint wondering about its history. Many afternoons in the library would be needed to complete that question. Tyrone drove through the hamlet, over a pack horse bridge and into the park, pausing for brief words with a gatekeeper beside a sign informing them that admission cost £2. Flint would happily wager that the entry fee would increase five or tenfold by the time the metamorphosis of Shadesmoor Castle was complete.

A drive of a quarter of a mile took the car past the manor and through sheep pasture, climbing up once more towards the ruined castle. A cinder car park occupied a sunny patch beyond the shadow of the towering sandstone keep.

"Welcome to Shadesmoor, lad." Flint laid on a thick Yorkshire accent, "Disneyland o't' north."

Two children's swings, a see-saw and a Donald Duck slide were the only visitor attractions visible from the car park. Flint and his assistant climbed out and walked up the switchback tarmac track which led to the top of the spur.

Shadesmoor Castle was more impressive as a back-drop than at close quarters. Its walls had suffered at the hands of the Roundheads and it had been abandoned at the end of the Civil War. A wooden plank bridge crossed the shallow dry moat, almost filled to glacis level by silt. They walked through the ruins of the gatehouse, where no stonework stood more than knee high, then into the bailey. Only the rear, eastern half of the bailey was still screened by a standing wall and all the internal buildings were lost and grassed-over. At the southern end of the bailey, the square keep and its four corner towers remained erect, its rippled, salmon-pink stonework sand-blasted by the centuries.

A golden-brown Jaguar drew into the car park. A figure dressed in a blue blazer slid out immediately, shielded his eyes from the sun, then spotted the two men amidst the ruins. Flint and Tyrone came back to the gatehouse to meet him.

"Doctor Flint?" The Yorkshireman looked up and

21

down the two archaeologists, deciding (correctly) that the one with the beard and John Lennon glasses looked as though he fitted the name.

"Bob Grimston." He delivered a hearty handshake.

"This is my assistant, Tyrone Drake."

Another handshake followed, Flint slyly watching to see whether Tyrone faked a mason's grip. He didn't.

"Welcome to our little kingdom." Intense brown eyes meant business and Grimston's authority was backed by the confidence of the self-made millionaire. Lean cheeks betrayed working-class roots despite his three decades of constructing and enjoying his fortune. "I'm afraid you can't meet my partner, Miss Balleron, as she's out of the country. That's her place down there," he nodded towards the manor. "Right lads, I'm going to ask you one question. You know our plans for the estate." His hands smoothed the air before them. "One question: what do you think?"

"Terrific!" Tyrone chimed. "This is the future of the past."

Flint groaned silently at the cliché, but Bob loved it, clapping his hands. "Grand. Now, I'm a bit tied up, so help yourselves after I've gone. I'll come up the keep and give you a five-minute preview of the show which will make us all famous."

Show?, thought Flint, as he followed Grimston up the reconstructed wooden staircase which dog-legged up the front of the building to the first floor level of the keep. Grimston halted momentarily within the guard room.

"We're going to build a battle scene in here, with model knights fighting off the attackers."

22

"Was the castle ever attacked?" Flint asked.

"Not until the Civil War," Tyrone replied, in lieu of an answer from Grimston. He was painting more of the scene, adding boiling oil and catapults, before leading into the main body of the keep.

"The floors are gone," Bob stood silhouetted in a doorway, leaning on a rail. They glanced down the centre of the hollow structure, which was cut in half by an arched cross-wall giving two rooms on each floor.

"This is the banqueting hall, and that means real banquets, lads; chickens over the shoulder and as much mead as you can sup. We've got to put the floor back and get heating and power in."

A dark doorway on the left led to a latrine.

"Lavs is our big problem, they didn't have any. They used to piss over the wall and we can't have our guests doing that, can we? We can't fit lavs, the clotheads won't let us."

He turned right and walked through the thickness of the wall. To the outside were a row of arrow slits broadened by time. To the inside, a yawning void protected by a handrail. Once at the south corner turret, Grimston began to climb, his voice echoing from ahead as they wound up a spiral staircase. He stopped at second floor level.

"We wanted to have this as a special suite, but fire regulations stopped us. Imagine honeymooners in there."

Bob pointed into a room thirty feet across, open to the sky above, with a sixty-foot drop to the ground below it.

"This level would have housed the private apartments," Tyrone said.

"Spot on! So we're going to have a bedroom scene

in one room. Lady Margaret de Balleron and her page discovered by the jealous lord of the castle."

"Doing what?

"Come on Flint, you're a man of the world. Guess what they were doing."

For a moment Flint feared a soft porn scene and frowned.

"It's all fit for kids, don't worry."

"But did it happen?"

"December 1478," Grimston said with a gleam in his eye, then led onwards. "In the next room, we depict the same bedroom a year later, with the master in his bed and the ghost of his murdered wife appearing through that door, up there!"

He pointed to an internal balcony part way to the roof.

"Ghost?"

"We have a real ghost, but she won't appear at the press of a button."

The thought sent Flint cold – and it was not fear of the supernatural.

"Isn't history rich?" Grimston added.

After a turn up the north staircase, they were at the summit, looking back towards moorland, down towards the park and the village, or across to where Shadesmoor again reared above the idyll.

"So, the castle is the centrepiece," Bob said, setting his hands downwards on the parapet. "The Middle Ages Adventure. Down at the bottom of the hill we're building a visitor centre: that's where all your evidence will be displayed. Now see the manor house over there? That's being done out as a hotel – forty rooms, with twenty chalets behind and we've turned all the old workers' cottages into little apartments – they're really beautiful, you should see 'em."

His hand swept up the valley. "Up there we're designing woodland walks with picnic spots – and we're going to have a railway built up to the waterfalls, with little Robin Hood scenes dotted around and Friar Tuck's Pantry right at the top. I tell you, it's a damn good job we're outside the National Park.

"You can't make money out of castles, so down by the river is where the big attractions go. We've got thirty rides at first, adding more over ten years. You get the picture?"

Flint nodded; his heart had been left somewhere in the car park and couldn't sink further. Tyrone was bouncing on his toes, asking questions without needing to feign enthusiasm. The answers involved computer this or laser that; screams, shrieks, thrills, horror and consumer-orientated history.

"Right! I'll leave the professionals to it," Grimston said, patting both on the back. As he vanished back down the staircase, a voice drifted up from the void. "Look out for the ghost!"

"Amazing, huh?" Tyrone said.

"It's bloody purgatory. It's worse than I imagined, I at least thought there was going to be some academic input into the display."

"But there will be! Just think of the opportunity, we're being given the chance to excavate an entire medieval estate."

"Not at first, that's for Phase II."

"Okay, but the potential is there." Tyrone ignored the objection and pointed to the locations on his specification, listing the areas of the site which needed to be investigated for archaeological potential.

"We have to survey the theme park area and make sure there's no archaeology getting in the way."

25

"Perish the thought."

Tyrone continued to list his tasks, but Flint became aware that even the grand Phase II would only be bread-and-butter work, intended to clear the site for development. It was not true archaeology in Flint's mind. This project was not designed to answer questions other than "Is it okay for us to build a toilet block here?". A troubled thought added itself to his disquiet.

"Remember the last field archaeology conference? Tom Aitken put forward a motion hostile to developer funding."

"So?"

"The only time I ever came into contact with him was at conferences. He was always very assertive, always pushing for rules and guidelines. He was one of those people who fought to get those committee posts that no-one else really wants. His academic work was politically naive, 1950s stuff, but when it came to professional standards, he was always very militant. He would have hated this."

"So why was his unit tendering for the contract?"

"Before we go any further with this game, I think that's one question we need answering."

Chapter Three

A twenty minute drive carried Flint and Tyrone back across a corner of Shadesmoor. First Archaeological Services operated from a Nissen hut on a trading estate outside Northallerton. It was the kind of location which belies the glamorous image of archaeology. For Ruth Hauxley, all the remaining gilding of the profession had vanished with the death of Tom Aitken.

At the far end of the hut, screened at first by haphazard Dexion racking stuffed with seed trays and cardboard boxes, sat a blonde-haired woman, a few years out of college. She sat amidst a series of trestle tables formed into two opposing L-shaped sets, head down, examining a sherd of pottery. At the far corner was an office, its unpainted ply door firmly closed. Ruth wore a shapeless off-yellow T-shirt, which her breasts pushed well away from her body. Short dreadlocks hung over her cheeks as she worked.

"Hello?" She was surprised by the intrusion, the dreadlocks flying back from her face as she snapped up her head.

"Excuse us, we're spying," Flint smiled. "The door was open."

"I know, its so hot . . ." she paused. "You're Jeffrey Flint," she said, in pleased surprise.

"I am, and this is my trusty assistant Tyrone Drake."

Tyrone said "Hi", then immediately took interest in a potsherd that Ruth was drawing. "Fourteenth century," he said.

"Or fifteenth," she commented, "we can't be that accurate."

Tyrone continued to mumble about pottery: the stuff always left Flint cold. Ruth dropped the sherd into a seed tray, then stood up with the tray, developed biceps rippling as she lifted the weight. Whilst not a classic beauty, Flint found her petite nose set in wide sunbaked cheeks gave her a hint of mystery. An array of cubic zirconia studs were in her ears, the jeans were ripped and she wore no make-up. Whilst not a uniform, her appearance marked her down as a circuit digger.

Ruth grunted as she stood on tip-toes to post the box onto a Dexion shelf. "So what can I do for you?" Ruth's accent had the nasal tones peculiar to West Yorkshire.

Flint avoided answering the question. "On your own?", he asked.

She grimaced, "I'm the last to go: I suppose you know why?"

"Tom," Flint used the familiar tone to assume the role of friend. "That's kind of why we're here."

Ruth became visibly tense.

"I guess you're out of a job?"

"Well, I might go freelance."

"Believe me, it's the same thing. Have you got a CV? If so, drop it in to me, I'll see what I can do."

"Are you digging?" Ruth's voice lifted, with a hint of hope.

"Hopefully – our unit is after Shadesmoor."

Her expression froze. "I wouldn't bother," she said after a few moments.

"It's the biggest contract going – Tom wanted it."

Without a further word, Ruth pushed open a plywood door into an office at the end of the hut. From within came the sound of a filing cabinet sliding open. Tyrone took the opportunity to poke around the shelves with the manner of a house-clearer, weighing up the value of the goods before he made a paltry offer.

Ruth returned with a file of press cuttings.

"This is what Tom thought of Shadesmoor."

With Ruth sitting in angry silence, Flint and Tyrone found a pair of rickety school chairs then speed-read some thirty clippings from local and national papers. In each one, Tom Aitken was named as spokesperson for the Save Shadesmoor Action Group. He issued quotes such as "Cultural Vandalism", "Trampling on History" and "Heritage for Sale". Bob Grimston was described variously as a "millionaire developer", "property speculator" and "visionary entrepreneur".

When they had finished reading, Ruth's opinion came unbidden, as if she would impose it on any stranger who happened to wander into the hut. "They killed him," she said coldly. "They hired a murderer fresh out of prison and they had him killed, because of this!"

Flint looked at Tyrone, who wrapped his cheeks into a grimace.

"The press reports said he disturbed a burglar."

"Burglar! What was stolen? Someone paid that man to kill Tom. I've told the police, but they don't believe me."

29

It was doubtful whether fiery rhetoric counted as admissible evidence, but the nagging doubts which had surfaced at Shadesmoor Castle had been shown to have solid foundations.

"So what made Tom want the university job?"

Ruth suddenly realised she was under interrogation and looked from one man to the other. "What's going on? What do you want?"

"Information," Flint intoned deeply. "Sorry, did you ever see a TV show called 'The Prisoner'?"

"It was before my time," she said, visibly confused.

"Look, as you know, I've got Tom's job, the one he would have had at the university."

"Oh, so you're a friend of the Welsh slag?"

"Dr Megan Preece?"

"Sorry, but it's hard to be charitable."

"Oh, I hardly know her."

"You will." Ruth's pale blue eyes fixed first on Flint, then on Tyrone.

Flint was curious, but had other avenues to follow. "If circumstances were different, and Tom were still alive, he'd have had my job. Presumably the plan was to merge your unit with the University Unit?"

Ruth nodded.

"As head of the University Unit, he'd have been expected to tender for Shadesmoor, but if he opposed the whole project . . .?"

"They changed his mind," Ruth said. "They corrupted him. There's too much money in that crazy scheme, it's not good and it's out of control."

"By 'they' do you mean Bob Grimston?"

"Yes, and his la-di-dah partner, or your Megan, she's in on it too. It's not what archaeology is about, money and history don't mix."

"You remind me of Tom," Flint said. "He used to say things like that."

A long slow nod greeted the observation. "Yes he did. But everyone has their price."

"He saw the light," Tyrone chipped in, "he saw the way the wind was blowing, that's what I think."

"And you knew him did you?"

Flint shot a glance at Tyrone, hoping he'd keep his ideas to himself. Ruth was also glaring at him. Her mood was rapidly deteriorating and she turned her simmering aggression against Flint. "I'd never have expected to find you involved with Shadesmoor. Aren't you supposed to be the last great Marxist archaeologist? Your papers are always so radical and anti-establishment, is all that just to fool the students?"

Either he softened his touch, or Flint knew he'd be ejected from the hut before he'd learned anything. "It's not crap," he said. "I believe all I write. So when it comes to Shadesmoor, I'm cautious. There's a whole bundle of implications for national heritage, and for my heritage. Many moons ago, I used to go there on school trips. We used to have wonderful times at that castle, running up the big bank, catching bullheads and sticklebacks in the river."

"Jam sandwiches on the grass?" Ruth even managed to smile. "My school did the same. Do you think children will be able to eat sandwiches on the concrete underneath the big dipper?"

Flint shrugged, suffering the same destruction of a childhood memory. "They'll have to go to Friar Tuck's Pantry for Hoodburgers and chips."

"Yeah, right, all the magic will be lost. When I got back from Syria, and I came to work for Tom, he dragged me into Marwood's Regiment of Foot

31

– we do civil war refights. Tom was a pikeman, but that was a bit rough for me, so he had me kitted out as a musketeer. It sounds mad, but it's brilliant fun, I've met all my friends through the regiment. Last November we went to Shadesmoor on the anniversary of the siege and performed a re-enactment. It was so cold, you wouldn't believe it!" Her smile slipped. "I don't suppose we'll be allowed to do that any more."

"You might – if it brings in the tourists. I'll have to whisper in Bob Grimston's ear."

Ruth's bosom heaved at the suggestion. "Don't go near him, I'm serious! You'll be in the same mess Tom got into."

Flint had to maintain his position, for now. "So, if we dig at Shadesmoor, I get the idea you won't be interested in a job."

When Ruth saw her warning was being disregarded, she sank back into her creaking chair. "No. No thanks. I wouldn't touch it with a fifteen-foot pike. And neither would you if you had any sense."

Tyrone pulled on his leather jacket before seating himself back behind the steering wheel. The open top could be breezy at eighty miles per hour.

"Shame we couldn't recruit that one Doc, she had muscles on her muscles. She'd have been handy for shifting spoil."

"Yes, shame," Flint said, without any sincerity. He had fallen into deep thought.

The engine grumbled into life. "Are we going straight back to London?" Tyrone asked.

"Yes – and we might just stay there."

"What?"

"I get the feeling we just made an enemy. If we take on this project, we could stir up a whole horde of them."

"We won't be intimidated, we can handle the flak; what can anyone do to stop us?" Tyrone pulled away from the Nissen hut with a roar of gravel beneath the tyres.

"They stopped Tom Aitken."

Chapter Four

Examinations slipped past and end-of-term parties occupied the energy of staff and students at Central College, London. The Archaeology and Classics departments held their usual joint party in the central quadrangle. Mythology was the theme and Jeffrey Flint strode around in green bathing costume, tinfoil crown and broom handle trident as Poseidon. The Sea God stood at the front of the assembled staff and students, whilst Jupiter (Professor Grant) rambled through a speech of farewell. Afterwards, Perseus (Tyrone) aided by two harpies, a cyclops and a crowd of demi-gods hurled Poseidon into the central fountain. The bathing suit had proved an act of foresight.

Vikki hated college parties and had no sympathy for the crushing hangover. She said she'd help Flint clear the houseboat, which had long since become too small for his books, videos and music collection. Whilst he pushed linen into a Sainsburys cardboard box, she loafed on his bunk, looking through a small pile of gifts and cards. Vikki picked up a small teddy bear, decked out as a prisoner with ball-and-chain, plus pickaxe.

"Who's Tania?" she asked, reading the sugary message tied to its ankle.

"Student." Flint avoided her eyes. "Dug with her once."

"Pretty?"

"Ish." The truthful word was "devastating". He had a golden rule about not seducing his own students, a rule that had lapsed just once. It had been a year ago, after all . . .

"Who's Molly?" Vikki had found another card.

"Cleaner: age fifty, married, five kids, sex appeal nil."

"You liar, I bet she's ravishing."

Flint pretended to ignore his guest and set about filling yet another box. Vikki had the figure of a fourteen-year-old and exhibited bursts of jealousy towards any woman for whom a bra was a practical necessity.

"Are you houseboating up north?" Vikki asked, when the cards had ceased to divert her.

"I may just look for a cottage, now I'm a man of substance."

"You're not buying a house? Is this the same Jeffrey Flint who preaches 'property is theft'?"

"Don't mock, I'm being practical. I need more space."

"A nice cottage," she mused. "With flowerbeds and a little path . . . I asked about your mate – he had a nice cottage."

"Which mate?"

"The one who got done in."

"Tom Aitken? I barely knew him, he was hardly a mate."

"Do you think there's a story in it? A story for me?"

"I doubt it."

Vikki left her recumbent position and laid one hand on each of his shoulders from behind. "Tell me the truth."

"Since when did the truth trouble you?"

"Ha ha. My stories just happen to move a little faster than yours."

He bent down to stow away another blanket. She grabbed him tightly as he stood.

"Hunky archaeologist murdered in the dead of night." Her voice dramatised the gory event. "A stone-age axe is used as the murder weapon, smashing down on the skull! Was it ritual, was it vengeance, was it a contract killing with a twist?"

He abandoned packing and turned swiftly to grab Vikki around the waist. "This is not one for your grisly satellite slot."

The reporter pouted her lips into a kissing action. "And why not?"

"They're people Vikki, real people who bleed and die in your stories."

"They're real people you dig up out of the ground – how would you like a bearded layabout scraping around your ribs with a trowel?"

"Layabout, huh?" He gripped her tighter, pulling her feet clear of the floor. Vikki weighed only eight stones fully clothed and would weigh somewhat less once he had removed those. This was a familiar game, and it usually ended horizontally.

Vikki gave one glance at the overcrowded cabin bunk. Flint spared a hand to push the farewell cards aside. Vikki gave the teddy bear a flick with the back of her hand and it bounced, unloved on to the floor.

"Sorry, Tania," she said.

Some cities loom in the distance, their spires and tower blocks advertising the metropolis from a dozen miles away. Leeds can therefore come as a shock. The

A64 shrinks in importance as it grows closer to the city, at last little more than a manic country lane, where traffic in both directions is unrestrained by a speed limit. The road sweeps past a derelict bus and up a wooded hill. At the crest, waiting in ambush, is Leeds.

Vikki had arranged to meet Flint at his new college, but had been almost an hour late. This was quite usual. He had come to accept Vikki as a random event in his life; sometimes there, sometimes not. She would display bursts of interest in him for three or four days in a row, then lapse into what she called her "friendly" mood for the rest of the month. It was often an arms-length or a long-distance affair and Flint was far too wary of entrenched relationships to try to alter things.

She drove her Rover a little too quickly for Flint's liking, turning sharply at his instruction, indicating too late to offer any benefit to drivers close to her bumper. He guided her through the legoland jungle of dual carriageways, roundabouts and council estates. One estate, no more remarkable than any other, was composed of a snaking pattern of post-war semi-detached houses set amongst grassy verges lined with poplar trees. The lower half of each house was faced in brown brick, the upper parts in cream-washed pebbledash, whilst the woodwork had all been replaced by white UPVC. Vikki braked to avoid a bouncing ball, then bumped into a high kerb where space between cars permitted.

"Home," said Flint, spreading his hands. "But not a castle."

Vikki seemed to take exceptional care in locking her doors, then looked around the crescent. A stray dog was just marking one of the trees opposite.

37

"It's a bit posher than where my mum lives," she said.

"No satire, please."

"Honest, you been to Lewisham?"

He gave her a once-up-and-down inspection at her request. The make-up was overdone, the maroon of the lipstick a little too deep, the dangling brass earrings perhaps a trifle large, the white blouse rather obviously expensive.

"How do I look?"

"Super."

A hastily wrapped present and a bouquet of flowers lay on the back seat of the car. Flint collected them, then stepped onto the brick path which led to the door of his family home. The wandering academic always felt a little nostalgic when he pushed open that gate: nostalgic for the people and the memories, rather than for the setting.

Mrs Flint was as tall as her son, her hair rather frizzy, almost totally grey, her eyes bagged by a decade of late nights behind the bar of the working men's club. She was sixty-two that week. He proffered the flowers and the present.

"Happy birthday, Mum."

Flint stiffened slightly at the inevitable embrace.

"Aw, Jeffrey, I love having you home . . . and this must be Lisa."

"Only when he's drunk," Vikki said softly and held out a hand. "Vikki."

"Oh Vikki, yes, I've seen you on the telly." Mrs Flint pointed up to the satellite dish which dangled below a bedroom window. "Come in love."

His father seemed to take to Vikki, wanting to resurrect all those gruesome true life murders she reported for a late-night TV show. Vikki perched on the corner of the settee, by the television, casting her eyes over a photograph of a much younger and hairier Flint in his graduation cap. Next to it, on the mantelpiece was a duo of weddings: Flint's parents in the centre, his sister to the left. Elsewhere were the photographs of a growing nephew and niece for "Uncle Jeffrey". He tried not to be self-conscious with his family so obviously on display, but Vikki was an expert at small talk on any level. Sometime later, he led his "girlfriend" outside, for the thirty second stroll along the garden path, past the greenhouse to the compost heap, with its view of the recreation field beyond the larch-lap fencing.

"Family Flint – sorry Dad went on about death and disaster. Since his back went, he seems to do nothing but watch the box."

"They're nice, and I'm glad he likes my show. It keeps me in work."

"I never wanted us to have to go through this meet-the-old-folks routine, but if I'm living on their doorstep, they're bound to bump into you sooner or later."

Vikki turned sharply at a shriek from the recreation field.

"Still on duty?" Flint asked.

"I'm always on the lookout for a good story – what's happening to your little mystery?"

"Nothing much."

"What about Ruth Hauxley? I think she's hiding something."

"And how would you know?"

"I met her."

"When?"

"Before I picked you up – that's why I was late."

"Vikki!"

39

"I know all your archaeology friends are a bit odd, but this Ruth . . ."

Flint was alarmed and cut her short with a burst of anger. "Vikki, this is nothing to do with you."

"I thought I'd help."

"Don't."

"Sorry – I just wanted to meet her."

"Were you checking up on me, or checking up on her?"

"Both. You have a reputation, and all your archaeology women must know about it by now." She folded her arms and stuck her nose in the air, defying him to justify himself.

"Leave it alone, Vikki."

"Someone has to look after you."

He began to calm down. "Not you. I'm a big boy now – ask my mum."

For a tiny woman, Vikki owned incredibly heavy feet, so the last thing that Flint wanted was Vikki stomping around on his patch. He had to quickly diffuse the idea that he had walked into a nest of vipers and obtain a sensible motive for the death of Tom Aitken.

Vikki went upstairs to unpack her overnight bag and "tidy up", by which she was being politic and allowing the argument to cool. Whilst she was showering, Flint took out the phone book and made a quick call to a Leeds solicitor. Vikki would be gone in the morning and then he would be free to dig a little deeper into the past.

Stubbs & Hare (Solicitors) occupied a first-floor office above a Leeds betting shop near the Kirkgate Market. Lincoln's Inn it was not.

He sought neither Stubbs, nor Hare, but Carrick;

obviously still toiling her way through Legal Aid sob-stories until she had won the status of partner. Flint's opinion of lawyers had never been high and recent experiences had eroded what confidence he had once held.

"Hello," she said, "Doctor Flint? Sue Carrick."

She was probably about the same age as him, opting for sober cardigan and skirt; a style of clothes where money is expended to no effect. He shook her hand, sensing the light grip and meeting serious, sunken and rather sad hazel eyes. "How can I help?"

Turn-of-century cheap wooden panelling gave the office a gloomy feel and its single dusty window looked out over market roofs. Shelves along one wall were lined with books of excruciating dullness.

"Jeff," he said, seating himself opposite the over-crowded desk.

Sue Carrick was obviously used to quickly judging personalities and adapting herself to meet them.

"Sue," she said, "and I've heard the joke."

"Joke?"

"Lawyer – Sue – never mind, how can I help?"

"I'd like to talk about Wayne Drabble."

"Are you a reporter?" she asked.

"No, I'm an archaeologist."

Dark-haired, her face took a tan, but it gave her a curious unwashed appearance. Sue sat back, repeating the word "archaeologist".

"I dig up bodies."

"I can't discuss my clients' affairs."

"I didn't expect you to. Could I meet Wayne, have a chat?"

"Why?"

"Call me curious."

41

"Given your profession, I assume you were an acquaintance of Mr Aitken?"

"Distant acquaintance: we met a few times, but I've got his job now and I'd be interested to hear what your client has to say."

"Don't meddle, Doctor Flint. These are complex . . ."

"Call me Jeff . . . and I know all about legal processes." He needed an angle, a hook to catch both solicitor and client. "I assume he's going to plead innocent?"

"I can't comment. What I would like to hear is one good reason why I should waste my time, and the taxpayers' money, allowing you to speak to Wayne."

"Perhaps I could get him off," Flint said lightly.

Sue had a humourless expression and it hardened further. "Don't joke, he deserves better than to have his hopes raised."

"No joke."

Every time he ceased speaking, Sue weighed up what had been said before replying. "What do you know?"

He put on a teasing face to hide his ignorance. "Let us say there are some interesting rumours circulating. Murderers kill for a reason. What was Wayne's reason?"

"I'd like to hear these rumours."

"And I'd like to hear Wayne's side of the story."

Sue paused for thought. "This is very irregular . . ."

"Pretend I'm a private detective, working for Wayne, trying to prove he's been set up."

"That's difficult – you don't look the part."

"I've got a raincoat at home and a Taiwanese .38 special that doesn't work."

"You seem to think you can charm me, Doctor Flint."

"Hope so."

"Why?"

"Prudence. I'm about to stick my neck into the same noose Tom Aitken wore. I need to make sure no-one is suddenly going to pull the rope."

"Or swing an axe?"

"You don't swing a hand-axe, you chop with it."

Smiling did not come easily, and Sue only suggested she was amused by the pedantry. "I'll have to talk to my client."

"Soon?"

A pause, a blink. "As soon as is practicable."

Chapter Five

Flint wanted to become acquainted with his new college before its staff scattered for the summer vacation. Shadesmoor Phase I had to be planned, courses had to be devised and the ghost of Tom Aitken had to be exorcised.

"Will I get away with recycling the courses I ran in London?" Flint was walking one of the endless corridors in the short but broad shadow of Keith Barnes.

Barney made histrionic thinking noises. "Our students are not up to the standard you've been used to – remember we're a poly in all but name. We get the oiks from comprehensives with exam grades so dismal they can't get in anywhere better. Archaeology, they say, soft arts, that's easy."

"They need to be disillusioned."

"Uh?"

"Stretched."

Barney led him into the Arts Faculty staff Common Room.

"We're a science," muttered Flint, knowing that if the government were to call archaeology a science, departments would expect higher funding.

"Megan!" Barney called to the back of a woman with short, red-tinted frizzy hair and a brown knitted waistcoat.

The broad-hipped, almost mumsy figure turned on her heels. Her glasses were almost identical to those worn by Flint, her face was a tall oval, her teeth just a little crooked and she was almost on his eye-line.

"Megan Preece; our new comrade."

"Jeff, yes, we've met a few times," Megan shook his hand. "You're the one who's going to win Shadesmoor for us?"

"With luck."

"Well I'm already on board – I'm on the Academic Advisory Committee steering the reconstruction, so I expect we'll be seeing a lot of each other, one way or another. Have you found anywhere to roost yet?"

"I'm squatting at my mum's in Leeds. Either I get a car, or I'm going to have to move closer. I keep experiencing an urge to find a little cottage, something rural, give me a change from London."

"They're expensive . . ." Barney began, but Megan stepped on him. "You could stay in my cottage." Her forehead creased to stress her sincerity. "Stay for a few weeks and see how you adapt to country life. I've a room at the back where I take in a postgraduate during term time. You could have that for the summer, and pillage my library at will. I've got all the references for Shadesmoor Castle."

The "Welsh slag" seemed keen to please. Only a patina of her accent remained and at that moment, she hardly deserved the insults that had been thrown at her by Ruth Hauxley. Megan continued to sell her room. "I'm only half a mile down the road, and my place is convenient for the A1, as the adverts say."

"Great." Flint was immediately convinced by the sales pitch.

"I'm only in Wetherby," Barney began to say, but

45

Megan had whipped a pen from her waistcoat pocket and scribbled her telephone number on the back of a car park ticket.

"Ring me, anytime." She smiled again, then breezed out of the Common Room. Flint imagined he could hear her singing.

Barney was shaking his head, watching her go. "Close to the A1," he said.

"What?"

"Like a spider drawing in a fly. However, think of it as a way of advancing your investigation."

Flint found himself becoming angry. "I'm here to teach, not conduct investigations."

"Fine, fine, just beware of our Megan. She'll suck you in and spit you out."

"There speaks a man of experience."

Barney flinched at the comment, but made no response. Flint was aware of having blundered into another minefield. Why was life never simple?

Wayne Drabble was a little large for a cat burglar: six-foot-two and fourteen stones probably explained complete failure in his chosen trade. His moon-like face carried a look of aggrieved surprise, his straight and greasy hair just touched the shoulders of his black T-shirt.

Armley gaol terrified and oppressed Flint from the moment he entered its forbidding gates. Even the bald interview rooms seemed designed to crush the spirit.

"This is Doctor Flint," Sue Carrick said gently.

"I'm not ill," he said.

"I explained all that, Wayne, no clowning, we don't have time."

Slack cheeks nodded in glum agreement and unexpected deep blue eyes met those of Flint. "You want to help me?"

Flint simply raised his eyebrows. He couldn't lie to someone this vulnerable.

"Why?" Wayne challenged, "What yer getting?"

"I like to beat the system," Flint stated, "and I don't like seeing the little guy get screwed by the cops."

Wayne was hardly little, but he clearly felt small, glancing around at his surroundings.

"I think you should tell him, Wayne," Sue said. She then explained her strategy to Flint. "At first we were going to put forward a plea of innocent on all counts. Then, I managed to find out what evidence the police were bringing forward. I'll give you a list, it's in my bag. Wayne was seen driving his girlfriend's car down the A1 at two in the morning; the police checked his record and presumed he was guilty of something. When they visited the flat he was staying in, they found enough evidence to connect him with the burglary. We've talked it over, but my advice to Wayne is that he plead guilty to the breaking and entering, and not guilty on the murder."

"Will they wear that?"

"I was put up," Wayne said. "I was out of the nick one week and this woman rang me bird's place. She said she had an easy job; it were easy money and I was straight out on the dole."

"Did you ever meet her?" Flint questioned.

"No, she was posh though, you could hear it in her voice."

"What did she want you to do?"

Wayne sighed, wanting support from his solicitor. "He's not going to tell on me is he?"

47

"If he does I'll sue him."

Hence the joke, thought Flint. "What did the 'posh' woman want?"

"I had to go to this big house called the Old Rectory, break in the back where there was a study, and get this gold necklace."

"The police have a picture of it," Sue stated.

"She posted it to me," said Wayne.

"Could you draw it?" Flint turned his notepad towards the burglar and pushed his biro across the table.

Another indolent sigh preceded the attempt at artistry. Wayne picked up the pen and drew an incomplete loop. Then he drew a circle at each end of the loop. After a few moments he began changing his loop into a crude representation of twisted rope.

"It looks like one of them rope chains, but as thick as your finger," Wayne said.

"It's a torc," Flint stated, "Pre-Roman Iron Age. A Celtic chieftain would wear one round his neck."

"Yeah, that's right. That's what she said."

"What were you being paid?"

"Five grand."

"See any money?"

"Five hundred – she posted it to me."

"Ever think of just keeping the money?"

"Yeah, but I reckoned she might get nasty. You know, she was just a voice, she said she had mates, they could be a mob, you know. They could be anyone."

Anyone, thought Flint. Or no-one.

"Wayne still had some of the money," Sue chipped in.

"The police say I nicked it."

48

"So," Flint said. "You drove up to the Old Rectory on April 15th – sorry it would be the 16th after midnight . . ."

"Half past one – she told me no-one would be in."

The "posh" woman had to be a close acquaintance, if this were true.

"So, I parked the car in a lane at the back, waited a bit, then went over the fence and up the garden past some sheds. The study is at the back with them big French windows. They can be real easy and there were no alarm."

"It was turned off," Sue added.

"I got in, looked around, then I tripped over this bloke on the floor by this desk."

"Dead?"

"The police can't be sure about the time of death," Sue said.

Flint had read his clippings. "No, the body wasn't found for what, three days?"

Sue pinched her nose with a grimace.

Wayne continued. "Well what could I do? What would you have done? There was blood everywhere, it was like a horror video. I just legged it."

"And that was it?"

"I went back to our girl's place . . . I was right shaken up, I had to have a few drinks before I went to bed. I cleaned up me clothes and thought I was all right. The cops came round on Monday after I got back from signing on. I was shopped, that posh woman shopped me."

A few weeks previously, when Flint had sat with Barney in the college bar, the other lecturer had made an offhand quip which now seemed oddly appropriate. Flint repeated the line.

"It's a capitalist plot."
"Eh?"

Sue wanted some time alone and Flint went outside to wait by her car. Either Wayne was a good fantasist, or Barney's words had been prophetic. It was possible that Wayne had accidentally stumbled on a murder and had invented the story in order to explain an otherwise unlikely coincidence.

Flint looked at the typed sheet Sue had handed him.

EVIDENCE – main points:

* Patrol car saw Wayne in girlfriend's car on A1 at 2.50 am on April 16th
* Aitken last heard of 10.30pm (approx) April 15th
* Intruder alarm at Aitken house turned OFF
* Aitken hit from above/behind with force; single blow with stone (i.e. killer had to be tall and fairly strong)
* Police question Wayne on 18th after body discovered
* Tyre marks behind Aitken house
* Gravel embedded in Wayne's boot
* Bloodstains on cuff of jacket and knee of trousers (both washed)
* Crowbar in boot of car matches marks on French windows
* Small bloodstain on rubber torch and seat of car
* Picture of torc necklace and £380 in Wayne's possession
* Nothing stolen

Sue emerged some ten minutes later. "So that's Wayne," she said, aiming an electronic key at her car. "He's in a mess, as you can see."

"Do you believe him?" Flint asked.

"That's a leading question – as his solicitor I have to believe him."

"A court won't swallow the story – it's too far-fetched."

"Perhaps – but Wayne is not a killer; he's got no history of violence. Unless the police disclose additional forensic evidence which links him to the actual killing, the whole case becomes circumstantial. Thank God he's a pro. and said nothing before I got to the station."

"So Wayne was just innocently burgling the Rectory and just happened to find a warm body? How the hell are you going to get him off?"

"Separate the burglary from the murder: we have to introduce doubt into the murder charge. Now what was the point of your joke about capitalist plots?"

"It was something I picked up from Nechayev, one of the Anarchist Philosophers. Essentially, the working class don't initiate plots, it's the middle class who pose the greatest obstacle to revolution."

"I don't quite see the relevance . . ."

"If there was some kind of plot to kill Tom Aitken, Wayne is too dim to have hatched it, he'd just be a pawn. I don't believe the coincidence, you don't believe that Wayne is lying, so the only alternative is to assume that some sort of intrigue is behind all this."

"Ah, I feel you may be building a dangerous argument now."

"Okay, I'm just kite-flying, it's a habit of mine. Do you happen to know who else the police have interviewed about this?"

"Several hundred people at least."

"Including Bob Grimston?"

"One of Mr Aitken's ex-girlfriends alleged that Grimston was behind the murder."

"That would be Ruth Hauxley?"

"Yes, I'm afraid she'll be on the receiving end of a writ unless she keeps clear of the case."

"The police don't believe her hit man theory then?"

"Wayne is not a hit man."

"No. Fancy lunch?"

"Yes, but I'm afraid it's with one of the partners. Can I drop you somewhere?"

Back in his office, Flint rummaged through his TA box file, which was now almost full. He took out a photocopy of the archaeological obituary of Tom Aitken. As is customary, and very useful, it listed his publications in date order. A busy man: 32 articles and two books in fifteen years, plus many mentions in the regional press. Following up these references in the library, he found a clipping from the Yorkshire Post dating to the previous autumn. The article included a rather dark oblique photograph of an object not unlike the sketch which Wayne had made. It was headed:

"IRON AGE GOLD AT FORM FARM DIG"

Three telephone calls confirmed what Flint had suspected: the torc had been given into the care of the Yorkshire Museum a few weeks after its discovery, and there it remained. Wayne had been cruelly deceived.

Flint furrowed his brow, doodling suggestions in his notebook. It was highly likely that Wayne had come across the newspaper report and made a naive assumption that archaeologists keep their best goodies locked in a bottom drawer of their desk. Okay, Flint knew one or two who did, but these were eccentric exceptions. Wayne could have fooled himself, or could have become involved in a plot by someone similarly deluded.

His gold-plated pen was sucked, long and thoughtfully. If the "posh" woman had the brains to arrange the theft, then sale, of an antiquity, surely she'd spot the flaw in the plot. Wayne's story began to look distinctly wobbly.

Chapter Six

"I'm going to run 'Approaches to the Past'," Flint said, over his loaded box, "plus 'Roman Britain,' 'Roman Architecture and Art' and 'Basic Dating Techniques'."

Megan Preece was just behind him, carrying a lighter box up the stairs of her cottage. She had discarded her glasses and donned a large pair of dungarees to assist in housemoving. "You're still Marxist, pledge me that."

"'fraid so, did you read my book on the third century?"

"No, Romans leave me cold. I heard you devoted only half a page to women."

The back room had a sloping ceiling with a view out over cow pasture and power lines. Flint dumped the box of books onto the candlewick bedspread. "Name six third-century women."

Megan deposited her box alongside his. "Julia thingy."

"Okay, Julia Domna, that's one. Any more? Name someone who wasn't an Empress."

"I'm not a Romanist – thank God – and it's not Empresses I want to read about. Where in your book are the ordinary women who raised their little boys to be your precious legionaries?"

"That was the thrust of my argument, that was what the half-page was about."

Megan puffed up her cheeks in mock disgust. "The Roman empire was run by men, for men, and its history is written by men for men."

"I know a number of very bright female Romanists who would take violent objection to that statement."

Megan made no attempt to press home her point as she led the way back down the fraying red stair carpet. "How are you doing on the Shadesmoor tender?"

"Tyrone finished it with a day to spare. He's a born capitalist, that lad; he's wasted in archaeology. He should be a land speculator, or a Tory MP."

"Or both?"

Only one more box lay in the back of the green Vauxhall van Flint had borrowed from his sister's husband. Flint disliked Carl intensely, he was literally a used car salesman. Were Carl not a broad Yorkshire lad, Tyrone and he would probably hit it off instantly.

The last box was one of the heaviest, Flint groaned as the bottom sagged, threatening to pour his books amongst the pansies which lined the brick path.

"Cup of coffee?" Megan asked as he passed her in the hall. For a die-hard feminist she had the domestic routine perfected. Little gingham curtains at the turn of the stair, crocheted drapes covering the bedside units and a multitude of nicknacks on the theme of cats decorated the bijou residence. Barney had warned him about the cats, black and white, Yin and Yang, which were lurking somewhere about the cottage. Barney had an allergy, apparently, and disliked cats almost as much as he appeared to dislike Megan.

*   *   *

July was a perfect month to move to the country and Flint spent his first ten days simply expanding into the space around him, savouring the sensible prices in the pubs and the ready humour of Yorkshire folk. Impersonal and squalid London was a distant country, left with only qualified regrets. Tyrone was lodging with friends on the edge of York: the region was thick with archaeologists and historians.

That first weekend he and Tyrone drove down to Marston Moor, the scene of Cromwell's famous victory in 1644. Civil War fanatics were out in strength, forming in scaled-down regiments for a near-bloodless refight. As loudspeakers blared a commentary, Parliamentarians defeated Royalists as the script demanded. Both armies were outnumbered by the ranks of tourists watching the spectacle. Tyrone was entranced and animated: Flint suspected he wanted to don a floppy hat and join Prince Rupert. Out in the scrimmage of pikemen and popping lines of musketeers would be Marwood's Regiment of Foot, and amongst them, Ruth Hauxley fighting for truth and justice, if not for God and Parliament. At one point in the action, Flint thought he saw one white-coated musketeer a little shorter than the rest, standing on her toes to reload her musket. After the gunsmoke had rolled away he wandered over to the encampment where the enthusiasts were congregating.

A couple of regiments were dressed in white, or near-white uniforms, but Marwood's were soon located. Laughing and joking, caulking bloody noses with cotton wool, they bore the appearance of a period rugby team. The regiment dispersed gradually, as members made for their cars or mini-vans. Flint and Tyrone moved amongst them, searching for

Ruth. She was in energetic, jovial conversation with two pikemen when Flint edged into her eyeline.

"Doctor Flint," she seemed surprised, possibly pleased.

"Good battle?"

"We won!" She responded.

Tyrone the Royalist objected. "You were supposed to win."

Ruth turned to her friends. "This is Doctor Jeffrey Flint, he runs the University Unit now."

"Were you a friend of Toms?" One of the pikemen asked, his head jerking up to ask the question.

"Not as close as I'd like to have been."

"Aye."

Tyrone asked if he could see Ruth's musket, which hung by her side. Her mouth broke into a petite smile at his request and handed over the reproduction piece, pointing out the detail. Tyrone put it to his shoulder, but it was too heavy to aim.

"Fancy coming for a drink with us?" Flint asked.

"Why don't you come for a drink with us?" Ruth replied. "We're going to the pub down the road. Just follow the vans."

Swords and firearms were left in the cars and many of the regiment had discarded their uniforms and kit before entering the pub. Tyrone and Flint crushed inside, where perhaps sixty hands craned for pints being handed out from the bar.

"We'll never get served!" Tyrone grumbled.

"I ordered for you," a voice said from behind him. "Is bitter all right?"

"Great!"

Two pints came over the crowd at shoulder height

and Flint found a handy corner to lean against. Ruth had changed down into a polo top and jeans.

"You changed your hair."

She pulled at a blonde, curling strand. "They didn't have dreadlocks in the seventeenth century. I always plait up my hair a few days before a muster, it gives it a curl."

"Ruth!"

She had been about to take her own pint away. "Don't ask me about Tom, not today, Jeff. I'm with my friends, I'm having a good time."

"Cheers!" Flint raised his beerglass and saw her vanish into the ranks. For the next hour he kept one eye on her as the crowd shifted. She held onto the single pint, drinking very slowly, refusing refills. Women were outnumbered by men and she stood with her back to the wall, laughing at their tall tales and always responding with one of her own. She could have been any graduate student in any bar in the country.

"What do you think of our Ruth?" Flint said, after analysing her body language at long range.

"Six out of ten, nose too small, crooked teeth and her eyes are too far apart."

"Oh God, Tyrone, it's not a cattle show. How do you think we get her on our side? I mean, she's avoiding us. She's being nice about it, but she's avoiding us."

Ruth now caught his eye and held it. As if to prove Flint wrong, she said something to her group, then made her way between bodies to join them. Her glass was now two-thirds empty.

"My ears are burning," her blue eyes flitted from one to the other as she looked up at them.

"Drink?"

58

"No thanks," she held up the glass as evidence.

He had her written down as a good-time girl, but had progressively reworked his opinion. She had moved amongst the men as friends, not flirting, not allowing any to monopolise her company.

"We need your help, Ruth. We need to get into the Rectory."

"Why?" She seemed to be bouncing on her heels as she asked the question, taking it in light heart.

"To square what happened to Tom – in our own minds."

In the far corner of the bar, a trio of men started singing. It may have been a country and western ballad; it may have been something more folksy and closer to Renaissance England.

"Excuse my friends," she said. She glanced back at them, wanting to be back amidst the antics.

"The Old Rectory?"

Ruth had ceased bouncing and the humour vanished from her slender lips. "If I say no, you won't give up, will you?"

"I saw Tom's place advertised in the property press. We could get the estate agent to show us around – I'd rather you did the honours, with you being Tom's friend. We'd feel less . . ."

"Ghoulish?"

"Awkward."

"I'm busy next weekend."

"Have you got another battle on?" Tyrone asked.

"Only with my mum."

"How about in the week?" Flint raised his eyebrows and used his pleading voice.

She shook her head, demanding sympathy as she wrinkled her face in pain. "My project is weeks behind schedule."

"Please?"

More facial pain. "I'll think about it, okay?"

"I'll ring you later in the week."

"Ruth sing us a song!" came a call from the far corner of the bar. She gave a forced cough of embarrassment and shielded her face with one hand.

"Excuse me," the smile returned to her face.

"Ruth! Ruth!" They called, men and women, in a mixture of modern and period dress. Ruth made a show of finding her way back to the group in the corner, who grew more raucous at her approach.

Over the hubbub, Flint could hear her voice, sweet yet slightly nasal, untrained with a strong hint of Yorkshire. She sang unaccompanied, putting notes to the poem, "She moves through the Fair". Odd lines carried across the room, of a dead love and of a wedding day.

"I hate folk music," Tyrone said.

It was time to leave.

At the western edge of Shadesmoor, its slopes become farmland, with fields lined by ancient hedges. The Norman church of St Barnabas sits at the top of Urethorpe, its weathered lych gate facing the redbrick rectory. Urethorpe shared a vicar with a neighbouring parish – the Church of England could no longer afford to maintain the rambling, tree-shrouded rectory. Quite how a field archaeologist could afford it was another puzzle. It had taken ten days of phone calls, hard sell and soft sell to persuade Ruth she had the time to spare.

Tyrone parked his Spitfire outside the gates on another bone dry day. A thin layer of dried cattle dung encrusted the lane and Tyrone idly kicked it into flakes with the toes of his boots. Flint looked around the beech hedge and down the rough dirt and gravel drive, trying to guess where Wayne had entered the garden. An estate agent's sign leaned crookedly against the hedge, inviting all enquiries.

A farm separated The Rectory and the village, one small field scattered with cow pats had isolated Tom Aitken on the night of his death. Around the pub at the bottom of the village came a short wheelbase Land Rover; it was an old model and bore the lettering "FIRST ARCHAEOLOGICAL SERVICES" on the door. Ruth Hauxley was behind the wheel, motioning Flint to open the gate as she approached. He obliged, then stepped back as Ruth swung into the drive with practised ease. She slammed on the handbrake, then slipped out of the door with a look of unease.

"I came," she said.

"And you have a key?"

"I've always had a key, if you get me."

Former mistress, or would-be widow, Ruth led them down the drive and past the house. Like Flint, she was dressed in the obligatory T-shirt and jeans. Tyrone cut a different figure in his camouflaged trousers and ex-DDR army shirt.

"Thanks for coming to open up for us," Flint said.

"I'm getting used to it. I'm up here a couple of times a week with the police, or the press, or with someone looking round the house."

"Any interest?"

"Not when they find out what happened here."

A small yard and a strip of unmown grass lay behind the back door, the waving heads of rye grass parched almost white by the drought.

"That used to be a stable." Ruth pointed to an

61

outbuilding which ran back down the hill. "We keep some of the unit equipment there."

Ruth led along the back, between house and stable, through an open gate onto a second, larger lawn, which dropped away to a hedge and a small copse of silver birch. Beyond the tree tops, Shadesmoor rose effortlessly towards the pure blue sky.

"I think the killer got in down there. A little lane runs along the back of the woods."

Flint walked across to the French windows which faced the lawn. A plank had been nailed across the damaged woodwork.

"Who owns the house now?" he asked.

"He had a sister in Zimbabwe: she inherits everything."

One motive had been dissolved by the question, another possibly introduced in its place. Ruth unlocked the kitchen door and allowed them to take in the dilapidated decor for a few moments. Some day, The Rectory would be bought as a country home by some solicitor or accountant and would then be progressively gentrified. The cracked post war enamel sink, the green tarnished taps, the ersatz kitchen units and bottled gas cooker would all go straight into a skip.

"Nice, isn't it?" Ruth asked, without a hint of sarcasm.

"Needs a bit of work," said Tyrone, hands pushed into his pockets.

Ruth noticed the criticism and moved on to the hallway.

"You'll never make an estate agent," Flint breathed. "The jargon is 'many original features, with potential for improvement'. Don't upset her."

The study was the only room of the house which

had been subjected to tender loving care. Its door was central, facing the French windows, with dark wood bookshelves filling the remaining wallspace. Someone, possibly Ruth, had cleaned the room since the events of that April night. The exposed and varnished floorboards carried no hint that they once bore darker stains.

"This used to be the dining room, but Tom had more books than dinner parties, so it became his library," Ruth explained. "I'm supposed to be cataloguing the books for sale."

Both archaeologists walked slowly past the bookcases, touching familiar volumes, pausing at the more unusual. Flint's eyes ran along the spines of the top shelf of books by the door, spotting Mortimer Wheeler's "Stanwix Excavations" report, then J.S. Curle's "Excavations at Newstead" and yet more books he would have to read to re-acquaint himself with northern archaeology.

"The hand-axe was here." Ruth pointed to a patch of desk to the left of the blotting pad. "Tom's father brought it back from Africa – it was one of the first artifacts that he owned."

"What about the Form Farm torc?"

"It's in the Yorkshire Museum."

"He didn't find two did he?" Tyrone asked.

"No, why?"

"That's what the burglar said he was looking for," Flint revealed.

"You met him?" Her face filled with anger.

Flint nodded. After a few moments, Ruth offered to make tea, possibly to diffuse her own temper. Flint made sure the door had closed after Ruth left.

"She's at home," Tyrone commented. "Was she his mistress then?"

63

"One of," Flint said, his mind elsewhere. "So Wayne broke in through the windows and began rummaging around. Play at being Wayne."

"Me?"

"No, the ghost of Tom Aitken, yes of course you."

Tyrone went over to the window, turned about and began to prowl.

"Torch in one hand, jemmy in the other." Flint walked to the door. "Okay, I'm Tom Aitken, in I come, what do you do?"

"Scarper."

Flint grunted agreement. "Okay – let's try a new scenario, come and rummage on the desk."

Tyrone came around in front of the door, put his back to Flint and began to imitate rummaging.

"I enter," Flint declared.

Tyrone spun round. "I cosh you with the hand-axe."

"What did you do with the jemmy?"

"I put it down to do the rummaging."

"And the torch?"

Tyrone pointed to a desk lamp. "I switched the lamp on; I need two hands for a good rummage."

"Do it again."

They repeated the charade. "In I come," said Flint.

Tyrone spun around. "Whap!" he said, knocking Flint on the forehead with the knuckle of his index finger.

Flint blinked, spotting the problem with this reconstruction. "Tom Aitken was struck on the back of the head."

Only a few moments thought brought out the brute thug in Tyrone. "Right! I kick you in the groin: double up Doc!"

Flint reluctantly doubled up.

"Whap!" Tyrone's knuckle came down right on the crown.

"Not so hard! Remember who's paying the wages!"

Flint straightened up, and looked into the dusty alcove between the door and the first bookcase. "Stand in there."

Tyrone moved a footstool out of the way and had just secreted himself behind the door when it swung open, squashing him against a bookcase.

"Sorry," said Ruth, fighting to regain control of the tea tray. "What are you doing?"

"Working out if the burglar was telling the truth," Flint said.

"What did he say?"

Dodgy ground loomed ahead. Flint chose a seat on the two seat sofa of button-down leather, made up some pseudo-legal excuse and declined a straight answer. Tyrone sat next to him, Ruth chose the reading chair next to the desk.

"What lies did he tell you?" Ruth narrowed her blue eyes.

"He said that Tom was dead when he arrived."

"He's lying, he was paid to kill Tom!"

Flint tried to cool down the conversation, taking his tea and taking his time. "By?"

"Bob Grimston and the ever-so-glamorous Eleanor Balleron."

"Who's she?" Tyrone asked.

"His partner. She's beautiful, rich, sophisticated . . ." Ruth twirled her hand in mockery, making no effort to conceal her disdain.

"Wayne said he was trying to steal the Form Farm Torc."

"Which any idiot knows is in the Museum. It's

something he's made up as an alibi. They told him to say that, it's obvious."

This could not be right, Flint thought. If Wayne wanted to distance himself from the plot, surely he would have omitted the "posh" woman part of the story. All sorts of intriguing possibilities opened up. Perhaps Wayne had been sent looking for something else, perhaps he really had killed Aitken on the spur of the moment and made up the conspiracy theory; perhaps he was telling the truth; perhaps he was telling part of the truth. He looked into the dusty alcove again, knowing that Wayne would have fitted even less well than Tyrone. It was the only place in the room from where a surprise attack could be launched.

"You weren't here that night?" Flint asked.

"No." Ruth stirred her tea energetically. "We had a fall-out and I moved out at the end of January. If I had been here, he would have killed both of us."

As she stirred, the muscles on her upper arm twitched to advertise the years that Ruth had spent heaving buckets and hauling wheelbarrows. This was no weak and feeble woman; she would pack a man-size punch.

"Come on Ruth, contract killers don't use hand-axes, they carry guns, or knives at least."

"Do they? I've never met one."

Tom Aitken had been a good six feet tall, perhaps taller. Flint guessed at Ruth's height, she had an inch or two on Vikki and was much sturdier in build. Say, five feet three, which would make her head level with Tom Aitken's shoulders. Too short, perhaps, to be the one to bring death down on her lover's head.

"Have you raised your suspicions with the police?" he asked.

66

"Oh yes, but I'm just a scruffy digger, what do I know? I wasn't even his wife, I don't count, I don't even inherit anything. But those Shadesmoor people have enough money to buy whatever they want. You know how corrupt the police are."

Even in his worst anti-police moments, Flint retained a sense of perspective. Ruth had clearly lost hers in a cycle of tragedy and paranoia.

"I can't believe this was a contract killing, Ruth, I simply can't. This is North Yorkshire not New York. Developers may be a bit crooked but they don't have people killed."

"Believe that if you like, but if you have anything else to do with Bob Grimston and his fancy lady, you'll end up the same way."

An embarrassed silence followed. Had she just warned them, or had she issued a threat? Tyrone must have read Flint's mind. "Is it public?" he asked Flint.

"Oh, yes, yes, it'll be in the local papers tomorrow. You're going to hate us for this Ruth, but we really had no choice. Our unit has won the Shadesmoor contract."

"Well." Her mouth set in a tight line. "I hope you make lots of money. You deserve everything you get."

Chapter Seven

York, Jorvik, Eorfwik, Eboracum, the key to northern England sits atop twenty feet of accumulated heritage. Castle Museum, Railway Museum, Yorkshire Museum, Viking Centre, Waxworks, Minster, saints, ghosts, and dead highwaymen suck in tourists by the million. From its atrocities to its odours, the past is re-enacted and re-interpreted for all levels of taste and learning, it can be touched, tasted and bought at every corner. For the historian, the city is the northern Mecca or at least, Babylon.

A free lunch was a free lunch and Flint was keen to go, braving both the A1 and the equally lethal A64 in the green van. He arrived two hours early and spent his time burrowing through secondhand bookshops in Fossgate, Gillygate, Petergate and any other gate he could find. With a couple of bargains swinging from a carrier bag, he met Bob Grimston in a glass roofed tea room facing St Helen's square. Grimston seemed hot in his suit and soon slipped his jacket onto the back of his chair.

"Bloody meetings," he complained. "Bloody councillors."

Outside, tourists sauntered past, enjoying, but also straining to ignore, the buskers. Some munched sandwiches on a pair of benches, unaware that medieval skeletons lay just a few inches below the honey brown paving slabs, and below those, a Roman fortress gate. Relics of the past stood all around, but many more lay deeply hidden.

"What'll you have?" Grimston asked.

Flint fell for an open tuna sandwich, but had more than an eye on an enormous Black Forest gateau which dominated the sweet trolley.

"Tuna sandwich please."

Grimston continued to grip the menu. "Don't piss me around," he said, without looking up.

"Sorry?" Flint was alarmed: what was wrong with tuna? Was it anything to do with killing dolphins?

Grimston glanced up, then withdrew a folded sheet of A4 paper from his jacket pocket. Flint accepted it and read the typed message:

FLINT KNOWS

"So you know," Grimston said.

"Apparently."

"Can I give you some free advice? Don't muck about with this Tom Aitken nonsense. This piece of rubbish came in the post yesterday."

"Do you know who from?"

"Ruth fucking stupid Hauxley – stupid bitch. Have you been messing about with her?"

Say nothing, Jeffrey old son. Flint moved his head ever so gently from side to side.

"Well don't. She's just a stupid kid who had a crush on Tom Aitken. I've got no time for schoolgirl fantasies. Right: bollocking over. Have you decided what you're eating?"

Flint was an archaeologist, not a hard-nosed executive. Bollockings were not forgotten in an instant. His pulse was up and his mind confused.

"Tuna," he repeated, trying to develop a tactic for dealing with Grimston's blunt edge. "Look, forgive me for being interested in Aitken, but archaeology is a small world, we all interact and what affects one, affects us all in some way."

"So?"

"Without over dramatising things, can I ask just one simple question about Tom Aitken?"

"Simple questions suit me."

"How come he was front-runner to win your contract, after he'd spent three years rubbishing the whole Shadesmoor project?"

Grimston's stare was hard, unyielding. "I bought him," he stated after some consideration. "Go on, tell me how shocked you are. I've spent seven years planning this, seven years. Some clever kid in a second-hand jersey wasn't going to beat me, so I made him an offer. Understand? If you can't beat 'em, get 'em on your side."

"Brown paper envelopes stuffed with cash?"

"No, no, that's another Ruth Hauxley fairy story."

Grimston's expression opened up and he twitched up his moustache in a smile. "You people don't see the world in terms of pounds and pence, you have some kind of mission. To you success is so many books published and so many lectures given, right?"

"Right." This was close enough to the truth.

"So let's say you win the Phase II contract. How many years will you be able to spend tripping round the country giving lectures about what we did at Shadesmoor? How many books and magazine articles will you write about what you find?"

"And this was the carrot dangled before Tom Aitken?"

"And he took it."

"So where did the university come in?"

70

"That was face-saving, all round. Me and Tom Aitken had spent three years telling the press that the other one was a complete pillock. Professor Vine agreed to play the broker and peace was made. The deal was that I would give your college the contract, they were to give Aitken a proper job and everyone would have been happy." He gesticulated to the waitress. "One tuna, one ham."

Grimston turned back to Flint with a satisfied smile. He had bought an archaeologist as easy as buying a tuna sandwich. Grimston touched his breast with both hands. "I've put my soul into this project. It's going ahead. They told me I needed an archaeologist, so I got one: I may as well have had Aitken as anyone else. At least it shut him up."

"There would have been other ways of shutting him up."

"Oh yeah, like clouting him with a rock? Bloody Ruth Hauxley again. She's caused us no end of trouble, I've had the police, I've had that cheap tart from the tabloids . . ."

"Not Vikki Corbett?"

"That's her, has she been pestering you? I've told her to stand clear, or my lawyers will nail her tits to the wall."

An unfortunate and sexist choice of words, thought Flint, and probably physically impossible. Vikki had been to visit him at the weekend, but had not mentioned any contact with Grimston: a damning silence. He would need to shunt the reporter firmly out of the scene if Vikki were not going to completely foul up his new appointment.

Grimston continued to grumble about Vikki, then about the police. "Everyone who Tom Aitken had breathed on was interviewed by detectives, but

Ruth Hauxley made things worse for us with her crazy stories. I had to spend half a day at the nick answering stupid questions, and who pays the solicitor's bill? Me.

"The thing that makes me really angry is that my partner got a grilling too. Eleanor Balleron is not the kind of lady who should be smeared by the press, or worried by the police. We're going to have Hauxley for something soon." Bob Grimston smiled the smile of a battered prize fighter. "There, that's Tom Aitken out of the way, so we can bury him now and deal with the job in hand."

For a moment Flint recalled several of the "Battle of Britain" movies he'd seen in which a pilot would walk into the mess and declare "Ginger bought it". The squadron would toast his name, then forget him and get back to the war.

"I can be a bit of a bastard to work with, but don't let it put you off. Treat me right and I'll treat you right. Get me?"

"You're the boss."

"Good attitude. York's a grand place, isn't it?" Grimston looked over his shoulder. "I've been round all the different exhibits, seeing how they do things."

Exhibits? Did he mean the museums, or some of the more downmarket attractions?

"I've been to the States a lot too, looking at what the Yanks do. I take the wife and kids when I can: they just love it all."

The merits of Williamsburg, Jamestown, Busch Gardens and Disneyland were expounded, whilst Flint shook his head and admitted he'd never crossed the Atlantic. "Have you seen my park outside Bridlington?" Grimston continued. "You must come along, I'll get you and your boys free tickets . . ."

"Great." Flint was bewildered, part excited by the opportunity opening up before him, part worried by Grimston's manner and method. Had he too become a tuna sandwich?

The discarded sign on the desk read "University of North Yorkshire Archaeological Field Unit": the title was as catchy as the slow movement of a Mahler symphony. Tyrone had removed the old sign from the door and sellotaped a piece of paper in its stead. From that day the Unit was re-named UNY-DIG.

Later that afternoon, Flint was assisting in the clearance and re-organisation of the UNY-DIG office, which meant scrounging furniture and equipment from elsewhere in the college.

"How was lunch?" Tyrone asked.

"The gateau was superb. Bob and I had a good chinwag about this and that. His ideas for Shadesmoor are eye-opening, really eye-opening. You two should get together sometime: he's a man you could learn things from."

"He's really going to make it big on Shadesmoor – the A1 motorised section is going to bring more people north, then there's the east coast motorway and Leeds is only what, half an hour away?"

"An hour – if I'm driving, half an hour if it's you or Vikki."

Tyrone smirked and presented a provisional list of diggers. Some thirty curriculum vitae had been sifted and Flint had made his final choice. He had the budget for a second excavation assistant and in former times he might have chosen a sensitive, probably attractive, female graduate but Tom Aitken had once had a woman at his right-hand and it had done him no good. Flint's growing wariness led him to opt for "Joss" Wardle, on the grounds that a beefy miner's son from Rotherham was the closest thing to a bodyguard he could hire.

Flint passed back the list. "How is the asset-stripping?"

"Finished, the unit's fully armed and ready for action."

"What are you doing at the weekend?"

"Staying in York, there's a big military vehicle rally on the Knavesmire. Do you want to come?"

"I'm going to Headingley to see England get thrashed by the tourists. In any case, I'm not into war."

"War is history!" Tyrone protested.

"There's history, and history. No thanks, you go and play tanks; pilae and ballistae are quite violent enough for me."

"Bodkins and trebuchets – we're going to have to think medieval from now on, Doc."

"Yes, well, Megan has pointed me towards a gross of medieval references we ought to digest. I'm working my way through it every chance I get."

"What about my thesis?"

"Ah." The vision of 100,000 words of dense Tyronespeak in two blue-bound volumes had begun to haunt Flint's conscience. "I've started it," he lied. "How's our research into Tom Aitken's background proceeding?"

"Oh, I've started it."

Touché, thought Flint. "Vikki hasn't been in touch with you has she?"

"Why?"

"It's just that she's going to lose both of us our jobs unless she stays well clear. This could be the end of a beautiful friendship, if you'll excuse the cliché. The next time she comes grubbing around for facts about Tom Aitken, keep mum and pass her onto me."

"Sure thing, boss."

Flint went back to his office, thinking of the weekend when Vikki had made a surprise foray northwards. He'd assumed she'd wanted to see him, but she'd protested that she was in a "friendly mood" – which meant a walk on the moor, a quiet meal at an obscure country pub, twin beds and strictly no intimate contact.

Now he doubted her motives. He took up the phone and tried to find his wayward friend at home, at her office and on her mobile phone. Which roadside corpse was she posing beside today? Which side of the English Channel offered the deepest deposits of sleaze to excavate and expose? He found her at her Docklands, London, number.

"Oh God, Jeff, what a day!" She sounded very distant.

"Ditto."

"Fancy speaking to *you*! I've tried ringing so many times since the weekend. What about this Welsh woman you're living with?"

"I'm not living with her, not in the biblical sense anyhow. She's my landlady."

"Doctor Megan Preece," Vikki stated with authority. "I've heard interesting things about her."

Flint had no time for catty comments, wanting to get straight to the point. "I need a serious chat, Vikki."

"How serious? I'm on the next flight to Brussels, if you'd rung five minutes later you'd have missed me."

"Okay, straight message, stop messing about on my patch."

Silence.

"You've been stirring up Bob Grimston, who happens to be the man paying my wages."

"Wage slave!" One of his own taunts was flung back.

"Grimston is not a man to mess with. Now, listen Vikki. There may be a story up here, full of sex and lies and gore and money, but I've only just scratched the topsoil on this one. Until I work out what the hell's going on, can you keep your paws out?"

"You know nothing about this case, dimwit!"

"So speaks the girl with fifteen degrees."

"Don't come the intellectual."

"And don't you come back north, unless you leave your reporter costume at home."

Vikki was clearly shaping another stratagem and when she spoke it was to taunt him. "So who did it, professor?"

"I don't know yet. I think there must have been someone controlling Wayne Drabble."

"Well who, clever dick? Was it your mate Grimston who rigged up the whole thing?"

"I don't know – it's possible, he's my favourite suspect so far."

The suggestion was met by a sigh of mocking despair. "Sorry professor, you're wrong. It was Ruth Hauxley."

"Ruth?"

"It's always the girlfriend who does it. I mean, look at her, she's butch, paranoid, bitter, she had all the motives and she was at The Rectory on the night of the murder. She's made up the whole plot and the police are just building up their case before they nab her."

"Did Ruth tell you she was there on the night of the murder?

"No, but my contact did."

Flint was feeling increasingly foolish. "Who? What's he called, your contact?"

"Must go now."

"Vikki!"

"Bye."

"Vikki!"

The phone went dead. Flint swore. After a few moments, he rummaged around his new desk for his telephone book and found the number of the Nissen hut where Ruth worked alone. Vikki's taunts had turned the murder hunt into a bizarre challenge. Academic logic had to triumph over the brute intuition of the gutter press.

"Hello, First Archaeological Services?" Ruth normally used a heavy West Yorkshire accent, but this was banished on the telephone.

"It's Jeffrey Flint here, I'm still grubbing around for facts about Tom Aitken: do you mind?"

"Do I have any choice?"

"I understand that you were at The Rectory when the murder took place."

"No." He could spin out a little line here. "But the police said. . ."

"They're wrong, I was gone by then."

Fact confirmed. Flint congratulated himself and ticked her off his mental list, but where to go from here? He asked her how her work on Form Farm was going, but as she replied, he was thinking of new angles to approach her from. He wished for James Bond's sex appeal to ease his way into her confidence, or at least the bait to lure her into a trap.

He made a few false starts towards arranging a

meeting, but Ruth named plausible-sounding prior engagements and pleaded an imminent deadline for completion of Form Farm. Flint realised she was stalling him, but he held no cards and Ruth called the trumps.

When she put down the phone, Flint was left in deep thought. The good old Yorkshire lass had sounded lonely but not without composure. She'd yielded one piece of information, but he was intrigued less by what she had said, more by how she'd said it. Ruth used a practised RP: what his mother would call a "telephone voice". Some might even call it posh.

Chapter Eight

Move north, the people are friendlier. Flint repeated this mantra over and over again, after finding that he was living in a cultural no-man's-land. The university had no attendant town and recruited refugee scholars from all over the country. Apart from a welcome shortage of public schoolboys and regrettably few overseas students, it could have been any college in England.

Flint was vaguely disappointed in the university library, but the British Library lending division was based at Boston Spa and he could make day trips to Leeds, Bradford, Sheffield or even London if necessary. He shunted open the glass doors, planning a further hunt around the shelves and almost walked into a stout figure concealed behind an impressive pile of books.

"Jeffrey!" Barney looked around his pile. "Well done on the contract, by the way. How is life with the Red Witch?"

"John Wayne," Flint responded. "*Wake of the Red Witch*: know it?"

Barney looked worried, as if he should know the film. He started to shift past Flint.

"I can't say I do."

Flint changed his plans and began to accompany Barney along the corridor. "You know, I don't understand what you've got against Megan, she's bending over backwards for me."

"Interesting posture," Barney puffed, "but not one of her favourites."

"Go on, Barney, tell me. What's all the departmental angst about?"

He shrugged the large, shapeless jacket shoulders and the pile of books lurched dangerously. "You'll learn. Comrade Megan is anything but comradely when she puts her mind to it."

Flint rescued the top two books from the heap and stuck them under his arm after glancing at the titles. "When did she have her fling with the late lamented Tom Aitken?"

The question caused more discomfort. "Megan is a predator, Aitken was another predator, they were a perfect couple. One can imagine them coming home each morning and then comparing conquests over jam and butties. 'How was yours, dear?' 'Who is it tonight, dear?'"

"When, when?"

They turned a corner, stepping around a cleaner, her floor polishing machine and its cable.

"Last year, this year? Who cares. She was all over him on the Easter field trip last year, but I don't know if it was just once, or once a night for six months. Some people never grow up."

"But that's part of the allure of college life, isn't it? We're all just students who won't grow up."

"Some of us might be."

Was there a hint of rue concealed within his words? Barney backed through a door and out under one of the covered walkways which ran towards the Mandela building.

"Have you noticed anything about this walkway?"

Barney switched subjects. "It's built perpendicular to the prevailing wind: it's completely ineffective in winter: your knees get wet if you don't sprint."

Outside, the sun burned the paved courts, with no threat of rain for as far as the forecasters could see. Flint moved the conversation back his way.

"Have you ever bumped into Ruth Hauxley?"

"She's another one of Tom Aitken's women. He deserved to have gone down with one of these dreadful diseases they keep inventing. I don't swallow this burglary idea, you know. My theory is that one of his monstrous regiment of women cracked him over the head when she found out about all the others."

Barney turned around to take the next pair of doors backwards. Flint held them open whilst he negotiated his way into the department.

"I know Aitken had a gregarious reputation, but were there that many women in his life? I've heard the gossip, but could you give me a reliable list? I mean, you were at college with him, you must have known him a bit. I know it sounds weird and voyeuristic, but I need help, I'm the new boy and I need allies to understand what's going on."

The medievalist stopped at the foot of the stairs, his murky eyes growing a little wider at the request. "A list? Of his girlfriends? Yes, I'll try."

That weekend, Flint drove to Leeds, collected his father and took him to the second test at Headingley. It was a throwback to his early teens when his father and his uncle would take the young Flint on the same pilgrimage to see Fred Trueman, and later, Geoffrey Boycott. For a few years he had been proud to be called Jeffrey, and wielded a competent cricket bat until his eyesight grew too bad to see the wicked red ball swinging his way. A couple of decades on, the sun beat down, the beer was warm and England lost three wickets before lunch.

He returned to Megan's cottage on Sunday, taking the back route through undulating farmland that passed as the hills of home. Comrade Megan offered to cook the student standard for dinner: spaghetti bolognaise, well prepared and attractively garnished. It was one step beyond Vikki's scorched beefburgers, microwave chips and frozen peas.

The last rays of the sun came through the kitchen window as Flint sat at the stripped pine table, opposite the stripped pine dresser and the stripped pine spice rack. Megan walked around her quarry tile floor barefoot as she cooked and chattered. Flint found her a little large to be wearing black leggings and his eyes tried to forget that one button too many had been left undone on her baggy denim shirt. She placed the meal before him.

"Delightful." Flint had bought in half a dozen bottles of wine so he could produce one when the moment was right. A bargain bin Lambrusco seemed to fit the occasion.

Megan was not wearing her glasses, bringing more prominence to her tall forehead and revealing sleepy academic hollows around her eyes. Her habitual choice of black mascara added to the weight of her half-closed eyelids. She would close them still further as she listened to him talk, leaning forward, ever forward. Flint poured the third glassful of wine and Megan winced only slightly as she tasted it. "Betty said she'd like to see you tomorrow – she and her husband are off to Hungary for the rest of the summer."

"Lucky Betty, rank has its privileges. She gets Hungary, I get Shadesmoor. Where are you going?"

"I'm staying here: there's no peace when you're the Admissions Tutor. At the end of August I have to sift the wheat from the chaff when the school results are out. It's complete bedlam for four weeks. Meanwhile, I've a paper to finish. It's in German, which is proving a real pig. Then of course, Shadesmoor is my bane too."

"And Barney's doing what? Digging?"

"Barney, digging? Are you mad, that's activity. He'll stay in his grubby little semi all summer and tell everyone he's finishing his book. He's been finishing that book for as long as anyone can remember: you could carbon date the opening pages."

"What's it on?"

"Vikings in the north. Original, huh? His problem is that better scholars than he are turning out papers faster than he can read them. He keeps having to re-write and spends half his time trying to scrounge research grants so he can update his fieldwork. By fieldwork he means jollies to Denmark and Norway. He'll never finish it, and if he does, he'll never find a publisher."

"Is that what's eating him, Megan? Do I detect an academic inferiority complex? He failed law, didn't he?"

"Yes, at Newcastle. I think someone told him that archaeology was easier. Poor Barney." She puffed out her cheeks. "I thought you two were old bosom pals?"

"No, he drifted through CCL when I was doing my doctorate: I think he had a one year fellowship researching something or other."

"Old English poems, I think, or was it Norse sagas? Dead languages are the only thing he proves to be any good at. He botched his Ph.D, you know? Letting him have an M.Phil was very humane."

"Is he pissed off he didn't get my Grade II?"

"Not if he's realistic. Betty doesn't like him because he doesn't pull his weight. We needed a senior Romanist, someone who was published, someone who could give the department a sharper profile: you were the choice. When we discussed what we were going to do after losing Tom, it was Barney who suggested we drag you in as last minute replacement."

"Did he now?"

Megan had a long, leisurely way of eating which Flint found oddly enthralling. She would reach forward her lips and almost suck the bolognaise sauce off the spoon. Did she practice this, he wondered, or was it subconscious?

"You are our murder man, Doctor Flint."

"I'm not a detective . . ."

"We're all detectives and Betty hates the shadiness of Shadesmoor – sorry, that was an awful line, you'll think I'm drunk."

"Let me get this right. Betty recruited me specifically to get to the bottom of Aitken's murder?"

Megan shook her head. "We're encountering tokenism here. Let us define Jeffrey Flint, let us investigate why he was appointed."

"Play," said a voice in his head, "play and learn."

Megan continued her game. "He's young at heart, attractive, radical." She closed her eyes to a slit, as if describing dish of the day at a restaurant. "He wears his reputation like a badge, everyone knows where he's coming from. He's honest . . ."

"No more flattery, please!"

Megan held up her finger in mock rebuke. "Wait!

There is a purpose to this eulogy. You are known to be what you are."

"Tokenism: you were right."

"Academia is a bitchy world and the Shadesmoor project is arousing so much jealousy and adverse comment. People are accusing the department of selling out. Betty helped form the advisory committee. I'm on that committee and you're digging our holes. The only person without soil on his hands is Barney; there are no Vikings up there."

"No Romans either," Flint said.

"Oh sod the Romans, boring fascists. You weren't hired because you know how to run an orgy, you were hired because you are what you are."

Flint now saw his role clearly. "So, Shadesmoor has this dodgy public relations problem, made worse by Tom Aitken's untimely end. But if the team includes bold, noble, Jeffrey Flint, he who is pure of heart . . .?"

"We're clean."

"What utter drivel," he said. "Sorry, no offence."

Megan pursed her lips to summon a further thrust in the intellectual fencing, but the spell of the Red Witch was broken by the telephone. Saved by the bell. She slipped from her chair and darted from the room.

As he listened to her voice echoing from the hall, Flint tried to understand Megan's part in the Tom Aitken saga, then Megan as a human being: Red Witch, Welsh slag, Admissions Tutor, indulgent landlady and Reader in Medieval Archaeology. She had been very cool, hardly wincing when she mentioned replacing Tom Aitken, yet they had been lovers (according to Barney). Was her remorse too deeply hidden, or had Barney simply opened a bout

85

of departmental in-fighting? The autumn term could prove awkward if he was unable to correctly judge the political climate.

"It's for you," Megan announced after a full minute's conversation. Her mood seemed to have altered. Flint was slightly puzzled as he took up the phone.

"You seem to be settling in nicely," Vikki's voice carried a familiar sharp edge.

"Yes, well, Megan is being . . . she's putting up with my idiosyncrasies."

Flint had one eye on his landlady, who winked at him from long distance. His pulse quickened.

"I thought I ought to let her know about a few of your habits."

"What habits? No, don't! Vikki, be reasonable. I'm a refugee, this is a refuge."

"Oh, yeah? I hear some pretty funny stories in my job, so I'll believe you, for today. When are you moving out? You said something about buying a house."

"It's early days, Vikki, things are complex up here and growing worse by the hour."

"Have you found the elusive lead yet?"

"I'm not looking for leads – and nor are you."

"It's a boring old crime anyway," Vikki retorted. "Who cares if a randy archaeologist is bumped off by his jealous girlfriend?"

"That's your theory and you're sticking to it?"

"It's plausible. Things like that happen every day, DON'T THEY?" Her voice swelled to ram home the point.

Megan was eagerly pouring out the dregs of the wine. Flint felt as if his head were in a vice, being screwed from two opposite directions.

"Look, you coming up soon?" he asked.

"Mmm, might be. I'll let you know."

"Bye then."

"Sleep tight. Mind the Welsh don't bite."

Flint made a deep, thoughtful, sucking sound with his lips to ease his anxiety as he replaced the phone. Vikki had never been heavily possessive, so why was her intuition suddenly working overtime? He'd have to dream up something special for her next visit. Pity she didn't like cricket. He paced thoughtfully back into the kitchen.

"Now, where were we?" Megan asked.

"Washing up, I think."

"There's more wine."

He rubbed his duodenum. "No, that rubbish I bought is wreaking merry hell down here."

She nodded, soon covering up with a smile. Close one, there Jeffrey, close one. Vikki might know more than she was letting on. Was it the black widow spider that invited males to her lair, then devoured them?

Chapter Nine

The university had been planned around a series of courts, some grassed, some paved and some landscaped with flowerbeds and benches. Professor Betty Vine walked slowly, gently deriding a twenty foot high, matt red metallic structure constructed at the centre of one of the courts. It resembled a crumpled paper dart which had struck the ground vertically.

"And we awarded him a Masters Degree." She shook her head. "I sometimes think we give them away. I had a good chat with Tyrone Drake yesterday, he was telling me about his thesis."

Ah, the thesis, yes, he must read it. Flint's conscience pricked him again.

"What is it called again?" she asked.

"'De-Romanisation in fourth and fifth century Britain'; he's got some novel ideas."

"Yes he has. I find him a strange choice for your assistant. He doesn't quite fit the mould for an archaeologist."

"Roman generals who rode into Rome in triumph would have a slave standing in the chariot beside them. As the crowds cheered, the slave would whisper, 'Remember thou art mortal'. That's Tyrone's role, he's my devil's advocate, he keeps my feet on the ground."

They left the court and entered an underpass. "Are you still researching urnfields in Hungary?" Flint knew that she was, but thought it polite to show interest.

Betty gave a slow affirmation. "Yes, after twenty years the work is still not finished; I often feel it never will be."

"Oh, you'll outlive us all."

"As I grow older, I realise I know less and less."

"That's rather like me and Shadesmoor. I thought I understood the whole affair when I first arrived, but it's simply exploding in all directions."

"Complications, complications," Betty said.

"Can I ask you an honest question?"

"Please do. This will be your last chance for a while."

"Was I recruited simply to put a gloss on the Tom Aitken affair?"

Betty stopped walking. "No."

"But you and the Shadesmoor people worked a face-saving deal to stop Aitken leading the protest movement."

"It was a *fait accompli*. We could no longer oppose the scheme, so I hoped that by forming the Academic Advisory Committee we could at least influence the plans and deflect some of the more tasteless ideas."

"Money changed hands?"

Betty put her hands together and almost gave a clap of delight. "No money changed hands, you have my solemn word. We won the contract, but that was only thanks to you and Tyrone. Now promise me something: you won't upset them, will you?"

Flint shrugged. "I'm just a pawn in this game. I'm a hired hand, I do as I'm told."

"That's m'boy. Keep out of trouble and let the police hunt murder suspects."

Betty bade him farewell for the summer, then walked on towards the car park. When she was out of site, Flint sprinted back to the Mandela building and up the stairs to the departmental office. The younger, blonder, more buxom of the two secretaries wanted everyone to call her Debs.

"Debs, can you remember the big hoo-hah when the police were here in April?"

"I won't forget it."

"Right, cast your mind back. Who was asking the questions?"

"Oh, there was a whole group of them."

"Ever watch cop shows on the box? There's always some wise-cracking detective who says something like 'if you hear anything, here's my number'."

Debs blinked, then turned towards her desk diary, flicking back towards April. Flint leaned over her shoulder, noticed how low-cut her pink top was, and tried to keep his eyes firmly on the diary. Megan and Vikki were conspiring to warp his mind.

The secretary hummed through pages looking for a name and a date. "Ah," she said after a few moments. "I knew it were here. Detective Inspector Simon Thorne and here's his number. The code is Northallerton."

Flint took out his pen and jotted down name and number, although he had already memorised both.

Warm and sticky beer was fit for a warm and sticky night. The following evening, Tyrone and Flint wedged themselves into a corner at The Green Man Free House, Urethorpe. Some happy coincidence meant that their investigations into the past normally involved a sequence of meetings in pubs and restaurants.

The detective did not look like a detective. D.I. Simon Thorne was a carrot-headed man of Flint's age, a little too plump for his ivory open-necked shirt and a little too tense as he peered around darts players' armpits to find the archaeologists.

"Doctor Flint?"

Thorne produced a ten pound note, obviously acquainted with the tradition whereby the detective lubricates his contact before squeezing out the information. Three pints of Castle Eden Ale soon stood beside the two half-empty glasses. Flint knew little about the career structure of the police force, but estimated that Thorne could not have been a Detective Inspector for more than a year or so.

"So," the policeman clasped both his hands together on the table edge and twiddled his thumbs. "You have information about the Aitken murder."

"I want to do a deal," Flint said.

"Go on."

"I want an information swap; what I know, in exchange for what you know."

"Sorry mate," Thorne sat back.

"We've done this before," Tyrone chipped in. "We're sort of freelance private investigators."

"Oh no – amateur sleuths! I thought you people died out with the steam engine."

"Come on, give us a break – what if I told you the wrong person is in custody?"

"So who should we have?"

Flint had planned to lure the policeman onto his own ground. "Ruth Hauxley: she had the motive and the opportunity to commit the murder."

Thorne shook his head. "No, sorry, we know

91

Wayne Drabble was at the Aitken house on the night of the murder."

"Have you got fingerprints?" Tyrone asked.

"Forensic," was his reply.

"But I've spoken to Drabble. He was set up," Flint said.

"That's a cock-and-bull story that wouldn't fool the station cat. Mysterious upper class women don't telephone third-rate villains like Wayne Drabble and he isn't part of an art smuggling ring."

"Ruth Hauxley says he was paid to kill Aitken."

The policeman held up his hands, "Drabble isn't the only one who can make up stories."

"So you think she's lying."

"Look, I won't say she's lying, but let's say she watches the wrong kind of TV programmes. Murders are usually very simple, lads, and this one is simple too. An old lag thought he'd found a way of getting rich quick and broke into The Rectory. The owner disturbed him and Drabble grabbed the first thing that came to hand."

"His jemmy, or his torch?"

"No, that rock."

"But Wayne's no killer."

"It was a panic reaction, all over in moments."

"Suppose Ruth is your mysterious 'posh' woman, faking the whole story in order to have someone to frame. She was there on the night of the murder, she admitted as much to me."

Thorne nodded, perhaps without knowing. His eyes carried a glitter of interest. "Go on, tell me the rest of it."

Flint and Tyrone had composed a number of stories, and one made more sense than most, one which could be rehearsed in front of Thorne to produce a reaction. "Okay, Ruth lived with Aitken for two years, then fell out with him: let's say he dumped her for another woman. She planned to kill him, asked around and found Wayne Drabble's name. Wayne was sold the fairy story about the torc, turned up at The Rectory only to find the body. Ruth had been there earlier to see Aitken and killed him when his back was turned."

"Have you any proof?"

"The alarm was turned off when Wayne arrived."

"And?"

"Presumably she used the hand-axe correctly, point first. Wayne wouldn't necessarily have recognised it as a weapon. We performed a reconstruction when we were up at The Rectory."

It was Tyrone's turn to colour the story. "I think the killer stood in the alcove behind the door. She could have hit Aitken as he walked towards the desk."

"How did you know where he fell?" the detective asked with interest. "Did Miss Hauxley tell you?"

"No, we guessed: were we right?"

"Are you sure she didn't tell you?" Thorne pressed the question, confirming that the guess was close to the mark. "I ask, because she wouldn't have known where the body lay. What else do you know?"

"Well, there's the use of the Form Farm torc as bait for Wayne Drabble. Ruth worked on Form Farm, in fact she's still writing it up. How many other people are familiar with it? There was one press article, and that is as far as the publicity went: the darned thing isn't even on display yet. It's not an obvious alibi for what you call a third-rate villain."

"That's just supposition."

"Okay, let's look at probabilities: domestic murders are far more common than murders during robberies," Flint stated. "More people are killed by acquaintances than by strangers, so statistics are on Wayne Drabble's side. Ruth regards herself as the unrecognised Mrs Aitken but he was a notorious rake: we've traced half-a-dozen former girlfriends."

"And we've traced half a dozen more." Thorne raised the stakes on behalf of the police. "You could pin the jealous lover tag on several of them."

"But Ruth had another reason to kill Aitken," Tyrone objected. "He sold out over Shadesmoor, and Ruth hates the project."

"Don't bring Shadesmoor into this," Thorne shook his head, a pained expression on his face.

"Lawyers?"

He raised a hand six inches above his head. "And Miss Hauxley is causing merry hell."

"With the freaky letters?"

"What freaky letters?"

So Grimston had not shown his letter to the police.

"What letters?" the policeman repeated.

"That's what I can trade with you," Flint was gambling now. "I mean, who else but the killer is going to send cryptic letters?"

"Who's received these letters?"

"Bob Grimston – just the one as far as I know, but don't for the life of you tell him that I told you!" Flint explained what the typed note had contained. "Grimston left it screwed up in an ash tray."

"It's probably a crank." The detective leaned forward, both his hands clenched together in a ball. "Look, I don't know what you two want out of all this, but I want to crack this case."

"Isn't there a great big team of detectives thrown at every murder?" Tyrone asked.

"There's fifteen of us working under the Super, different teams looking at different parts of the case. Ruth Hauxley is mine."

Warmer and warmer, thought Flint, sensing how excited the policeman was at the prospect of a dramatic solution of the case. "She was at The Rectory, wasn't she?"

"It mustn't go beyond this table," Thorne confided. "We have independent evidence that Ruth Hauxley was at the house on the night of the murder, but she denied it at first, when we interviewed her. She said it had to be someone else, some other woman."

"Did she say which other woman?"

Thorne nodded, clearly keeping the secret to himself. He licked his beer-tinged lips and broke into a smile. "The age of the amateur sleuth is dead; the lone copper can't make his mark any more, unless he takes risks. Do you know, we've taken eight hundred statements and cross-checked them all?"

"And you've got the wrong man."

"My Super has got the wrong man; I can sense it, I know there's something else going on."

"So you're going to pin it on Ruth?"

"You might be amateurs, but you've latched onto the same track as me. That's sort of comforting."

"Circular reinforcement," Flint said.

"Come again?"

Flint supposed that Vikki had somehow extracted the detective's suspicions and presented them as her own. By a circular process this had then become his own firm conviction. He in turn was now pressing the recycled idea back onto D.I. Thorne. It had to be bad science.

"Your forensic evidence must give you some clues. Our labs back in London can do wonders with a two thousand year old corpse; you guys must be able to do better with a body that's fresh."

Thorne became increasingly incautious. His lust for fast promotion ran strong. "Miss Hauxley's prints were everywhere."

"On the bloody flint?" Tyrone asked. "Sorry for the pun, doc."

Jeffrey Flint smiled at the play on words.

"Sadly, the rock was clean. The other knock we've taken is that a leading professor of forensic science tells us that Ruth is too short to have killed Tom Aitken. His lab reports were clear, the blow came from above. Wayne Drabble happened to be just about the right height to have done the job."

"If she'd kneed him in the goolies, height wouldn't matter," Tyrone said. "It had to have been Ruth; if she's told you one lie, she's probably making it all up." Tyrone continued expanding the hypothesis. "So, either you lock her in a cell and beat her into confessing, or you try and entrap her."

"We're not allowed to do either of those."

"But we are," Tyrone said.

"I never heard that." The policeman looked around the room.

A few moments pause followed, filled immediately by a din of gossip, clanking beermugs, the clunk of darts and raucous cheers from the players.

"Seriously lads, if we don't play by the book, the defence lawyers will kill us in court."

"But if we can set something up," Tyrone said. "You could surround us with squad cars and pounce at the critical moment."

Flint looked at Tyrone, questioning his idea, but D.I. Thorne seemed in the throes of indecision.

"We're on the inside, so to speak." Flint added

tentative support for Tyrone's enthusiasm. Something had come into his mind as the pint glass had become emptier. It all revolved around that alcove, and relative heights. His mind verged on the photographic. Now he mentally re-read the titles of the books on the top shelf. He had a null hypothesis and knew how it could be tested.

"What I need is a lever," Thorne said. "If Miss Hauxley makes one little mistake, one contradiction, we're halfway to a confession. That's how we solve most murders; the villain makes a daft mistake, we trip him up and then the truth comes out, bit by bit."

"I know how we can do it," Flint stated quietly.

"Will it screw up my case?"

"No, it shouldn't. It's just a way of giving you that lever. I don't think it would produce new evidence, but might give you the moral ascendancy."

"She mustn't suspect we're after her."

"Ruth's paranoid, she thinks everyone is after her."

Thorne sat back on his stool, rocking it on two legs, the image of fiery confidence. "This case is going cold," he said. "My Super is going to court to convict the wrong man and he's going to get egg on his face. Drabble's lawyer is a sneaky cow and we don't have the evidence to make the murder charge stick."

"So you have to act fast," Tyrone said. "Or Drabble walks free. Ruth walks free and you guys end up looking stupid."

"Maybe." The detective stood up to leave. "I'd better shoot off. Allow me to sleep on this, I'll ring you tomorrow. If this goes wrong, the Super gets my badge." He pointed at the beer glasses now crowding the table top. "I hope neither of you will be driving?"

Once he had gone, lecturer and assistant pondered empty glasses and a clouded future. A trap had to be sprung, then a site had to be surveyed.

Chapter Ten

Three miles of red cones marked the twisting lanes of a contraflow. Tyrone impatiently tapped the wheel of his Spitfire as they crawled along in the traffic queue. Flint composed a little ditty and recited aloud:

> "The A1 is a splendid road,
> we all have come to love it,
> I wish I had an aeroplane,
> so I could fly above it."

His student passed him a questioning glance. Flint had no qualms about appearing cranky and strived to keep one step ahead of his reputation.

Ruth had mentioned that she was cataloguing Aitken's library so it could be sold. The morning after the meeting at The Green Man, Flint had telephoned Ruth to express interest in buying a few titles. He'd mentioned a couple of out of print volumes in which he was interested, only later realising how expensive the ruse might turn out to be.

"I'm running out of petrol," Tyrone moaned.

This was his habitual cry and Flint, as usual, dipped into his own back pocket when they pulled into a service station just behind the First Archaeological

Services Land Rover. Ruth Hauxley paused by the door as she went to pay at the kiosk for her own petrol.

"I've got to drive the Form Farm stuff down to York afterwards," she explained. "You don't get far on a tank of petrol in one of these things. I'll see you at the house."

Flint noticed the large brass crucifixes which dangled from her ear lobes. Those artifacts would long linger in his mind.

"Sorry to put you to this trouble – I'll buy you lunch sometime," he said.

"That would be great."

Yes. Ruth did own a smile. For a moment, Flint felt guilty about the entrapment, but murder was too ugly to overlook, even in his most liberal of moods. He needed a clear field, free from the doubts that a murderess was stalking his project. He needed to remove the claims of culpability which had been flung at Bob Grimston before he could work for such a man. He needed to satisfy the confidence that Betty, Megan and Barney placed in his abilities and, most of all, he longed to beat Vikki at her own game.

Ruth smiled again as she returned to her Land Rover.

"Got her in our sights," Tyrone said, petrol pump in hand.

"Yes, but we've not got *her* yet, she's a clever girl, our Ruth. She's not going to fall into our clutches without a struggle."

The Land Rover left a minute or two before them, but once on the lanes, Tyrone soon caught it up. It was the last Friday of July, the last weekend before UNY-DIG made its debut excavation. The sun blistered the landscape and, ahead of them, Shadesmoor bore the scars of drought. Grey smoke hung in the windless sky above Urethorpe. Some thousand feet above the earth it met an inversion layer and was swept sideways, creating a curious L-shaped pall. "Look North," on the BBC, had carried variations on the same story each day that week, a wildfire on one heath or another. Today, it was the turn of Shadesmoor.

Ruth parked in the drive of The Old Rectory. Tyrone deliberately boxed in the gateway before he and Flint dismounted. An innocuous blue Rover had been seen loitering in the car park of The Green Man Public House. Thorne should be in position.

"Hope this doesn't put you out," Flint repeated his concern while walking down the drive.

"I was coming out here anyway," Ruth explained. "There's a box of Form Farm material in the shed."

"I bet you're happy it wasn't a kiln site." Tyrone said.

"Why?"

"Think of the pottery: Form Five from Form Farm, it would make lectures tricky."

"Aha." Ruth gave a faint acknowledgement of Tyrone's clumsy humour.

Flint noticed there were now three estate agents' signs cluttering the front garden. He paused to buy time. "Still having trouble?"

"Say 'murder' and people want thirty thousand pounds knocked off the price."

"What's it going for now?"

"A hundred and fifty-five. Fancy it?"

"It's a little out of my range."

"The book's in the study."

They followed her through the front door of The Old Rectory. She put one key from her keyring into the study door and unlocked it. Flint tried to stall her once more, walking to the French windows and discussing the garden, suggesting she have the lawn mowed to make it more attractive.

Ruth glanced over her shoulder at a noise from inside the house. Flint's pulse increased.

"Books, books," he said, "mustn't keep you."

"So, what are you after again?"

"Ah, Mortimer Wheeler – *Stanwix Report*." He looked up at the top shelf. "And, yes, Curle – the *Newstead Report*."

She glanced up at the maroon book jacket. "That book's pretty rare now, isn't it?"

"Expensive?"

"We can work something out."

Flint found himself talking to cover his own nerves. "I must read up on the northern frontier, I've been too long down south. Let me have a look and we'll talk prices."

Ruth was used to being ordered to fetch and carry. She turned into the alcove behind the door and drew out the footstool. Raised nine inches, she stretched for Sir Mortimer Wheeler's report on the excavation of the Iron Age hill fort at Stanwix.

Flint tried to control his trembling. Perched on that stool, Ruth would have been in a perfect position to deal the killing blow. He felt vindicated, no longer guilty about his deception.

Ruth pulled out the thicker, heavier copy of Curle's *Newstead Report*.

"When we were here the other day," Flint began,

with Ruth still airborne, "Tyrone and I tried to re-enact the crime."

"What?" she asked, clearly outraged.

Flint strode to the centre of the room. "Pretend I'm Tom Aitken and Tyrone is the burglar."

"This is disgusting."

Tyrone pretended to cosh Flint and he buckled to the floor. After playing dead for five seconds, he rolled to his knees. "Now, our demonstration has proved that Wayne Drabble could not have killed . . ."

"Tom was over here," Ruth said, pointing down at her feet. "You know nothing about it, Jeffrey Flint."

The study door shot open and D.I. Thorne strode in, almost a caricature of the parlour scene detective.

"'Allo, Ruth," he began, in an imperious voice that quavered at the edges. "Would you like to explain how you know where the body lay?"

Flint cursed, the entry had been too soon, off cue.

Thorne nodded towards the footstool. "We wondered why the stool was found in that position after the murder. Perhaps you could explain it for us . . ."

"Shadesmoor," she murmured. "You all work for Shadesmoor now."

"I have to caution you . . ." D.I. Thorne began the familiar line, but the combined force of John Curle and Sir Mortimer Wheeler cut him short. Five hundred pages of hardbacked archaeology caught him on the side of the temple. Ruth swung the books with two-handed force and the policeman collapsed against the desk, then rolled floorwards, entangled in an anglepoise.

Flint was still on his knees, Tyrone was the far side of the sofa and Ruth was out of the door, pulling it closed behind her. It was locked before Tyrone reached it. Flint crawled over to where the detective was now rising to his knees, holding his head.

"Will you live?"

D.I. Thorne groaned affirmation. Tyrone pulled at the door, then ran towards the French windows, which were still nailed closed. He kicked half a dozen times before the repair splintered, a pane broke and the doors swung open. Flint followed Tyrone, with the dazed policeman last. An engine revved noisily as they ran around the building.

"She can't get past my car!" Tyrone shouted over his shoulder.

Ruth had no need to. She engaged four-wheel drive and made straight for Tyrone as he sprinted down the path towards her. He skidded to a halt, then ducked behind the corner of the house. Flint ran into him and the pair were farcically sprawling on the ground as the Land Rover gained speed. It swung across the yard, through the hedge and into the cow pasture. The ground was hard and Ruth was heading downhill.

The policeman cursed and took the lead in chasing the retreating vehicle. Tyrone and Flint disentangled themselves, then ran the opposite way towards the Spitfire.

"We'll get her!" Tyrone said, vaulting over the door. "She doesn't stand a chance of getting away in that old bucket."

Flint copied his student, landing rather awkwardly in his seat. He pulled an OS map out of the glove compartment and by the time Tyrone had turned the car around, he had his bearings.

"A lane runs behind that field and comes into the village just below the pub."

Scattering pats of dried cow dung, they reached the pub before Ruth did. Tyrone threw the Spitfire around the bend and Flint closed his eyes. He hoped the chase would be mercifully short, but imagined the Spitfire ending up on its back in a ditch, its wheels still spinning in the air. His eyes avoided the rushing hedges to either side and fell on the white road marked on the map. It described a half-loop around the top of the village and rejoined the yellow line marking the main lane. Thereafter it climbed towards Shadesmoor.

When they rejoined the lane, having travelled almost in a circle, Ruth was still out of sight, but they had seen the point where she had charged the stunted hedgerow to escape from the cow pasture. Tyrone hit fifty before Flint shrieked. A red Fiesta swerved out of their way and an overhanging branch whipped Flint's protruding elbow.

The sun was lost from view as they entered the pyre of the grouse moors. Blue smoke was on the air, stinging the nostrils. Smoke banks would come and go as the road twisted upwards. Then came a junction.

"Minor road, left!" Flint guessed. If he were Ruth, he'd head for the smoke and a snaking lane where speed was no advantage.

"There she is!"

For one moment, a green back door could be seen around a bend, then a fine curtain of smoke shrouded the view. In another moment, it was as though they had burst onto another world. The top of the moors was revealed as an undulating patchwork of browns, with a sheer wall of grey rising a mile to the left. Running imps of flame could be seen darting into and out of the smoke. With a fitful wind, the fire was its own master, wandering the moor at will.

The Land Rover roof could be seen above dry-stone walls, only a few hundred yards ahead, snaking back and forth around the bends. Then the road straightened. One foolhardy white car pulled out of a side road, but Tyrone streaked past, two-tone klaxon blaring. Flint's map was caught in the slipstream and torn from his grip. He watched it flutter over a wall and vanish.

The distance had halved. Flint saw the needle strike 70 and wondered what Tyrone would do when he brought himself level with one ton of wayward Land Rover. Ruth obviously saw them coming, the brake lights on the green vehicle suddenly flashed on.

"Oh, she's not!" Tyrone said.

Only fifty yards away, the Land Rover swung across the road, then bumped over the grassy kerb, bounced out of a ditch, then began to labour painfully towards the smoke.

The Spitfire left a long streak of black rubber on the tarmac, and Flint found his nose only inches from the dashboard as Tyrone jammed the brakes on hard. Straightening himself, he saw his student was grinning.

"Come on Doc."

Two men on foot darted after the receding Land Rover.

"She can't get far!" Tyrone shouted, "She'll bog down in no time."

Ruth was making little more progress than her two pursuers. As they ran, she was reversing to avoid some obstacle. Then the wind freshened, tongues of flame leaped higher on the slopes and the world became a rolling cloudbank.

"She's crazy!" Tyrone said.

"We know that."

The sirens of fire engines could be heard somewhere behind them. Both men stood, hands on hips, weighing risks and advantages.

"Are these fires dangerous?" Tyrone asked.

"Only if you run about in them – I can't remember anyone ever being killed," Flint broke into a cough. "Until now."

The wind shifted and for a moment they savoured clear air. Ruth's Land Rover could be seen again. It had passed one isolated clump of burning heather and was heading towards a coomb, the roof of which was a coiled dome worked in blues and greys. After they had jogged another hundred yards in pursuit, the vehicle was seen to stop, then cant over onto one side. A moment later, the breeze shifted again, blowing hot in their faces and sweeping the scene from sight. A dry-stone wall seemed to offer shelter so Flint rested his hand upon it, his eyes watering. Minutes ticked by, and with each shift of the wind, a regiment of little red flames could be seen, advancing, halting, then running forward again, like the Duke of York's army.

An unexpected, hollow roar fixed their attention on the coomb. A ball of yellow flame burst from the feeble flickers amongst the heather and forced its way into the sky. Black, oily smoke followed.

Groans came to both throats at once and Flint

recalled one of his last sights of Ruth, dutifully filling her Land Rover's petrol tanks for the drive to York. The petrol had sent her rather further than she had planned.

Chapter Eleven

Scarred black, with grey-white bands of ash, Shades-moor smouldered under a haze of idle smoke. The big fire had moved on then expired, leaving tiny rearguard actions to be fought in clumps of heather or gorse. Firemen took second place to a cordon of police keeping the ghoulish back from the buckled metal spider that had once been the FAS Land Rover.

Flint and Tyrone had returned the following morning, to be kept back at the tape by policemen in their shirtsleeves. The ground was still warm beneath their feet. D.I. Thorne noticed them there and led them closer to the scene of the tragedy. What had pretended to be a shallow coomb in the side of the moor was revealed as a sharp-sided ravine some forty feet deep. The Land Rover had rolled or fallen down the side and landed on its roof.

"She's burned to a crisp," Thorne said. "It's right horrible. We'll never identify her."

"Teeth?" Flint asked.

Thorne grimaced. "Aye, teeth, but hardly owt else. The fire was burning all night and they only got to her an hour ago."

Men in blue boiler suits fussed around the cremated remains.

"Was she still in the car?"

"Yes, poor cow."

Flint had been hoping that Ruth had made a miraculous escape. Murderesses deserved at least a trial and a humane sentence: burning sinners alive had been abandoned in the Middle Ages, as to be demonstrated in a holographic display at the Shadesmoor Centre. Somehow, the passage of five hundred years turned unspeakable agony into acceptable public entertainment. He remembered the crucifix earrings, and mentioned them.

"We'll be asking her parents along to identify her possessions: she wore quite a bit of jewellery, that should make it easy."

Thorne's right cheek was puffier and redder than normal and his eye had swollen. "I've had a bit of a hard time with the Super this morning, but I think I've talked him round to our way of thinking. It's obvious now that Drabble was telling the truth about the 'posh' woman, and the 'posh' woman was Ruth."

Flint nodded, lost in personal recrimination. If only the policeman had been more alert, this could have been avoided.

"So every cloud of smoke has a silver lining: presumably Wayne will be out on bail?"

"No way – he stays inside for breaking his parole. We can still stick the burglary on him."

Flint's introspection was suddenly erased by the sight of two figures. One was an Indian woman taking photographs of the scene. Directing her was a smaller, more familiar, figure in toffee-brown skirt and jacket, with incongruous yellow wellington boots smeared by drifting ash. The figure saw him and began to slowly make her way towards him, struggling to step over the tussocks of blackened heather, her eyes invisible behind sunglasses as black as Whitby jet.

"Hello, Jeff," Vikki said, not removing the glasses, not revealing her thoughts. Her lips were painted a purple shade, her jaw locked into a defiant pose.

He took her firmly by the arm. "I need a drink," was all he could say.

Vikki drove a silent Jeffrey Flint away from smouldering Shadesmoor to the calm of The Green Man, Urethorpe. The barman greeted them and commented on the soot. Flint ordered a pint of Conqueror Ale.

"What do you want, Vikki?"

"Gin and tonic."

"You can't come into a Free House in Yorkshire and drink G and Ts."

Vikki nodded. "Okay, slimline bitter lemon."

He despaired, and made the order.

"You're chatty today," Vikki said, as he chose his corner by the dart board.

"I'm avoiding saying anything I'd regret."

"So let's talk regrets."

"Like?"

"Like I don't know why I put up with the procession of women who float into your life."

Flint had been composing an attack, but was thrown onto the defensive.

"You're not denying anything," she stated.

"Should I? What's all this about?"

"You still haven't told me what went on in Greece, with the luscious Lisa. You still haven't explained about Tania."

"Hang on, I don't have to explain anything. Just like you don't have to explain your lunches with the

111

editor of the Daily Scum or your jaunts to Brussels
to meet the Euro-prats."

"I want to know what's going on between you and
Megan Preece."

"Nothing. And I want to know what the hell you're
doing up here." Got her! Switched the tables, now
he could play the injured party. "What are you
doing out on the moor, taking pictures, stomping
around . . ."

"It's my job, I was sent here."

"I read that crime is on the increase; this can't be
the only murder case in Britain."

"I had a lead."

"And look where it got us! Okay, so you were
right, Ruth probably rigged up the whole event,
but did she deserve to die? No, not like that. If
you hadn't prodded me, I could have kept out of
things."

"Don't blame me."

"Who do I blame then?"

"It was your dumb idea to try and trap her, you
chased her into that fire."

"Look. Yesterday, in Brixton, a four-year-old child
was strangled by its nanny. Now, isn't that gruesome
enough for you? Why don't you go and interview the
parents, get a few pictures of the corpse . . ."

Two thirds of a pint of 'Conqueror Ale' splashed
across the front of his glasses. Flint was blinded, and
soaked from fringe to crotch. He shrieked aloud.

"There you are! Real ale! Get your Welsh tart to
lick it off!"

Vikki swept out of the pub, perhaps out of his
life. A dozen faces stared at Flint, someone giggled,
but most fell silent. A bar towel was thrown in his
direction, then the hubbub resumed. Flint wiped his

glasses, so could at least see how many people were laughing at him. He dabbed at his beard, gave up on his shirt, then limped to the Gents to find a gross of paper towels.

Urethorpe was, in many senses, the middle of nowhere. Vikki had marooned him at The Green Man. Tyrone had been abandoned on the moor, and could be anywhere. Flint hung around the bar, accosting those people jangling car keys, making five attempts at bumming a lift. People were suspicious of this man whose beard stank of beer and whose clothes were stained by ash. A young couple in a GTi finally gave him a ride as far as a transport café near the A1 and, running out of alternatives, he telephoned Megan.

His landlady drove up some twenty minutes later. She was behind the wheel of one of those nondescript small hatchbacks, which Flint found impossible to distinguish on grounds of typology.

"Jeffrey, my dear, what a crisis! Come on home – the shower's working again."

Shower, yes, great. He counted the minutes until he was home. Get out the ash and rinse off the beer (no assistance required). He hung his head beneath the feeble jet until water ran from his nose and his beard spouted a waterfall. He had always known that a gulf existed between himself and Vikki, but now realised how wide it was. He could never become part of her world: she peddled a new form of pornography which disgusted him.

"Have you eaten?" The singsong Welsh voice came from behind the door.

"No," he bubbled through the waterfall.

"Is Indian food okay?"

113

"Wonderful – I'll bring down a crate of wine."

With luck, she wouldn't throw it at him.

Dinner came, as did the bottle of Merlot, as did the bottle of Chilean Chardonnay, as did the soft looks and the not-so-subtle hints. Vikki had gone, Vikki had never existed. Flint was a man of the world, wasn't he? He was a no sentiment, no strings, freewheeling romantic. He was a perpetual student, a college rake, a campus lecher, wasn't that the way Vikki read his character? It was time he lived up to the act.

Megan had fallen into the corner of her settee, laughing at one of his oldest digger's tales.

"I've had a bad, bad day," he said, falling next to her.

"Make it better," she mumbled.

"Ample" was a word he might use to describe Megan. Pretty no, shapely, no, ample, yes. He let his head fall onto her shoulder. "I'm not being very professional now," he said.

She pulled him tighter. "So you're an amateur?"

For half an hour he'd known exactly where he was going to place his hand. "No," he said. "I am NOT an amateur."

"Goodie, goodie."

Flint let out a long groan. It was a groan of satisfaction, a groan of exhaustion, it was a what-the-hell-am-I-doing-here sort of groan.

Megan's bedroom had a pink ceiling – he'd seen a lot of that since dawn. She also had ivory pillows, with co-ordinated rose trim. He'd seen a fair amount of that too.

He rolled away from her and looked at the clock – ten forty-five. A time machine had whisked him back a dozen years to the mornings-after of college parties. He didn't do this kind of thing any more. He was out of practice.

A hand placed itself in the centre of his back. This would complicate college life enormously and he was not quite sure he even liked Megan. Like Everest, she had just been there.

"Shall I make breakfast?" He asked.

"Make love, make lunch, it's a free world."

He rolled onto his back again and she lurched onto his chest. Her limp white skin was damp with perspiration. Without her glasses, without her clothes, Megan looked even older than he'd remembered her. He began to feel stronger pangs of guilt.

"One favour," she said, touching his lips with her finger.

"I'm in your power."

"Don't say anything at college about this."

"I'm past bragging in the tea room."

"Good. I just don't want people to get the wrong impression. Don't assume anything, will you? Don't think you're moving in permanently."

This was getting better by the moment. "No. I won't assume anything."

"You see, I can't be owned. I can't have any man thinking he owns me."

"Property is theft."

"Yeah. Sorry, but I've had men around, I've been married, I don't need the aggro. No strings, right? Sorry, that sounded so swinging sixties didn't it?" Megan swallowed heavily.

The silence needed filling by something.

"Lunch?"

"No." She gripped him. "It's too early for lunch."

Another groan, this one silent. She was right.

Lunch came around in due course. Megan chattered almost nonstop, nervously, as if she was embarrassed. And why not? Flint was embarrassed. Bungle a stakeout, smash a friendship, make a fool of himself in a pub, hitch-hike halfway across the county, put away a bottle of wine and round off the day by seducing the landlady three and a half times. Okay, perhaps she had seduced him and it may have been only two and a half, but he was still embarrassed.

Sex and death had always walked hand in hand, perhaps Megan too, had been reacting to the moorland tragedy. It had, after all, put the lid on the death of Tom Aitken. Perhaps she had needed the excuse to come out of mourning, if she had ever mourned. Perhaps she was rediscovering her sexuality after her affair with Aitken. Flint had not yet tried to understand Megan, and maybe he never would. Modern life had become too complex and he wanted to escape. He'd make his excuses like a gentleman, he'd start looking earnestly for a new place to stay. He would go to Shadesmoor Castle, take out his rusty old trowel and dig his way back to the Middle Ages.

Chapter Twelve

Diggers were loosely distributed in a semicircle as Doctor Flint strode into the inner bailey of Shadesmoor Castle. There was no formality and most of the youngsters remained seated on the stump of the old bakehouse wall. The unit director's eyes ran over the motley bunch: two supervisors on inadequate salaries, eight UNY students on subsistence allowance, four over-forties unpaid volunteers, two Americans paying their way.

Down below was his concession to the age of the petrol engine – Carl had sold the green van to the university unit at a "good price": it was the closest most archaeologists come to a company car.

Shadesmoor Phase I had seemed an awesome task on paper but, from the battlements of the castle, even paper plans looked optimistic. Flint would have to lead from the front if the contract was going to be fulfilled.

Grimston's proposed prostitution of the castle would require every square metre to be surveyed and photographed. Phase I would consist of a preliminary survey, giving details (and costs) of what archaeological work needed to be performed before the project could see its monstrous birth.

The photographer and the sharpest surveyor shouldered their equipment and sauntered off towards the keep to record the standing structure. Tyrone chose the prettiest three female students and went down to survey a suspected area of earthworks in the meadow where the million-pound rides would stand. He'd taken the two Americans on the flimsy pretext that he would be "training" them. Joss from Rotherham, with five experienced diggers, would sink a series of small test trenches within the inner Bailey. Flint would be taking the remainder down to the manor house. By Tyrone's reckoning, the whole team would be able to re-group after four weeks and assault the castle ditches.

Conflicting emotions accompanied Flint in his short drive to the manor. As he handed out surveying tapes and ranging rods, he asked himself whether the project had been worth two lives. Next, he asked himself whether it had in fact cost two lives, given that Ruth Hauxley's motives would remain unknown indefinitely. Flint focused on the word sex, with a presumption that some kind of pathological jealousy had prompted the plot. Aitken had been a determined womaniser, thriving on ephemeral conquests, but Ruth struck him as someone who would have desired a solid relationship. He would have to ask Megan if he could catch her at a vulnerable moment. A little colour came to his cheeks.

"Are you all right, Doctor?" one of the volunteers asked.

"Yes, yes. I didn't get much sleep last night."

Sex, yes. The sheer boredom of archaeological excavation can be assuaged by liberal doses of sex, alcohol, coffee or roll-your-own fags. Stick a dozen students in a campsite miles from civilisation and there is little else to do. Sex, yes. It took his mind off the immolation of Ruth Hauxley. He repeatedly tossed his trowel in his hand as he daydreamed, seated on a wall beside the bird garden.

"Doctor Flint!"

Blonde hair had been coiffured into a clubbed 1920s style and the blue-green eyes smiled down at him. She was gorgeous, and his mind focussed more strongly on sex.

"Hello, I'm Eleanor Balleron." The horse was tall, slim and chestnut. The rider was equally slim, equally well groomed, wearing a well developed suntan to set off her jodhpurs and wide-necked, white blouse. She wore no hat.

"I was told you wanted to speak with me." Eleanor dismounted and gave her horse a pat. "I'm sorry we haven't been able to meet before."

"We have now." He stood up and checked for dirt before he shook hands.

"Welcome to my home. I'm sorry I've been away in Antigua – travelling can be so tiresome."

The trowel, inscribed with the monogram "JSF" slid back into the pocket of his cut-down jeans.

"Perhaps you would like to show me around – have you found any gold yet?"

Why does everyone ask the same question? "Not yet," he replied with tact. "We're still laying out our survey grids. I wanted to ask you about your garden."

"May I show you around, or have you seen everything?"

"Please, I'd love a tour." Flint had seen everything he could, but the company of the enchanting lady of the manor could not be, indeed should not be, passed up.

The manor had been begun at the end of the

119

seventeenth century, but most of the extant building had been the responsibility of Eleanor's great-great-grandfather, and so it had been completed in the Victorian style. Its front was asymmetrical, the main entrance being in a three storeyed, crenellated structure to the left. The other half of the frontage was older, less mock Gothic, two storeyed with a sloping slate roof feeding sad, eroded gargoyles.

"Anything you're not intending touching, we can leave alone," Flint said. "I've got the architect's plans and I think I can follow them."

Eleanor led her horse around the Restoration south wing. Flint was as another willing beast, equally tethered. He listened with care to the husky words speaking gently of generations past.

"I don't know anything about architecture," she confessed, having made clumsy attempts to explain the various improvements and additions to the building by her ancestors.

Flint sometimes found it comforting to be in the company of someone who was not an expert in one field or another. That was what had drawn him towards Vikki. What was Eleanor saying?

Eleanor had called a lad who had emerged from the stable block. He took the horse away and she thanked him. He called her ma'am; it was very feudal but, oddly, did not seem out of place. A certain strand of English gentry has been bred to merge with the country in a way that city-born plebeians like Flint never could.

The public was now admitted to the south side of the house. A dozen parents and children queued for ice creams at a courtyard kiosk and beyond was the turnstile leading into the bird garden.

"This was the manor farm?" Flint asked. "And it's all being changed?"

"Yes: it's a little . . ." She looked back at the barn, shabbily converted to deal in ice cream. "It's a little cheap. All the barns and stables will become apartments."

Flint tapped the cobbled courtyard. "This coming up?"

"I hope not, but we're having a fountain put in the centre."

"Okay, well that's a watching brief for Phase II."

"A what?"

"Watching brief: when your contractors turn up to dig out the cobblestones, one of my team stands and watches what they're doing, and stops them if they find anything important."

"Oh," Eleanor frowned, perhaps worried by the word "stops", but not saying so. She led on, past the turnstile and into the bird garden. A concrete path, cracked in places, weaved between a succession of cages and wire-fronted enclosures. Trees and shrubs attempted to add a natural feel, but Shadesmoor was too wild in winter to support extensive exotic plant life.

"Are you keeping the birds?"

"For a few years. I quite like the birds, but they don't make very much money."

"Does any of it?"

She smiled. "Keep to the digging; don't involve yourself in money."

"Money's not something that's ever interested me."

"Nor me."

Ah, thought Flint, there is a difference between not having to worry about money and not having any money to worry about. He stopped and remarked on the flamingoes: exotic birds caged in pampered security. A little like Eleanor, it seemed to him.

"We might have to dig up your croquet lawn."

"Of course, I hate the game."

"And the extension to the manor will mean we ought to check this end of the formal gardens. We don't know how far north the original manor buildings went."

"Just dig where you like – where you have to."

"Will do."

"I say, I'm clearing a dinner date at the end of the month. It won't be much, just ten or twelve of us. I'd be very pleased if you could come."

"Black tie?" Flint asked cautiously. Where would he find a dinner suit?

"No, no, I hate too much formality, wear what you like."

He spread his hands and drew attention down to his fraying denims and the "I love Napoleon" T-shirt.

When she smiled she revealed a perfect set of teeth. "Not that informal: you do own a suit?"

"Yes, of course. Please excuse the scruffy togs: it's a kind of digger's uniform, it bonds us together and we can recognise each other in a crowd."

"I say, I ought to leave you to your digging. I hope I haven't wasted too much of your time."

"No, not at all. Any time, delighted."

As Eleanor walked back towards the manor, Flint knew he had meant what he said.

It was high season for tourists at Shadesmoor. As Flint moved between groups of his workers, he made a mental note of visitor numbers: up to half a dozen coaches per day, a hundred cars at weekends less in midweek. People would make straight for the castle, spend twenty minutes looking for something of interest or climbing the keep. Next they would head for the bird gardens, the ice cream kiosk and picnic area by the river. That was the Shadesmoor experience as he remembered it from childhood, down to the perfect blue bowl of sky and the simmering, sweet-smelling pastures. The memory was as a painting suspended in a dusty gallery; the picture remained unchanged as the building crumbled around it. Shadesmoor Castle, and its estate, was crumbling through lack of money. Flint knew that it could not survive unchanged but Bob Grimston would transform it beyond recognition.

Joss Wardle was a big lad with rampant brown hair which dangled well down his shoulders. His roughly shaved, piggy face would often snort good humoured curses and his store of excavation anecdotes was unrivalled. Joss had graduated from UNY five years before, when it was still a polytechnic, and he'd never managed to find employment for longer than six months in a row. He and Tyrone did not make a good double act; arch socialist and arch Tory respectively. Flint often thought of people in a historical context. Were this 1916, Joss would have made a good NCO, down in the trenches with the pals' battalions, inspiring the lads by hard work. Tyrone, on the other hand, would have been quite happy back at headquarters, sticking flags in maps and masterminding the whole show by clever, callous paperwork. The diggers heard Flint refer to him as "Biggles" and the nickname stuck.

Joss soon made a mattock-swinging impression on the castle interior, cutting away square areas of turf to expose the foundations of buildings. Away by

123

the river, Tyrone directed his chosen women with military precision. One was English and she soon demanded to join Flint's team, complaining bitterly about the way "Biggles" treated her. The American pair stuck with Tyrone and Flint was impressed by the results. What the lad lacked in compassion, he made up for in attention to detail.

Bob Grimston dropped by on the first Wednesday, hands on hips, always ready with questions concerning how much, how long and how significant. He gave Joss a cigar, and won a friend. He let Tyrone demonstrate his computer, and won another. He would take Flint aside and let him into some confidence about how the plans were progressing. The archaeologist would nod, and agree and file this tactic away as a good managerial tool. Bob would lay a hand on his shoulder and let Flint in on the conspiracy. Flint felt part of the team and even his cynicism began to wane.

Once he had managed to separate Joss and Tyrone, Flint found he loved every minute on site. Excavation and discovery was his life and he wouldn't swap it for any of Grimston's millions. Eleanor would visit almost every day. Sometimes she would be with "someone she knew" (male, female or a couple). Sometimes she would be walking her Dalmatian, sometimes riding her gelding. Tyrone was always embarrassingly civil; Joss would try to pull her leg, which seemed to unsettle her. The diggers secretly referred to her as "Lady Godiva", but the director was at her beck and call. This was her land, Flint would explain in response to knowing looks, and Eleanor was paying the bills.

After a week of spade work, he was able to lead the lady of the manor around three long, shallow scars which radiated away from the manor house and ruined the croquet pitch. He pointed out the lines of walls, marking earlier plans of the house and its outbuildings. Eleanor crouched beside an area of tiled floor whilst Flint told her of the guesses made at its date and function (kitchen? eighteenth century?).

"And when you're finished?" she asked.

"We start again."

Eleanor frowned deeply and revealed her true age: more forty-four than the apparent thirty-four. "You're going to take a long time?"

"It's a big site. It looks like there are three phases of manor house here, and probably at least five major phases of castle construction. Come round the front and I'll show you something really exciting."

A short cut led through the formal garden and across the access road which led up the hill. One of the oaks which lined the road had been felled and Flint leaped up onto its stump.

"See down there," he pointed to the meadow by the river.

Eleanor held out a hand and he hoisted her beside him, thrilling at the soft and graceful touch. Her perfume had to be as expensive as it was powerful.

"See those people of mine?"

She covered her eyes to discern Tyrone and an American girl.

"The orange tripod supports what we call an EDM, they're using it to record slight differences in the level of the meadow."

"If they're slight, why measure them?"

"Perhaps I should have said 'subtle'. A bump a few centimetres high might be the only sign that there's a structure concealed beneath the soil. As it happens, I think we've found what looks like your DMV."

"Pardon?"

"Deserted Medieval Village. Four or five hundred years ago, landowners found they could get more money from sheep than from people, so the peasants were simply evicted. The records we have put your DMV over on the west side of the stream."

He pointed to beyond the area doomed to be the main car park. "It's early days, but Tyrone thinks the village was actually in the meadow east of the stream. It's possible the stream line has moved since the last records were made."

Eleanor was helped down, "You must think me ever so stupid, I really don't know anything about archaeology." She paused, looking hesitant. "Is what you have found *important?*"

"Possibly, one never knows. We've got another seven weeks to find out."

"But if there's a whole village under the low meadow, how long would it take you to dig it out?"

Flint winced at her terminology, thinking that DMVs were not bodkin arrowheads to be plucked at the earliest opportunity.

"Wharram Percy took two decades to excavate."

"You're joking."

He wished he was, and when Flint saw her expression collapse, he immediately saw the extent of problems ahead. He'd hoped the archaeological work was planned to embellish the project, and give Bob Grimston something to boast about before a skeptical world. True, Bob had a keen interest in the past, but it was interest with a cash limit. At that moment Flint became convinced he was being employed as a surgeon, cutting out unwanted barbs from the flesh of the theme park. He wondered how deep Tom Aitken had been prepared to cut.

Chapter Thirteen

Castles no longer protected the realm from attack. Flint turned at the sound of the low-pitched whistle. Green woodland led up through a cleft in the moors, and it was from this cleft that a dot descended, skimming the trees, drooping below the skyline. Too slowly, it seemed, the dark green jet whined along the line of the river, with another a hundred yards on its tail. Once at the bridge, the first oddly distended aircraft flipped its wings almost vertical, displaying its egg-like engines atop the fuselage. Incredibly agile, it swooped around the manor, around the castle and vanished into the next coomb. A moment later it was followed by its wingman.

"A10s!" Tyrone said, straining for a better view. "Look at 'em turn!"

"Waste of bloody money," Joss remarked, watching with equal interest.

"You've got air cover," Flint said to Eleanor as she stood beside the portakabin. "Makes you feel safe, eh?"

"They frighten the horses," she replied, not noticing his irony.

"Come into the command bunker," Flint said, keeping the conversation in theme and mounting the steps into the grey hut.

Eleanor's feet grated on the grime-streaked floor

and she looked around at the dangling rolls of plans which were costing her thousands of pounds to produce. Flint hoped she'd see value for money. The plans meant nothing to her, so Eleanor ran a thumb down the line of postcards affixed by the window by masking tape.

One was of a Viking Longship. It was from Barney, in Denmark, apparently engaged in field-work, despite whatever Megan might have said about his lethargy. Another was of two killer whales breaking surface, from Tania. Flint's favourite ex-student was diving on a shipwreck off Vancouver Island.

"Are these all from archaeologists?" Eleanor asked.

"Most."

"It must be fascinating to travel."

"Haven't you just come back from Antigua?"

"Oh that. It's not the same," she shook her head. "It must be quite fun, all camping together by the river."

"Ah, I must admit, I've chickened out on the camping. Rank has its privileges."

Flint immediately regretted what he'd just said. Had he just destroyed his rugged down-to-earth appeal?

Eleanor poked a finger into a tray of washed late medieval pottery. "This is all very interesting. It feels like I'm . . ."

"Touching the past?"

"Yes."

"Careful – it's addictive."

"Once, Tom . . ." she began, then stopped herself.

"Tom Aitken?" Flint latched on to the word immediately.

Nervously flicking eyelashes gave away Eleanor's

regret at having mentioned the name. "Yes, he once said that, about excavating being addictive."

"Wasn't he a thorn in the side of the project?"

"Only at first, at the end he was on our side." A gold wristwatch was checked, almost too fast for Eleanor to have read the time. "People for lunch." She winced. "Tiresome people."

From the door of the Portakabin, Flint watched her stride off with purpose down towards the manor. Eleanor had of course been the "posh" woman that Ruth had intended to frame. The thought of Ruth chilled the warm glow he'd enjoyed whilst showing Eleanor the pottery. The following day, he would be called to give evidence at the inquest.

When Flint testified he stated he had last seen Ruth Hauxley alive when she had charged past them in her Land Rover. He supported the story told by Tyrone and by D.I. Thorne that Ruth had been chased to the moor where her vehicle had overturned and caught fire. She had been alone and nobody had been seen to escape the fire. Opinion was expressed that the human remains had been too badly burned for easy identification, but her jewellery and personal effects enabled the blackened fragments of bone to be identified as the mortal remains of Ruth Hauxley. No foul play was suspected, no *post mortem* had been requested and the Coroner returned a verdict of misadventure.

A few days later, the act of cremation was completed at a municipal cemetary in Halifax. Flint was driven there by guilt and hoped to hide amongst the mourners in order to avoid accusing eyes from family and friends. He had half expected a guard of honour from her Civil War Regiment, as had apparently attended Tom Aitken's funeral, but all shunned the burial. Two of her friends, a couple of former colleagues and six of her family barely filled a pew. Ruth was mourned by the press, by television, by rubbernecking townsfolk and by a watchful D.I. Thorne. Vikki Corbett was over the far side of the crematorium chapel, but did not once glance in Flint's direction. A relationship was also buried that day.

Flint returned to Megan's cottage in a state of gloom. In theory, the life of a middle-ranking lecturer is a life of ease, but he felt emotionally, physically and intellectually overstretched by the drama, and by his obligations. He wanted to be on site every day: that was what archaeology was all about, prizing the past from the soil. Even when he came back to the cottage at night, there were courses to prepare, Tyrone's thesis to mark and he had to complete his background reading on Shadesmoor Castle.

In her wide-hipped jeans and home-knit canary cardigan, Megan was clearing away supper and talking Medieval sources. "I can let you have anything you want."

Flint assumed she was still talking Shadesmoor. His domestic arrangements had taken a strange turn. Megan would make no show of affection and accept no sign of possession. Both suited Flint completely as he could return neither. Megan was happy to discuss him moving out and would push the weekly property press under his nose, even drive out with him to give instant pronouncement on whether a house was suitable. Some nights she would ask him if he wanted a game of Scrabble. On two or three other occasions, using the same tone of voice and same depth of intimacy, he would be invited to her room. He had always thought of himself as amoral, but never this amoral. Perhaps it was the simplicity of casual sex which appealed to him.

"Do you know about the ghost of Margaret de Balleron?" Megan asked, tea towel in hand.

"Unfortunately, yes; she's appearing to order as a hologram."

"I'm consultant on the costume – medieval women, see: that's where being an expert gets you. Poor old Margaret was murdered by her husband: he caught her astride his groom, half strangled the poor girl and pushed her down the well. It was the price of liberation in 1478 and the husband walked away scot free; that's feudalism for you."

"It seems to be the only thing that ever happened at the castle."

"Apart from the civil war siege, but that only lasted five days; they have some kind of pageant there every year. I've never been, it's perishing bleak up there in November."

"Ruth Hauxley was involved in that last year, apparently. So too was Tom Aitken. Did he never try to drag you into the civil war fanatics?"

"Not my scene."

As Tom Aitken had been mentioned, it was perhaps time to trawl. "Can I be very insensitive and very personal for a moment?"

She ceased wiping and leant back against the stainless steel drainer. "I've been expecting this – go on, be insensitive."

"Call me a nosy blighter, but I've heard all sorts of stories linking you and Tom."

Megan looked across at her blue china collection, giving each plate a few moments consideration before she decided to reply. "Oh, it was last year, he taught

132

our Excavation Processes course in the spring term. We both went on the Easter field trip to Whitby and became friendly."

"A little like you and I?"

Very deliberately, she said "No."

Meaning what, that emotions ran deeper? That the affair was more than an alternative to Scrabble?

"Oh," said Flint.

"You are rather like him, has anyone ever told you?"

"I thought he was big, butch and macho?"

"Well, he was. He was rather rougher than you, and rather more conventional."

"We're talking bedrooms here?"

"Aha," she confirmed, her face defiantly asserting her right to be so candid.

Flint felt the blood rising to his cheeks at the thought that he was being compared.

"Tom wasn't a sex maniac," Megan continued, "but he liked the company of women, and he liked to keep himself intact."

"Emotionally intact?"

"Exactly. He used the word 'love' as a lubricant, without any idea of commitment. He was the archetypal womaniser."

"And that's how he and I are similar?"

"I'm not being judgmental, you're honest and you don't pretend."

"But he did, and he hurt you, didn't he?"

Now it was the quarry tiled floor that received her scrutiny. "It's no secret, all college knows. I fell for the whole act like I was still an undergraduate, we girls never learn."

"Who did he move onto next?"

"Anyone who came along. I was silly to blame him, of course, I'm an old hag, he was the Yorkshire super-stud, what could I expect?"

"Do you think Ruth felt the same way?"

"Dear Ruth, always trying to be one of the boys. I felt so sorry for her, he used her cruelly."

If only Megan knew what Ruth's opinion of her had been, she might not use the words "dear Ruth". Or, on second thoughts, perhaps she would.

"Was there ever any hint that she might kill him? Did she ever threaten you, or Tom?"

"No, one day her nerves must simply have snapped. Everyone has their limits. Some women always expect too much of men."

Flint had to nod in agreement, amazed at the brazen manner in which Megan could disregard her own role in the tragedy.

"What do you fancy doing now?" she asked quickly.

"The fifth century beckons – I'm only a third of the way through Tyrone's bloated thesis. He's done a hatchet job on the origins of the King Arthur myth and I want to check how many of the ideas are his own."

"You can't want to work again, it's too late for bloody Romans."

"Owt on the box?"

"Is there ever?"

He sighed, looking at her tired academic eyes, her age lines, her dyed hair and her appealing mouth. For a moment, a different image came to him, a model of the English damsel on horseback, a woman who inhabited a different universe from his. Megan had inclined her head in a highly suggestive manner.

"I'm not in the mood for Scrabble," she added.

Neither was he. The vision of Eleanor faded and Megan was waiting for a reply. This is your world, Jeffrey, he thought, better make the best of it.

Sinning for recreation matched sinning for a living. The Reverend Peter Bright and Mrs Augusta Dawson knew nothing of how Flint spent his nights, but cast damning words on how he spent his days. The weather had broken and a fine rain fell over Shadesmoor, ending the drought and bringing relief to the tortured grouse moors. Flint walked briskly away from the manor, with the spindly Reverend on one side and the matronly woman on the other. Well-spoken criticism was being directed at him from two angles. In the distance, he could see Tyrone approaching downhill from the castle, giving him an excuse to be impolite and feign pressing business.

"Look!" He turned, displaying his impatience. "I'm very busy."

"But people say you're someone who listens," the Reverend pleaded.

"They say you are the sort who would oppose this abomination," the woman added.

Flint had been bombarded with mail and phone calls from half a dozen groups with objections to the project. This pair represented one of the factions.

"It's over," Flint said. "The protesting is over."

"Yes, Tom Aitken sold all our souls to Mammon," the Reverend retorted.

"We relied on that man, don't you know?" The woman echoed the dismay. "We gave him all our information, they let him chair the Action Group and then what did he say at the public enquiry?"

"That he thought it was a jolly good thing," Flint said dryly. Yes, that had worried him too, but he was damned and jobless if he admitted it.

"He must have been bribed: have you been bribed?" Mrs Dawson continued.

"I'm only doing my job," was a better answer than "yes".

"That's what the Nazis said," she continued. "They were only following orders, and look where that led them."

"Look. If I resign, another archaeologist pops up in my place. We're like Space Invaders – there's an inexhaustible supply of us out there. You can't stop the project, so learn to live with it. Talk nicely to Bob Grimston and perhaps you'll be able to have some input."

"Bob Grimston, Bob Grimston!" The Reverend displayed a distinct lack of Christian charity. "A showman, a slum landlord, a mean hearted land-grabber. Do you know he's wormed his way onto half the committees in the county? He's buying his way into favour, he's poison . . ."

"Excuse me."

Tyrone was shouting to attract attention, giving Flint the perfect excuse to break away. He had been unsettled by the jibes, but this was modern archaeology; he who pays the digger calls the tune.

"Doc," Tyrone panted, "Someone's taken the EDM."

This was the apparatus with which Tyrone and his Americans were surveying the lower meadow. Flint asked, "Are you sure?" and "Have you checked?" and other obvious questions.

"It's gone!" Tyrone repeated. "The hut's been burgled."

Flint had no need to feign urgency. He ignored the two protesters and broke into a jog.

"Anything else taken?", he panted.

"I dunno," Tyrone panted back.

The Portakabin rested in the car park just below the castle walls. Tyrone paused on its steps and pointed to the splintered plywood around the door frame.

"Who was here first?"

"I was," Joss replied from within. "Bastards did it in the night."

Joss made liberal use of the word "bastard" as Flint looked around the hut. It had been perfunctorily ransacked. He was looking for a large, plastic, art folder which held the site plans.

"Where is the plan case?" Flint asked, kicking the side of the desk.

"It were down here last night," Joss said. "Bastards must've took it."

"It's sabotage, it's sabotage," Tyrone kept repeating.

Flint nodded, glumly. "If this is Phase I, Phase II is not going to be easy."

"Any ideas who the bastards are?" Joss asked, as Flint took up the mobile phone.

"Well, there are two suspects at the bottom of the hill, but I don't think burglary is quite their style."

He tapped in Bob Grimston's ex-directory phone number. The millionaire owned a house in the leafy northern fringes of Leeds and could be at the castle in little more than half an hour.

When Grimston arrived, and had been told the news in more detail, he was far from amused. "How much did it cost?" he asked, "Was it insured?"

137

Flint was sitting on the desk, Tyrone at his side, literally backing him up.

"The EDM was insured," Tyrone said.

"But the cost is beside the point," Flint said wearily. "They took one of the plan folders. That's about three weeks work by our castle team down the drain."

Bob blasphemed and shot an angry glance out at the rain.

"All my work's safe," Tyrone said. "The survey was input onto my laptop computer and I always take it home."

"I'm glad to see someone's thinking straight. Well Flint, you'd better get more people up here and do it again: we can't let the twats screw up our schedule. I'll see about a dog patrol."

"No, please, that's not the way we do things."

"It's the way I do things."

"Look, we'll move the diggers' camp up here, then someone will always be around. We'll organise a rota and have one person sleep in here each night."

"But can you trust your people?" Grimston pointed a finger at Tyrone. "Are there any clotheads who think this sort of thing is funny?"

Tyrone shook a nervous head. Like Flint, he was unused to discipline.

"You haven't received any threats have you?" Grimston asked.

"Who from?"

"The Action Group, Historical Society, Archaeological Society, Civil War Society, Friends of the flipping Trees; the hills are full of nutters, take your pick. I heard that you had visitors this morning."

Grimston was always well informed. Possibly the gateman owned keener eyes and carried a sharper

138

brief than would be expected. Flint nudged the conversation off balance. "This isn't a popular project, is it?"

"Ask the kids in Leeds, or Sheffield, or Hull – they think it's amazing. There's only a few clotheads who live in the past who want this castle to be left to fall down and the estate to go to ruin. Forget them, and don't mess with them. The future is ours."

Bob made for the door, then turned. "Sort out this shambles today and keep in touch. You're coming up to dinner on Saturday – it means you can meet some more of my people. Have it all squared before then."

Grimston allowed no discussion, or dissent. "Oh, Tyrone. I'd like you to come to lunch, meet me at twelve in front of the manor."

No choice was offered. Orders had been issued. Flint closed the door on Grimston, and the rain. "Lunch, eh? I hope you brought your best frock."

"I've got some clean stuff in the car."

"Watch him, kid."

"It's just lunch, okay? You're going to the banquet at the manor. I wasn't invited to that. You could have asked me along as your guest."

"I'm escorting Doctor Evans along."

"Old Megan? Everyone says she's after you."

Flint flinched in discomfort. "Who is everyone?"

Tyrone poked a thumb out of the window, presumably indicating the digging team.

Such gossip had to be squashed immediately, if two reputations were not to be compromised. "Doctor Evans is a very capable medievalist – she's helping me sort out my tyggs from my tythes. She's also advising this set of jokers, although I don't think Bob Grimston takes advice from anyone."

The way Tyrone put his tongue into one cheek revealed he believed none of Flint's plea of defence.

"Right!" Flint re-asserted his control. "From now on, ensure no original material is kept on site – duplicate everything. I also want you to re-open all the enquiry files."

"Tom Aitken?"

Flint nodded. "We've got another motive, and another suspect."

"Who?"

"A thief would have nicked the EDM, but not the plans. Lots of people out there want to sink this project. At least one of them is prepared to take things too far."

Chapter Fourteen

An addition of £3,500 to the UNY-DIG budget bought the services of four more circuit diggers and paid for the hire of a new EDM. Eleanor was "taking a break" and not back until the Thursday before the promised dinner at the manor. The August Bank Holiday drew near and, as tradition demanded, the forecast was for rain.

Flint could feel Phase II closer to his grasp. The project was beginning to excite him, he was becoming attached to his team, his Portakabin and his castle. A book was already written, mentally at least, and he had begun to idly plan lectures with a medieval slant. Ideas began to form about the way his data could be displayed and interpreted; ideas that Bob Grimston would surely leap at.

Joss was tapping data into the computer, with Flint watching over his shoulder. A rat-tat at the Portakabin door sent his pulse leaping. It might be Eleanor, she was due back, she would surely want to come up and see the progress.

The door had swelled in the rain and opened with a heavy creak. Around it came a hand, then a familiar, flabby round face.

"Jeffrey old bean!"

"Hello, Barney," said Flint, not hiding his disappointment. "How were the fleshpots of Denmark?"

"Fleshy and potty."

Lucky dog, thought Flint. "So what are you doing here? Come to volunteer, we need every trowel we can muster."

"No fear, no way. I'm just being a tourist, you won't find me on your chain gang. I mean, Good Lord, this is the first decent day this week, the weather's been filthy. How do you boys stand it?"

"We were brung up tough," Joss intoned, then gave a deep guttural laugh.

Barney flinched just slightly. "I say, if you're not busy, could you show a fellow student around your site? Say no, you must have a hundred things to do."

What Flint had planned to do was hang around the hut looking busy in the hope that Eleanor would drop by. Instead, he obliged and led Barney on a site tour. Just to rub home how squalid excavation could be, he began with a walk to the Low Meadow. What had been hard ground in June now squelched underfoot and the line of the old stream was clearly visible as a snaking puddle. Tyrone slopped towards them, with dark-haired Loretta waving hello from behind the new EDM.

"Tyrone always chooses the pretty ones," Flint observed.

Tyrone was no longer easily needled. "He thinks pretty students are his prerogative, that right Doc? Where is Tania these days?"

Flint deserved this riposte. "Diving off Vancouver when last heard of, why?"

"I want her whole underwater team out here: aqualungs, flippers, shark knives, flotation bags, everything."

"Is it that bad?"

142

"No, I just thought you might want an excuse to call Tania."

"Who's Tania?" Barney asked.

"Don't ask," Flint replied, annoyed at being teased about the Canadian student. She'd only sent him a postcard, dammit.

Tyrone grew bored of the game. "If we work Monday, we'll be finished on schedule."

"Isn't it a bank holiday?" Barney objected.

"It is," Flint said, "but this is the cutting edge of contract archaeology; we stop for nothing; not holidays, not weather, not sabotage."

"Sabotage?"

Barney was always the last to hear gossip. Flint told Tyrone to blow his whistle and he'd explain the saga over tea.

On Saturday evening, Megan called heads, the reproduction Cross Ha'penny fell with the face of King Edward uppermost, and Flint ended up driving to the Manor.

"This mustn't look too domestic," she had warned.

"Perish the thought."

Two BMWs, one Jaguar, a white Mercedes sports car and a green Vauxhall van stood outside the manor. The green van had a greater mileage than all the other vehicles combined. Tyrone had suggested a new colour scheme, but all Flint had allowed him to paint was the unit logo in white on each door. This was a clenched fist holding aloft a trowel, rather like an AK-47 on a revolutionary banner. The letters UNY-DIG were stencilled below.

Flint had attended a pair of brief meetings within Shadesmoor manor and found it an unloved, undistinguished place. Only one suit of armour stood in

143

the hall, and this was incomplete. Oil paintings of eminent and obscure members of the Balleron family were badly cracked and called out for a clean. Two spaces on the oak panelling revealed where paintings had been removed, possibly sold. Flint the leveller had always approved of swinging death duties on the estates of the rich, but Flint the protector of national heritage found the consequences distressing. Eleanor Balleron's motives in so earnestly embracing the theme park became clear.

Megan's library had given Flint a sketch of the Balleron family. The castle itself had been founded by a Norman knight, Jules de Balleron, during the "harrying of the north" which followed the Battle of Hastings. That line had long since died out and the estate had changed owners on several occasions. The castle had been slighted at the end of the Civil War and the manor constructed in its stead. In 1914, the estate had been owned by a branch of the von Lissel family: wealthy German textile merchants. In a fit of grief, Eleanor's great-grandfather had changed the family name to Balleron after his eldest son (her grandfather) was killed in the retreat from Mons.

Eleanor welcomed Flint graciously, with a soft, patrician handshake. The colour of her dress was a deep crimson, its high, buttoned collar only serving to heighten her exquisite neck. She had arrived back from her holiday with a shorter hairstyle and a fresh selection of scents. Flint took the gentle hand, self-conscious in his suit, unable to escape the impression that despite the haircut and freshly trimmed beard, he was still the beggar at the feast.

The summer dining room was modest, oak-panelled and could seat perhaps twenty around a visibly worn, long table. Eight guests were ranged down each side,

Eleanor taking place of honour with her back to the window. To right and left sat Bob Grimston and his wife, who had found a "little black number" that seemed a little too little. Megan sat beside Grimston in a dress she'd made herself, its fabric an English jungle of cornflowers and poppies. Flint sat opposite, paying little attention to the rest of the crowd: a lawyer, Hugh Thurlscote and one of Grimston's thrusting young underlings, both with their wives firmly in tow.

Doctors Flint and Preece were very much on show. Grimston enthused about the project, the lawyer would often add the names of people who were "happy" about it, the thrusting young man would use jargon like "projections" and "cash flow". Mrs Grimston began to talk shopping and Eleanor woke up from the trance which had settled upon her whilst finance was being discussed. Salmon en croute followed broccoli and walnut soup and arrived to a hubbub of polite delight. Whilst Flint's tongue treasured the dish, the women hatched a conspiracy to bring horses into the conversation.

"Do you hunt?" Eleanor asked Flint, when the topic was at its height.

"I went on a hunt once," he said cautiously, not revealing that he had been the one with the aerosol and the balaclava.

"So you ride?" asked the lawyer's wife.

"Camels, seaside donkeys and the odd horse."

"Camels?"

Flint found his cue to steer chat away from the slaughter of furry mammals and trotted out his standard digger's yarn about an expedition to Jordan. The women nodded politely. Megan cut across with a few comments, but the men seemed bored and soon switched back to talking money (and its proper disposal).

TiramiSu was a desert Flint had always skipped in favour of heavy gateaux or profiteroles. His education had improved with every course. Quality wines glugged into glasses on all sides and he regretted losing the toss to Megan. Then again, perhaps he was better with his wits unimpaired by drink.

"I can't make you archaeology boys out," Grimston said, his merriment improving with each glass of wine. "We've had a few round here and I must have met a hundred during the planning of this project, but honestly, you don't have a clue."

"How do you mean?" Megan asked.

Flint had heard her use that knife-edge tone before. He was sober and hoped Megan wouldn't launch into one of her tirades. Grimston waved his glass and continued to generalise.

"All your energy goes into whingeing and whining, stabbing each other in the back. It's a cut-throat world you're in."

"It's because there's not enough money," Flint stated. "Everyone scrabbles for what there is and everyone ends up under resourced. Projects are rushed, sites are incompletely excavated, other sites are never published, post-excavation research is neglected. It's easy for a rival academic to stick his dagger into your work because you can never do a subject justice."

"So my project is your golden opportunity, right?"

"Our budget is heavily constrained . . ."

"That's it with your bunch, never satisfied! You academics have no concept of schedules or deadlines, or budgets, or management. You all live in cloud-cuckoo land." He smiled at Megan, "Most of you."

146

Flint said nothing, his silence had been bought. Perhaps he should have stayed in London. Encounters with drunks asleep in doorways and punks shouting abuse on the tube suddenly acquired nostalgia status.

"But I like your lad Tyrone," Grimston continued. "He's got his head screwed on right – for a southerner. You're a Leeds lad, aren't you Flint?"

"Aye, I am that," Flint added just a trifle more accent than he normally employed.

"You know the old saying "where there's muck there's brass"? That's a good motto for an archaeologist."

"*ubi sterans ibi aes*" Flint added.

"Isn't that a film?" Mrs Grimston exclaimed.

"You're thinking of *Quo Vadis*."

"Aren't I awful?" Mrs Grimston burst into a fit of giggles and lowered her head towards her plate. A shared thought shot between her husband and Eleanor as Flint made a mental calculation of the number of wine glasses emptied. Grimston whispered something to his wife and she corrected her behaviour, flicking her eyes across at Flint, then turning them to study her half-empty glass.

It was all positively feudal. Grimston the lord, surrounded by his retainers and each keeping the women in their allotted place. The nobles would make plans for the future of the common people, distributing boons and administering punishment, ensuring always that power and wealth remained in their hands. The castle, of course, was the key. It was a statement of the power of the lord, it was his sanctuary against his enemies, it was the base from which he would sally forth and do battle. It was Bob Grimston who held court at Shadesmoor, not Eleanor Balleron.

Eleanor made motions towards the waitress, who hovered silently in regulation black-and-white. The cheese arrived, then the port, then Flint found that he and Eleanor were the only non-smokers in the room. Cigars busily stained the ceiling whilst the maid returned with a tray of coffee cups.

Sober and alert, Flint had learned so much about the people seated around the table. Eleanor continued to intrigue him, laughing at the jokes without seeming to enjoy them. She'd been served with a tiny portion of food and only picked at it. Her second glass of white wine was almost untouched and she sniffed uncomfortably at the smoke. When she gave orders to the waitress they were hesitant, lacking the true authority of aristocracy. Flint, the knight errant, identified his damsel in distress.

Most of the wall behind where Eleanor sat was taken up by a pair of tall windows, each of twenty panes. The curtains were open to reveal a bright southern sky. Flint thought he saw motion outside; no, it had to be a reflection. Someone made a quip and his attention shifted for a moment. When he again looked back the ghostly figure was still there, an orange object now raised in its hand.

The window shattered.

Eleanor shot upright and shrieked as a heavy object spun into the room and bounced onto the carpet. A glass shard skipped down the table, another hit the shoulder of her crimson dress. The waitress dropped her tray onto the table. Cups, coffee pot and wine glasses scattered in confusion. From outside came a peal of shrill laughter.

"What the bloody hell!" Grimston roared and made a dash for the window. Flint was the next man to recover his senses. Four of the panes of one window was broken and at his feet lay a familiar orange object the size of a house brick: the EDM ranging scope.

Grimston was barking orders, but only his underling responded to his command. Both set off towards the front door in pursuit of the laughter.

"What's that?" Megan asked as Flint picked up the battered object.

"It's the business end of our EDM. The ghost of Shadesmoor strikes again."

From across the table, Mrs Grimston dissolved into another attack of nervous giggles. The party was over.

He turned to Eleanor, who was still sitting upright, tears running down her cheeks. He dared put a soft hand on her shoulder.

"It's all right," seemed a useful stock phrase in times of crisis.

She clasped his hand and squeezed tight. "Tom!" she whispered.

Chapter Fifteen

"Do I hunt!" Flint scoffed as he drove home from the manor. "No, and I don't whip my negro slaves either."

"Tsk tsk, don't be a class snob," Megan chided.

"But honestly, all that crap Mrs Lawyer came out with about Covent Garden opera tickets being such stunning value: what is she on?"

"About a hundred thousand a year, or her husband is."

"You're very sanguine, whatever happened to Red Megan?"

"Red Megan has drunk a bottle of red *Bordeaux* and only wants her pink pillowcase. Lady Godiva took the poltergeist attack very badly."

"Do you blame her? How would you feel if someone lobbed half an EDM through your front window?"

"I wouldn't sit and sob. I wouldn't simper whilst a handsome young man patted me on the head and said 'there, there'. Goodness Jeff, did you have to be so comforting? I know she's filthy rich and ravishing . . ."

"She's not my type."

Megan scoffed. "You would have eaten off her feet, you were all over her."

"I hate aristocracy, period, no matter how well packaged."

"You hide it well. Keep it up, boyo, don't let your prejudice show, we all need the money."

"Is that where your new car came from?"

"Yes, yes, my lovely consultancy fee."

"You too can be a tuna sandwich."

"Pardon?"

"Nothing."

Flint was back at Shadesmoor Castle soon after nine the next morning. The team always worked Sundays so it could make full use of part-time volunteers. This Sunday the team stood around in huddles, expanding on the drama of the night before. Policemen and glaziers moved around the manor house and Eleanor was refusing to see anyone, even Flint. She had been frightened by the attack, and so had he, in a different way. He was frightened that he no longer understood what was happening.

Tyrone had been assigned to the Portakabin that night and reported hearing nothing unusual.

"I hate this," he said. "We can't just sit here and wait for the police to find this lunatic."

"Yes we can." The memory of Ruth's immolation still haunted him. The police had to be left to earn their salt.

"I've been putting a lot of time into the Aitken case but I'm getting nowhere."

"Blow your whistle," Flint said, watching the gossiping groups of diggers eating up his budget.

"What?"

"Your whistle, blow it."

Tyrone blew, and Flint clapped his hands. "Work!" he shouted. "Now!"

Some looked shocked, others hurt, but the diggers

151

got the message and began to disperse towards their trenches.

"Fascist," Tyrone said.

"Takes one to know one."

Monday found Flint moving house. Megan had begun to drop heavy hints. She was deeply involved in filtering the new intake of students and they had played their last game of Scrabble. She would not be owned and not become attached and although Flint had become quite fond of her, it was the fondness one might feel for an indulgent aunt. The prospect of taking up permanent residence with a militant homemaker was enough to set him searching the property press in earnest. Megan's curiosity seemed satisfied, he had completed his rites of passage into the department and it was time to move on.

So many of the northern academics seemed to own houses, a novelty to someone who had spent a decade in London. Everyone urged Flint to buy, but he hung back. Suspicion of lawyers, estate agents and banks continued to keep him out of the housing market.

"Prices will only go up," said Megan the socialist.

"Rent is dead money," Barney said, with no originality.

"Get your foot on the property ladder!" urged Tyrone, dead on form.

No, the spectre of the tuna sandwich still haunted him. Once he had invested in a house, he was trapped and at the mercy of Betty, the University and the fickle whims of Bob Grimston and Eleanor. He did not want to fall further under their thrall.

There was a cottage to rent at the edge of Urethorpe; fifteen minute's drive either way to Shadesmoor Castle, or college. Two minute's walk from The Green Man Free House and right on the late Tom Aitken's doorstep.

Yes, the moth was edging closer to the flame. Tom's job, Tom's site, Tom's village, Tom's lover. Eleanor had gripped his hand and called him Tom: the transmigration was almost complete. Looking around the terraced cottage, every room a jumble of cardboard boxes, Flint found himself trembling. Perhaps the flame was closing on the moth.

Joss Wardle rode a 250cc Honda. Its angry insect buzz could be heard even over the engine rattle of the green van. Flint followed the moped over the cattle grid and up towards the castle. Another day, another denarius.

With a fit of bravado, Joss opened the throttle on the tree-lined park road and drew away from Flint with a wave. Seconds later, his hand shot back to take control of the handlebars. Right, left, right, the motorbike slewed across the road. Flint kicked the brakes and brought his van to a skidding halt, the seat belt digging into his shoulders. Joss stuck out a leg like a speedway star and his bike regained a wobbling stability until it rolled past a tree and onto the grass.

Flint closed his eyes, counted to ten, then opened them. Joss was alive, he was alive. How he hated cars. When he opened the door and stepped out, his legs still quivered.

"You okay, Joss?"

Joss had removed his helmet to inspect the damage to his machine. "Bastard tyre blew."

On instinct, Flint looked down at the tarmac. A carpet of heavy duty tin-tacks began just in front of the green van and scattered twenty yards up the road.

"See what the bastards have done?" Joss pointed to the tin-tacks. "There must be two hundred bastard nails." He seemed to be limping.

"You hurt?"

Joss rubbed his leg. "No. Who's paying for my tyre?"

"Petty cash." Flint imagined Tyrone cringing. "And don't breathe a word to Bob Grimston. He had the police combing the moors for the idiot that broke the manor window. Tell him about this and he'll bring in armed guards with Dobermanns."

His thoughts were clearer now. "I'll sweep these up; I don't want the diggers to know either. Understand?"

"Yes, boss. I ran over some glass."

"You had a flat, full stop."

"Yes, boss."

It took Flint and Tyrone the best part of an hour to sweep up the tacks.

"You said you were getting nowhere," Flint said, broom in hand.

"My suspect file is enormous," Tyrone replied. "All those girlfriends Barney found us for starters. Then Aitken clocked up a long list of enemies in various local groups, all the other units he beat for contracts, all the diggers he sacked, all the academics who he fell out with, treasure hunters he reported to the police. The list is infinite and the list of motives is also infinite, so we can't find the suspect via the motive."

Flint leaned on his broom. "You know, in my wilder moments I've described excavation as detective work, but the analogy isn't perfect is it? Archaeological sites sit still, with all the evidence waiting to be found. When it comes to a murder, the situation remains dynamic, things keep changing. We're confused, the police are confused and meanwhile, some lunatic is working his or her way towards the grand objective."

"If Ruth wasn't dead, she'd be my favourite suspect for this." Tyrone shovelled a few more tacks into a rubber bucket.

"I have this awful, awful feeling that Ruth must have been innocent."

"Nobody is innocent," Tyrone said with gravity, "we have only to assess the extent of their guilt."

Flint frowned. "Let me guess: Dostoevsky, *Crime and Punishment*?"

"No – *Judge Dread, 2000 AD magazine*."

He had always recommended that his students read widely. "As I see things, it's pointless using a technique of investigation which works from clue to suspect, because there ain't enough clues and there's too many suspects. So we have to think laterally and dream up scenarios which fit the known parameters."

This gave Tyrone another excuse to stop work and make a show of deep thought. "Scenario one is that Aitken's murder was part of this campaign of harassment. He double-crossed the action group and he paid the price."

"You're assuming the murder and the sabotage are connected."

"They are, directly or indirectly, everything's connected."

"Have you been reading *Zen*, or is that Judge Dredd too?"

"Logic."

"If we accept your scenario, it means Ruth must have had at least one accomplice. I suppose it would explain why the police had so much trouble pinning the murder on Ruth exclusively."

"Uh-ho, here comes Megan," Tyrone chirped.

The metallic grey car belonged to Flint's former landlady and former bedmate. It slowed to a halt as they signalled with the brooms. Megan wound down her window.

"I've come about the loo," she said, strengthening her Welsh. "I have to look at the *garde-robes*."

"Is this for the Medieval Dysentery Experience or the Shit Chute Super Slide?"

"Ladies present," Megan blinked deliberately.

"Sorry, excavation humour."

"You may crack lavatorial jokes, but they do actually want a display about the *garde-robes*."

"In smell-around?"

"Yes; the designer is obsessed by the Viking toilet at the Jorvik Centre. If they have a toilet, we must have a toilet."

"We can't be out-toiletted can we? Joss has a nice cesspit you can see, he's found some real sixteenth century cess."

"No thank you."

"What's wrong with the road?"

"Nothing," Flint said, checking that the way was now safe.

"Tyrone, would you be a darling and help me find the *garde-robes*?"

"That okay, Doc?"

Flint assented, and Tyrone won a lift to the top of the hill. Flint swept up the last few tacks from the roadside, then loaded the tools into the van. The sun shone, birds sang, he was in the heart of peaceful England, yet danger haunted Shadesmoor. For a while he was tempted to pull out of the project to shield his team; a Mickey Mouse castle was not worth a life.

Late in the day, Flint stood upon the top of the keep, ninety feet above the bailey, watching his worker ants below. Everything and everyone has a history. The towering keep had a history, as did the manor, the low meadow and all the characters who were moving across the landscape, playing their tiny and transient parts in the tale. The castle would remain standing when all the human components of the scene were dead. Looming grey under the autumn sky, the moor would endure long after the keep had tumbled into ruin and its stones had become entombed by grass. Monstrous as the theme park might be, it would only be a transitory scar on the landscape. After a few decades, it would be a deserted shell; after a century, an overgrown skeleton thick with wildlife; after five centuries it would be as inoffensive as the medieval village which slumbered under the low meadow.

The darkest secrets are deepest buried and often cleverly concealed. Flint had become too embroiled in the mire to see clearly. He'd fallen for all the promises, half-truths and deliberate lies thrown his way and his responses had been logical, indeed predictable. Flint the anarchist needed to be rediscovered: believe no-one, trust no-one and always think the unthinkable. He'd take a new look at Ruth, Eleanor, Megan and the girlfriends, whilst Bob Grimston deserved a little more covert disrespect. With his impromptu visits and his insidious talent for befriending and influencing people, Bob could stifle any investigation which offended his interests. Flint pictured the millionaire and Tyrone over the table of a small wine bar in Ripon or York, leaning close, talking figures and prospects. It was time to put space between Tyrone and temptation.

Chapter Sixteen

The trial excavation of the castle ditches could be completed without Tyrone. Joss was a workhorse on site and Flint dare not put the pair in a trench together without risking class war. The two American students had taken to surveying almost as well as they had resisted Tyrone's chat-up lines; they could finish the task on their own. Flint and his team would hold the fort, quite literally, leaving Tyrone free to be a latter-day black knight roaming the land in the name of justice.

Tyrone was sent back to college, to down-load his data onto a PC and expand his file on Tom Aitken. The major task (as he saw it) was to identify the lunatic who was haunting the castle. Delving into the life of Ruth Hauxley might uncover the vital clues. The newspapers had been full of her life story the day after her involuntary suttee on the moorland, which had also been carried on Vikki's satellite crime show. Tyrone was now able to distil the data from the press cuttings, filter out the numerous factual errors and suppositions and add them to the computer.

Ruth had been twenty-six years old, born near Halifax, taken Archaeology and Anthropology at Sheffield University, then set about globe-trotting after graduation. She had met Tom Aitken in Syria two years previously and returned to work for him and "serve as his mistress", in the words of one reporter. She moved out of The Old Rectory about ten weeks before the demise of her lover and found refuge with a schoolfriend who lived on the outskirts of Ripon.

Okay, that was the obvious suspect dealt with. Scheming Ruth, motivated by a broken heart and a demolished set of values. But what of her accomplice, the one who was still free? How closely had his/her motives been linked to those of Ruth?

Tyrone began to work back through the archaeological record of the work of Tom Aitken and FAS, looking for names of assistants who might be Ruth's confederates. Having advanced scenario one as a postulate, he began to doubt his own off-the-cuff idea: one anti-Shadesmoor terrorist was just conceivable, two strained credulity. He believed in Bob Grimston's vision and could not construe the Shadesmoor project as being evil, unlike the unswervingly right-on Jeffrey Flint. If scenario one were to be true, he had to find a plausible ally for Ruth and a credible motive for the string of crimes.

The university library was not a patch on the one he'd been used to in London, but was still uncluttered by undergraduates. Tyrone checked through local journals and newsletters looking for any mention of Form Farm, the site where Aitken had found the golden torc, the site which Ruth had been working on when she died. The excavation had been aimed at recording remains of a moated manor which would be destroyed in construction of one of the A1 link roads. The discovery of an earlier, Iron Age settlement and warrior burial had been unexpected.

He remembered Ruth saying something about

going to York to deliver the Form Farm material. It was likely that much, if not all, of the site records and finds had been destroyed in the exploding Land Rover. If so, the site would remain a site of mystery, as Aitken had published little information, apart from the note on the torc.

If Tyrone had been a cartoon character, dollar signs would have slid into his eyes to the tune of ringing cash tills. The research had reaped its first profit, although not of the sort Flint intended. Flint would have to pull strings and Professor Betty Vine would have to throw her professorial weight around; Tyrone needed to lay his hands on the surviving archives of First Archaeological Services. Someone had to complete their work, someone had to inherit their contracts: why not UNY-DIG?

Flint was glad to see Tyrone leave the site and he seemed happy to go. He had even dropped a few hints that he was tired of camping. Rejection by both the Americans probably contributed something to his disillusionment with the glamour of field archaeology.

The terraced cottage Flint had rented at the foot of Church Hill, Urethorpe, was still an uninhabitable shambles. Boxes which had been half unpacked at Megan's had been hastily re-packed and everything was in utmost confusion. After an hour of sorting through piles that Saturday, Flint could bear no more. He found his sleeping bag and his hiking tent, and moved into the diggers' camp at Shadesmoor.

The campsite had been moved adjacent to the car park and Portakabin, to enhance the security of the site. Half the diggers camped, whilst the rest shared cars to homes in nearby towns. Evenings were most often spent in The Three Tuns, a farmers' watering hole where muddy boots and wet jeans were accepted without a murmur. Diggers would spin out pints of John Smith's bitter to buy time out of the rain. Each time one counted out coins to the barman, Flint was painfully aware of how little he was paying them. The contrast with the banquet at the manor was profound.

A convention arose whereby Flint normally drove back to site with the whole team squashed illegally into the back of the green van. Warm, close, damp and steaming, the team bonded and grew together. Back on site, students and ex-students would crowd into the Portakabin for tea before taking turns at the portable toilet in the car park. It was squalid, but Flint loved it, wishing he'd moved up there a month earlier.

"Night, momma." "Night, grampa!" "Night John-boy!" The nightly ritual of calls from tent to tent would roll on until boredom set in. It would often be midnight, or beyond, before the games ceased. Flint would take his turn that night in the Portakabin. He pulled his sleeping bag from his tent, hoisted it onto his shoulder and trudged towards the hut, torch playing at his feet. The earth was dark, the sky a low, scudding canopy of deepest grey. Down in the village, a dozen lights showed. A black shape moved across them.

Up flicked the torch, feebly stabbing at the night.

"Okay wise guy." His voice contained fibre his spirit lacked.

"Doctor Flint!" A voice shrieked from the dark.

"Eleanor – Miss Balleron?"

The shape rushed towards him, grasping his shoulders.

"Doctor Flint, I'm sorry."

He shifted the weight of his sleeping bag, and took hold of her arm, steering Eleanor towards the Portakabin. In a few moments, she was inside and he had lit the gas lamp.

Eleanor was deathly white and wore a green wax jacket over lilac silk pyjamas. A single muddy moccasin stuck to her left foot.

"I'm sorry, you must think I'm stupid."

"No, what's wrong?"

"He tried to get me."

"Who?"

"Him, out there! He got into the manor and broke into the study."

Flint lit the gas stove and set the kettle in place. "Don't you have a burglar alarm?"

"I turned it off. I didn't want the police up here again. Don't tell Bob will you? He'll call the police."

Someone else had once turned off a burglar alarm, Flint thought. "Don't you have people down there? Maids and things?"

"Bob pays them. Bob pays for everything, he owns everything."

"I thought you were partners."

"Oh yes," she seemed to correct herself, then sniffed.

Flint offered her the sleeping bag and wrapped it around her shoulders. "We haven't seen you on site for what, ten days."

"I went to London, after that night . . . I hate this place."

"Sell it to Bob."

Eleanor simply gave a derisive laugh.

"Do you want me to check out your house? I can

163

bring some of the lads down – we come cheaper than policemen and we're more politically correct."

"I'm sorry for this, I just didn't know who else to come to. I'm going to go back to London tomorrow, I've got a flat in Chelsea, I like it there."

"No, don't," he said hastily. "Don't run, or they'll win."

She sniffled into the sleeping bag.

The kettle began to bubble. "Cheap tea or instant coffee?"

"Coffee please, black, no sugar."

Convenient, as the milk was a little cheesy and the sugar had coalesced into a single grey-brown mass. Flint looked for clean crockery and gave Eleanor his own *Greenpeace Rainbow Warrior* mug. He made her coffee and she held it close for warmth. Flint chose the Eric Bloodaxe mug, threw in a lump of coffee, filled the mug with water, sniffed at the milk once more and also opted to take it black.

"At the manor house, when the window broke, you called me Tom."

"No," she said.

"I beg to differ."

"I suppose I do confuse the two of you some-times."

"Tom Aitken and me? He's dead, I'm not."

"But you're both . . . similar."

"He was six foot, black-haired, clean shaven, hunky . . ."

"Stop it! Okay?"

She still had not tasted the coffee.

"Can I help?" he ventured. The look of alarm was telling, as was the rejection. "I'm a very charitable soul, a good samaritan at heart. I like to help people."

164

"I'll be fine soon. I'll go back to my room, if you'll walk with me."

His pulse leaped, then gradually subsided as common sense took over from fantasy. Ahead of him lay a path strewn with things far more dangerous than tin-tacks. "Better still, how would you like company? There's a pair of American girls working for me who would just love a fortnight in an English stately home. Find them a room next to your own: they know how to take care of themselves, one of them is a New Yorker. If there's any more hassle, one of them can run up here for help."

Eleanor's eyes gazed at him in an odd, distant, almost childish wonder. She was a decade older than Flint, older even than Megan, yet despite all her grooming and her wealth she was frightened of the world.

They talked of things of no consequence and the coffee went cold in her hand. Flint took the untasted liquid and set the mug on the desk. He checked outside the hut and made a short foray to the campsite, but encountered nothing sinister. Next he guided Eleanor to the green van and drove the short distance to the manor. It was fully lit and one of the groundsmen was frowning in the porch, shotgun in hand.

"Miss Balleron? Is that you?"

"Yes Hughes."

Hughes threatened Flint with a stare. Any explanation would compromise the lady, so none was offered. A maid appeared and Eleanor whispered goodnight.

"You should watch yourself," Hughes said, once his mistress had gone.

"Pardon?"

"You heard. Watch yourself."

"I shall."

It may have been to make a point that Eleanor visited the site the following morning. The sun was out, making the Low Meadow steam. Hettie the Dalmatian sniffed around the spoil heap as Eleanor chatted to Flint without mentioning the midnight melodrama. The trench through the castle ditch was half-complete and she seemed fascinated as the archaeologist pointed out the succession of bow-shaped lines visible in the section.

"These tell us the whole history of the ditch," he was explaining. "Each of these soil lines represents an episode of silting or rubbish dumping."

"What would the black be?"

A large triangle of black soil interrupted the smooth pattern of bows.

"That seems to be a midden – a rubbish dump. We've got a heap of pottery out of it." He turned to shout to his finds assistant over the baulk. "What's the black layer date to Julie?"

"Seventeenth," the woman shouted back.

"The midden post-dates the 1644 destruction deposit, so it seems that after the castle went out of use, your ancestors dumped their rubbish up here."

"Not my ancestors," she laughed. "We're impostors here, my family were German."

Suddenly her face fell. Flint climbed out of the trench to see a bronze Jaguar approaching the car park at some speed. Eleanor called to Hettie, then without more than a glance of farewell, found the metalled path and began to walk to meet Bob Grimston.

Grimston called first at the Portakabin, then met

166

Eleanor at the edge of the car park. They talked, Flint watched. Eleanor threw back her hair in a show of nerves then, after a minute, Grimston seemed satisfied and renewed his progress towards the castle. The haste with which Eleanor made for the manor was telling.

Flint held his position in the trench, wanting to appear busy. "Morning Bob."

Grimston was dressed in a grey flannel jogging suit. His hair had not been combed that morning. "Could I have a word, Jeff?"

Flint dug his trowel into an uncleaned stretch of ditch section and went as summoned. Grimston walked swiftly up the scenic track which ran along the spine of the hill from castle to moor. Nothing was said until well beyond earshot of the diggers.

"Where's Tyrone?"

"He's back at college for a few days catching up on the paperwork."

Grimston grunted. "So what went on last night?"

Flint had seen this coming but had failed to plan a satisfactory answer. "I think someone broke into the manor."

"Someone did: now I find two of your gippo's moving in. What's going on?"

"One of those gypsies is an oil heiress; the other is the daughter of a Yale professor. Eleanor seemed to want company and they were tired of being rained on."

Grimston halted and poked a finger within an inch of his chest. "Look, you're not employed as a security man and you're not her bloody nanny. This is not some airy-fairy college where everyone can come and cry on your shoulder, this is a business venture."

"Ease up, Bob."

167

"What?"

"Ease up on the pressure, it's not the way we work. We do this job because it's a vocation, because we want to do it, because we care about the past. We don't do it for the money."

"Then why do I keep hearing that this will cost more, and that will cost more? Don't you know what you're digging up?"

"No, that's why we're digging it up. It's why we're here, costing you so much money. We want to discover and we want to rescue the past before it ends up in a dumper truck."

"Don't get smart."

"I'm just doing my job."

That finger came back again. "Right! Just do your job. And as for my partner . . ." He seemed reluctant to smear Eleanor, or even consider she had been at fault. "Don't get high ideas, she's too good for the likes of you. In her circle, the three most important things are money, money and money. Remember that."

Grimston stalked off, leaving the path, moving directly downhill towards his Jaguar. Halfway down the greasy slope, he slipped onto his backside and slithered a few years before regaining his dignity. From up in the castle, somebody laughed.

Chapter Seventeen

A sea-grey van bore the logo *Stronghold Security*. Three men climbed out into the car park. Two wore ill-fitting uniforms and peaked caps the same shade as the van.

"Bloody Nazis," Joss commented.

The third man was in his shirtsleeves, hugged a clipboard and carried a mobile phone hooked to his belt. Bob Grimston met the trio and led them around the site with much pointing and serious emphasis. Flint was introduced to Mr Heggarty, the man in the shirtsleeves. Heggarty had been in the Marines, he said, had served in Northern Ireland, he said, he knew about sabotage, he said.

"Bloody Nazi," Joss said when he-man Heggarty had climbed aboard Grimston's Jaguar to be whisked away to lunch.

"Oh he's all right," said the younger of the guards in a slow monotone.

"No he's not, he's a wanker," his colleague corrected.

"So," Flint said, rubbing his hands together. "You're going to guard the castle like knights of old?"

"Yeah," said the slow one.

"All bloody night for three-fifty an hour," said the other with a strong Geordie accent.

"That's less than we get!" Joss said.

Both sets of eyes fastened onto the mud-smeared digger.

"And we don't have to face raving loonies in the dead of night." Joss disappeared into the trench, chuckling.

"How long have you been doing this?" Flint asked gently.

"He's new," said the militant one.

"It's better than being on t' dole," the slow one replied in his own defence.

Grimston had sent these men on site, but Flint moved swiftly to assert his control on their movements. "Okay guys. It may look like a mud bath, but this is an archaeological excavation; complex, sensitive and expensive. These are the ground rules . . ."

He led the pair around the site, warning them of trench positions, surveying lines and barrow boards. He told them what he could of the sabotage campaign and offered them tea in the Portakabin.

"Tell 'em about the ghost!" The disembodied voice of Joss drifted from the trench.

"Ghost?" the slow one said.

"I'll introduce her when it gets dark."

The diggers christened the security guards Bill and Ben. They worked seven day weeks, twelve hours a night, which had Joss handing out the phone numbers of friends in the unions. The arrival of the guards should have allowed Flint to relax his own watch on the site, but his confidence in them was nil. The guards were a psychological deterrent, not SAS-trained supermen as Heggarty had implied. The test would be whether "Margaret" (as the intruder was known) would be deterred by two lads fresh off the unemployment register.

Monday was rest day on site, so Flint gave himself and the team a break by organising a gentle ramble over Shadesmoor. With six others, he strode out in strong sunshine, following a trail which began at the manor, north along the river and into the woods. Amongst the birch and oaks there were significant signs that "progress" was about to be made: white tapes strung from tree to tree mapped the planned line of the light railway. Yellow crosses on the trunks marked inconvenient trees for summary execution.

The waterfall at Valley Head was only just recovering strength after the drought. Pretty, but not rating any stars in the guidebooks, it would need considerable work by Grimston's landscape engineers to turn it into Robin Hood's den.

Over Valley Head they climbed, into the National Park and into an open world of yellow grass and russet heather where no man was master. Most of the moor had escaped the fire which had ravaged the top above Urethorpe. Rabbit paths cut down to the sandy bedrock and Flint chose one which led to the Whinstones – five oddly proportioned red sandstone pillars abandoned by topsoil and left to be whirled into fantastic shapes by the wind. These at least were beyond Grimston's grasp.

The party sat on an outcrop of sandstone opposite the last and smallest Whinstone. Another fifteen minute's walk would bring them to the highest point on the moor, a rounded hill known as Wade's Seat.

"This Wade was a giant, right?" Loretta, one of the American volunteers broke the reflective silence.

"You'll be able to see him at the castle next year, holding up the helter-skelter," Flint said.

"You don't like this theme park do you, Doc?"

"I'm paid to like it. I'm told we must move with

the times and give people what they want. Heritage must pay its way."

"Do you think anyone can stop it? You know, those people who keep sneaking up to the camp?" "Margaret," one of the lads chipped in.

"No, they can't stop it, they're doing the cause no good at all. They'll be caught." He tried not to sound rueful, but the harder he thought about Bob Grimston, his aims, his methods and the people he chose to do his work, the more uncomfortable Flint became. If he could hire macho ex-commandos, who else would he hire in extremis?

"So who's going to catch them, Doc?"

"Bill and Ben!" chimed the others. "Hard men!"

Flint's eyes came to rest on a stone building on the skyline. The moor was dotted with abandoned lead workings, derelict farms and shepherds' huts. Any one of them could house a small team of dedicated fanatics. He stood up and stretched, knowing that to the north and east there was little but rolling moorland between Wade's Seat and the North Sea. Only a massive and expensive police sweep would stand any chance of hunting down the saboteurs. Flint allowed himself an ironic smile. For the while "Margaret" was safe.

Tyrone was whistling as he stepped into the Porta-kabin that Tuesday afternoon.

"Where have you been?" Flint demanded.

"Where you sent me – North Pole Polytechnic."

"What about in the evenings? Every time I ring, you're not at home."

Tyrone shrugged. "It's my life."

"Fair enough – what did Bob want?"

"Bob?"

"I saw you talking by the manor, just before you drove up."

Flint waggled a pair of binoculars. "I like to keep an eye on my workers."

"Oh he just, you know."

Tyrone was overdressed for site, wearing a pure white shirt (badly ironed) and his plum jacket. Flint pointed to a tiny red blob on the shirt. "Is that red wine or tomato ketchup? Lunch in York perhaps?"

"Harrogate," he said. "And it's Gypsy Rose sauce. Bob wanted an insight into how contract archaeology worked."

"So you gave him the benefit of your six weeks' experience?"

"Yes – I think he found it useful and it might have done us some good."

"How?"

"I'm selling him on my ideas for Phase II."

"Your ideas?"

"Our ideas."

"Bit of fatherly advice, Tyrone. Don't get too pally with Bob, he bites, and when he bites, he swallows whole."

"With respect, I think you misjudge him."

In academic circles, "with respect" translates as "don't be a pillock".

Flint absorbed the insult. "I assume from that you haven't managed to link him to the murder?"

"It's pointless, Doc. The police have done eight hundred interviews, they've assembled far more data than we have and it's got them nowhere. I'm halfway to laying hands on the FAS material though – that will allow us to gain access to their archives."

"What you mean is it will allow us to get access to their funding."

"That too – we've got to eat. We're not in the 1970s any more, nobody owes us a living"

"Yes, yes, sorry for playing the militant socialist all the time, but understand my worries about Bob."

Tyrone looked away in his usual, almost insolent, way.

"Pack your toothbrush, I need you back on site for the rest of the month. Joss will be hard pressed to finish the big holes and have them backfilled. I need you to start wrapping up the site and start on the Phase II spec."

"Mothball, not wrap up. We're going to win Phase II, we could just leave the equipment here."

"You're that confident?"

The way in which Tyrone nodded caused Flint to feel even greater unease.

Night blew in from Russia. A cold, intensely black night, reminding the campers what winter would be like if they were so foolish as to remain. Flint listened to the wind tearing at the flaps of his two-man hiking tent. One week to go and eight days work to somehow squeeze into seven.

Tyrone was on night watch duty in the Portakabin, the Americans were body-guarding Eleanor and half the volunteers had driven home to soft, sensible beds. Flint lay awake: Tyrone worried him. More precisely, Tyrone's moral outlook worried him. Since coming back on site, he had been perceptibly evasive about quite where he was going, or who he was meeting, or what he was working on. Perhaps the lad was asserting his independence and perhaps Flint should let him go.

He'd never heard a wind wail so much!

The tent pulled at its ropes, then fell slack, but the wailing repeated itself. That was no wind. Flint was still mostly dressed and within moments had pulled on a greatcoat and wellingtons, seized a flashlight and pushed himself out into the night.

Gaunt and tall, the keep frowned down on the excavators, laughing at their efforts to reduce its secrets to a few pages of text. A light was briefly seen through an arrow slit, then through a second, further up the tower. Another shriek of laughter joined the wind as Flint ran to the Portakabin and banged on its door. Within a minute, two flashlights were leading the way to the keep.

"Shit!" Tyrone's flashlight suddenly crashed to the ground, and he stumbled to his knees.

Flint thrust out a hand to arrest his fall.

"I tripped."

In the beam of Flint's torch, a tangled string could be seen on the turf. Tyrone gave a curse. "It's one of our section lines! Someone's unpegged it."

An object bounced off the reinforced foot of the keep and crashed to the ground.

"There's someone up there, Doc."

"Our friend Margaret the poltergeist, and it sounds like she's wrecking the place. Tell me the camera is in the hut."

"It's in the hut."

"But the tripod was left in the keep?" Flint had managed to find the fallen object in the beam of his torch. "Scratch another fifty quid off the budget."

"It's worth it – we've got her now," Tyrone said, reaching the door of the forebuilding.

"Her?"

"Listen!"

175

The laugh had to be a woman's laugh. Flint's mind flicked over the list of mad women he knew and came to the total zero.

Tyrone had a plan, and it did not sound like a good one. "Okay, one of us can work up each staircase and we're bound to trap her."

"Are you serious? I thought you were in Britain's top one per cent? There's a hundred-foot drop inside there."

"Ninety."

"Pedant! It still hurts when you hit the ground."

The equinoctial gale whirled around them as they stood impotent and out of ideas.

"Where are Bill and Ben when we really need them?"

"I'll stand guard if you go back for reinforcements, Tyrone offered. "She won't get out."

"Unless she's armed with a hand-axe."

"What? You think that this is . . .?"

"Yeah, I do. And I can think of at least two other ways out of the keep if you don't count walking through walls. I'll lurk over there – you call out the guard."

Tyrone raced off downwind and downhill. Flint turned off his flashlight and fell back into the deepest shadow he could find: a niche within the main curtain wall. The wind was bitter, howling through an archer slit, but that was not why he shivered. The ghost of Margaret de Balleron might be stalking the ruins, but the ghosts of Tom Aitken and Ruth Hauxley were closer at hand. He had no intention of joining the celestial party.

An object fell down the central void of the castle with a clatter. Mentally he took stock of equipment that might have been left up there, knowing that most

176

would now be scattered in buckled heaps around the base of the tower.

"Come on!" he whispered.

Loud and sharp, the noise by his right ear sent Flint into a spasm of surprise. Something ricocheted off the base of the keep and flashed past in the dark, smacking into the curtain wall. He swept the torch beam skyward, but it scarcely reached halfway up the sheer, dark face.

Flint ducked back into the protecting niche, then used the beam to find the fallen object. It was a surveying tape, its circular case now split and spewing its contents onto the grass. A similar fate would have befallen Flint's skull had he been standing three feet further forward.

Lights and voices accompanied a posse of diggers to the keep door. Tyrone came up to the niche, mobile phone in his hand.

"We can't find Bill and Ben, so I think we should call the cops."

A forlorn hope of diggers surged towards the castle, but Flint stepped in front of them and reached out a hand. "Stand back team, we don't get paid danger money. Bob Grimston said, and I quote, that we're not employed as bloody security men. For once, I agree with him. It's time we got some value out of our income tax."

Chapter Eighteen

One hour and twenty minutes elapsed before a pair of policemen reached Shadesmoor Castle. The diggers were cold, rebellious and convinced of having seen the ghost on half a dozen occasions. Flint kept them all well back. With its staircases, wells, half excavated buildings and fully excavated trenches, the castle was a lethal place to wander around at night, even when spectres were not hurling surveying equipment from the sky.

The second siege of Shadesmoor Castle got off to a pathetic start, with the eight diggers cowering under the ramparts and the policemen falling over tapes and wheelbarrows as they tried to put sense into the story they were being told. D.I. Thorne was called, but never put in an appearance. Bill and Ben stuck their hands in their pockets and cadged fags off Joss. Diggers drifted off to bed as more police arrived (Flint had pulled Bob Grimston out of bed and had him call the police). Flint and a trio of die-hards kept a distant watch from the Portakabin, fuelled by continuous cups of coffee. The hut now had three brands on offer, with percolator, brown sugar and a ready stockpile of condensed milk in cans. Flint was prepared for all eventualities.

Dawn came slowly and was cold. The police presence had swelled to two dozen officers, plus dogs, minus the sergeant who had sprained an ankle chasing shadows.

"It's like the bloody pit strike out there," Joss commented.

The police caught no-one in the castle, but they found a short rope dangling down one of the *garde-robes*; "Margaret" was not only cunning but conducted thorough research. Alsatians rushed away barking across the moor, but with a hundred square miles of wet heather to choose from, they did little but frighten the grouse who had survived the summer. Flint exchanged a few subdued words with D.I. Thorne on the mobile phone. The policeman had just finished talking to Bob Grimston, who had been somewhat less subdued. The sun sneaked up behind scudding cloud and all thought of sleep was abandoned.

Bill and Ben, plus their van, vanished from the site that day. The lost equipment had to be accounted for and the excavated trench checked for damage. The diggers were bemused, some even unnerved by the events of the night, so Flint urged Joss to hurry the completion of the excavation before the site was attacked again.

Flint drove over to the Nissen hut once used by the now defunct First Archaeological Services. In a matter of days, Tyrone had obtained leave to clear up the mess left by the collapse of the unit. Contracts had been partly filled, and organisations ranging from road construction companies to the County Council to English Heritage were owed reports in return for their funding and museums awaited delivery of archives and finds.

Tyrone poked his fingers into a tray of unwashed

pottery on one of the racks. "With so many units going bust these days, I'm sure there's money in excavating their leftovers. Most contracts have a final payment on completion: we could cream them all off."

A fine film of dust betrayed the fact that no-one had been in the hut since Ruth Hauxley's premature departure. Tyrone showed Flint a locked metal cabinet at the back of the office, to which no key had been found.

"We'll have to bust it open," Tyrone said.

"Vandal!"

"Ruth probably had the key, so it will be a molten blob by now."

Flint acquiesced and they found a tool box in the unit's equipment store.

"I'm negotiating to lay our hands on this stuff too," Tyrone said casually.

A hammer and a chisel broke open the secure cupboard after a short battle. The cupboard was empty.

"All the goodies are gone," Flint mused. "But when, and to where?"

He knew that a careful programme of detective work amongst the unit's paperwork should uncover answers to both these questions. Tyrone planned to re-employ a former FAS finds' assistant to clarify precisely what FAS had excavated and what of this had been sent to museums. Anything missing was likely to have gone skywards in Ruth's pyre.

"Form Farm!" Tyrone found a set of red hard-backed exercise books, each with mud dried on their covers. "Site notebooks."

The pair sat and sifted through the rough notes. All other archival material for the site seemed to be missing. Ruth had had a very neat hand and an organised mind. Every box of artifacts had been given a unique serial number and was keyed to a shelf location in the storeroom. Boxes 1237 through 1390 contained material found at Form Farm. The unit's accessions register had all these boxes ticked as returned to the museum.

A phone call followed. Yes, all the boxes were in the museum bar – the first thirteen, which had been expected on the day of Ruth's death.

"What was in them?" Flint asked Tyrone, setting down the receiver.

"Their early finds, all the post-medieval crap."

Flint checked the brief list of box contents and stopped at box 1241. "Skeleton," he said.

"So?"

"I think we need to talk to our friendly neighbourhood policeman."

D.I. Thorne had been harassed by Bob Grimston's lawyer and was looking for any activity which could pose as progress. Flint's request was granted with enthusiasm and minimal red tape. Everything found in the wreckage of the Land Rover was to be laid out at the forensic science laboratory at Wetherby.

"We've interviewed just about all Ruth Hauxley's known associates," Thorne said glumly, "including the action group, but we can't put precious resources into a case of vandalism."

"And theft, and burglary, and harassment, and assault."

"Yes, well Miss Balleron didn't come clean on all that."

"You know the sabotage and the murder are connected?"

"That's a point of view."

The police can be less thorough than archaeologists and not every object found could be connected with the precise part of the vehicle in which it was found.

From the cab of the Land Rover had come the remains of Ruth's keys, a zipper, a trio of "Levi" studs, one pound fifty-six pence in change and fragmentary objects which probably represented the junk stuffed into all glove compartments. A heavily tarnished crucifix earring also remained, with other brassy blobs that would have been her circle of studs.

"Pity they had her cremated," Flint said. "I'd like to have seen her remains."

Thorne went to a side bench and produced a set of large colour photographs. "I hope you've got a strong stomach."

"Bodies is my business," Flint said, sifting the pictures one by one.

All that had remained was a pitiful set of bones; all were in fragments, all burned, many calcined to a white powdery state or congealed with a black residue which may have been the molten remains of the steering wheel or seat back or windscreen glass. Some of the grey-black matter still clinging to the bones must have been flesh. The skull was a mess of thin pieces of cranium plus a pile of loose teeth.

Flint came to a picture resembling a lump of coal: foot bones embedded in a mat of rubber from the soles of her heavy digging boots. The eyes of the boots formed green tangled blobs within the debris. An image came back to him of Ruth aloft on that footstool. She had been wearing trainers.

"What did the pathologist think to all this?"

Thorne wrenched one of his cheeks into an expression of pain. "Cutbacks."

"Pardon?"

"Look, it was Ruth's Land Rover, we all saw her get into it and there's no question that she was dead and no doubt in anyone's mind as to how she died."

"Did the pathologist examine her?"

"No – as I said, we're strapped for cash, I have to fight for my budget these days. Technically, this was a traffic accident, nobody else was involved, we had sufficient personal effects to identify the remains . . ."

"Did you check the dental records?" Flint asked.

"We tried, but she'd been out of the country for most of the last seven years, in Syria and Africa."

"What about when she was a kid?"

"Her school dentist is dead and I don't know where this is leading us. Laying all this out again took time you know. Time is money."

Amongst the pile of sundry metal fragments were three twisted lengths of grey metal, the length of a finger. Each had a double row of perforations and each had once been bent into a right-angle.

"Know what these are?" Flint asked.

"No."

"Corner re-enforcers from a skelly box."

"What's a skelly box?"

"A heavy brown cardboard box that FAS used to store their finds in. Okay, this is my postulate, shoot me down if you like, but here goes. Ruth Hauxley was travelling to York, taking thirteen boxes of post-medieval material to the museum."

"This stuff?" The detective pointed to the piles of

overcooked pottery and shattered clay pipes found in the rear of the wrecked vehicle.

"Yes. Now, in the footwell of the Land Rover she had her digging boots, her scruffy digging jeans and on the front seat, nice and safe, skelly box 1241 containing an eighteenth-century woman's skeleton. I've seen the site records; the skelly was intact, but the skull was found in the section edge and was crushed by a mattock during excavation."

The detective's eyes opened wide. "So you're saying this isn't Ruth Hauxley?"

"Ruth's quite a bright girl, she could have worked this scheme out in a couple of minutes. She throws us off the trail, but gets stuck in that ravine. So, she pours the skelly into her boots, piles the rest in her seat, takes off her earrings, then pushes the truck over the edge of the ravine and into the fire. Perhaps she even had time to set fire to the thing, just to make sure."

Thorne found a chair and dropped into it. "Oh Gawd, I'm going to look a right prat when the Super hears about this."

"He rubber-stamps your cases, though. Where does the buck stop?"

"Don't breathe a word!" Thorne said, pointing a warning finger and trying to think.

"Tell him it was your discovery. I mean, who'd have guessed it? If you'd ordered an autopsy, the pathologist would have spotted the trick in no time. I doubt if even Ruth expected to fool you for more than a day or two."

"So if Ruth is still alive, what's she up to? As you seem to be the expert, tell a poor copper what's behind all this. What about that torc thing, what was it worth?"

"God knows – twenty thousand pounds? But it's in a museum, so the question is irrelevant."

"There isn't more than one is there? Don't think I'm daft asking this, I never went to college, but, just suppose Mr Aitken and Ruth only handed one bit of gold to the museum and kept the rest."

Flint's thoughts turned to the empty cabinet at the Nissen hut and a whole new spectrum of motives opened up.

"Again, don't think I'm daft for asking, but do you find these things on their own, or in piles?"

"Singly in a burial, but a hoard could contain anything up to two hundred pieces."

Thorne's eyes widened. "Two hundred times twenty thousand – now that's worth a bit of risk. We're going to have to find Ruth before she flits to Brazil."

"I don't think theft is her motivation."

"So what is?"

"Shadesmoor."

"No, I'm not having conspiracies behind murders."

Flint formed his hands into a fist. "Look, this case of yours is hideously complex. Shadesmoor is a moral mire and there are a score of people who have been contaminated."

"Don't you work for them?"

"I'm one of the contaminated ones."

The policeman spread his hands in appeal. "I can't just wander up there and arrest everyone, can I? Wayne Drabble is back inside, we have this story about a 'posh' woman, but there were no other clues at the scene of the crime."

"You need another death."

"Don't tell me there's a serial killer loose on Shadesmoor."

"No, but there's a systematic campaign of sabotage. People could get hurt, probably my people. Ruth, for whatever reason, has got a pathological hatred for this project."

It was clear that Thorne believed the theory, and might even have dreamed it up himself given a little more time. "Do you mind if I put one of my men onto your site? We could disguise him as a digger."

Flint was far from sure, the spectre of Bob Grimston bore down on every decision he made. "Better clear it with Grimston first."

The policeman looked slightly sheepish. "It was Mr Grimston that insisted we do it."

Chapter Nineteen

Newspaper headlines reported the resurrection of Ruth Hauxley in sensational terms. If only Vikki were here, she could really go to town on this one, thought Flint, but Vikki did not reappear. She had done what he had demanded, she had stayed well clear of the case. What hurt was that she had stayed well clear of him, too.

The Police confirmed that "new evidence" (Flint was not mentioned) indicated that resourceful Ruth had found a way off Shadesmoor in the smoke.

She now seemed to come and go with ease, striking the castle at night like a Scots raiding party.

Within the Portakabin, Flint looked through Tyrone's computer file on Ruth, knowing that the police had far more information at their disposal and more resources than one laptop PC and one (admittedly brilliant) research student. Ruth was again the obvious suspect for all the crimes, but Flint had grown wary of the obvious.

"Tell me about Eleanor," he said.

Tyrone typed her first name and the computer searched for her file. Flint inwardly wanted her history to be dishwasher clean. She seemed too vulnerable to leave in the cast list of potential villains, but she was too deeply enmeshed in the web to be omitted.

"Aged forty-four. Educated at Roedean to age 18, then seems to have had a string of nothing jobs until married to Roger, Marquis of Thryburgh. That lasted three years, the divorce made the tacky end of the gossip columns."

"Why?" Flint asked.

"They used to have screaming fights at parties. She left him."

"Next?"

"Bits of scandal, then vanished for a while. Married again at thirty-one to a Harley Street doctor."

". . . of?"

"Psychiatry."

"Ah," Flint's mind recalled the frightened face of a woman who barely touched her food.

"I think we know where she vanished to," Tyrone said, with his tongue lolling at the corner of his mouth. "I bet she was sent to a Swiss nuthouse."

"Don't be uncharitable, she's not mad. Unhappy yes."

Tyrone was unable to accept the sympathetic viewpoint.

"If Ruth had remained dead, Eleanor could have been your screaming lunatic. You once told me the aristocracy are all mad due to in-breeding."

An image of a distraught face in the dark came back to Flint. He hated the idea and rejected it. "I talk rubbish some times. Is she still married to the quack?"

"No, they were together for six or seven years. He went bust after some scam went wrong and the marriage went at the same time."

"Since then?"

"She's harder to follow – probably back in the loony bin."

Flint sometimes wished he didn't need Tyrone. Sacking him would be so easy. He shifted the subject away from Eleanor. "By the way, where have you been the last couple of nights?"

"Oh, just out." Tyrone shifted sharply back. "Now Eleanor's father was called Edward and died of a stroke just before her second marriage broke up. Her mother died of something horrible when she was twenty. Eleanor has no kids, no siblings, and the nearest relative is her uncle Bernard."

Flint noted the evasion, adding it to a catalogue of odd behaviour by Tyrone. "Uncle Bernie, eh? He's a new one – can you chase him up next?"

"Okay, but we have to write up our preliminary results and prepare a presentation for Bob in only two weeks."

Grief, the presentation! It was the main chance to bid for the Phase II contract. That and the new term too. Flint was allowed a minute to fret and make *ad hoc* suggestions whilst Tyrone let him sweat.

"Don't worry, I've got it all under control," Tyrone soothed. "Want to see the cost breakdown? I've got it on a spreadsheet."

"Just tell me, simply. Will we win the contract?"

"Bob wants to make the assessment report available to our competitors, so they can all tender for Phase II."

"They can have it."

"No, he's bluffing."

"They can still have it: Shadesmoor is a pit of vipers."

"No, Doc, we can win it. I've been talking Bob round."

"Have you?" And it was "Bob" was it?

"You know, selling him on aspects of what we can do for Phase II."

"He's only interested in what we don't do."

"No, no, trust me. He's buying our ideas. Megan's with us too, she's working on him from a different flank. We'll catch him in the crossfire."

Conspiracies were building up on all sides. "I hope you both know what you're doing. Coming to the party tonight?"

The party was to close Phase I and wish the diggers on their way.

"Might as well." Tyrone curled his lip. "But why is it at Barney's house? He's a nerd, he's been crawling round Denmark all summer and he hasn't lifted a finger to help the project."

"This is his contribution, right? Come on, be generous, he's giving up his house and I'm told he's a decent cook. Barney offered to run the party and I said yes. It makes him feel wanted."

"It's one way of buying friends – I bet Megan isn't coming."

Flint narrowed his eyes. "Find out about their feud, could you? Just ask around, when you're compiling your files."

"Why?"

"I'm up to here with intrigue and the last thing I want is to spend the autumn term playing departmental politics."

Barney owned a suburbia-style semi-detached house in Wetherby. It was good and central: diggers from Leeds, York, Harrogate or college could reach it with equal ease. Others from the department could drop in, but as college was still quiet, only a few postgraduates turned up.

The host was indeed a practised cook. Flint thought his mushroom quiche superb and found a *humous* dip that was unusually palatable. He enjoyed parties, whether laid back and mellow or red-hot and hip, but the evening in Wetherby was a flat and unrewarding experience. The house was only half-full of people and Barney proved an incomplete host, choosing hackneyed '70 music for the CD player, then settling down to bore the American girls with details of his trip to Denmark. The Americans left early, reducing Tyrone's opinion of Barney even further.

"Where are the coats?" Tyrone ventured into the back bedroom and snapped on the light.

"Barney told me to dump them on the bed."

"He needs a personality transplant. Who wants to listen to Fleetwood Mac all night? Even your Bob Dylan's better."

Flint was only half listening, browsing the white DIY racking which held several hundred paperbacks and a few textbooks. "I collect Dylan records, I collect Bogart videos, but I don't inflict them on people at parties."

"Right, as I said, he's a charisma donor. I mean, tonight was our last chance."

"Our last chance?"

"Loretta is really keen on you."

Flint flicked the pages of an *Inspector Morse* novel, then replaced it. Barney was a keen consumer of detective stories and legal biographies: perhaps he had chosen the wrong assistant. When his investigation stalled, he might just pick the failed lawyer's brains: Barney would enjoy that.

"Hmm?"

"Loretta?" Tyrone repeated, pulling on his car coat.

"I don't seduce my diggers, or my students, it's a rule."

"What about Tania, last year?"

"You don't know about Tania, nobody knows about Tania."

"Everybody knows."

"Everybody is wrong."

The new term crashed over Flint's head before he was aware of the incoming tide. In London, he had only to learn the names of half the new intake each year. In Yorkshire, he had also to become acquainted with years two and three, plus the postgraduates and occasional students and a legion of staff, from learned professors to tea ladies. He was, of course, on show. He was the new boy, a fresher all over again. The absurd rituals and unwritten rules of a new institution had to be learned from scratch.

Seminar room E47 was booked for the presentation of the grandly titled *Shadesmoor Castle Archaeological Evaluation Project (Phase I)*. Flint had proposed a guest list of 20, including the local Inspector of Ancient Monuments and several leading academics. Bob Grimston vetoed the list and substituted his own. Flint and Tyrone would deliver the results, but the only academics present would be Megan and two others retained on the Shadesmoor payroll. Bob Grimston, his designer, his thrusting sidekick, his lawyer and the constantly immaculate Eleanor Balleron represented the philistines.

Flint talked about the castle, the manor, and the DMV.

"The what?" Grimston asked.

"DMV, sorry for the jargon. The Deserted Medieval Village."

Tyrone operated the slide projector and positioned overhead projector charts in tune to the performance. At times, Grimston would interrupt. Flint had just described the evidence relating to a Civil War earthwork inconveniently situated beneath the planned visitor centre.

"Civil War?" Grimston asked. "Isn't that too late to be archaeology?"

"No, it's never too late: everything's a potential monument. If English Heritage don't decide to schedule the earthwork, we would have to excavate it in entirety. That is, unless you could re-locate your visitor centre fifty yards downhill."

"That's possible," the designer whispered.

Grimston seemed satisfied. "Don't dig it, we'll move the building."

Flint arrived at his conclusions, aware that Eleanor was watching his act, watching every move. Somehow, this made him more nervous than Grimston's aggressive challenges. Tyrone completed the seminar by running through an outline costing for Phase II. "We can work up a detailed spec. for your second tender, once we know what options you're taking."

"You do it," Grimston said after only a few moments' silence. "The whole job is yours."

No bids. No chance for rivals to snatch the prize away from UNY-DIG. Tyrone had been correct, but Flint could hardly believe it.

"But I don't like this DDT," Grimston said.

"DMV," Flint corrected.

"I know what I don't like. It's only a few shit-and-stick huts and everyone thinks it's on the opposite side of the river."

"We can't just bulldoze it."

"Why? Who's to know?"

Flint swept his arm around the room, "We would."

Grimston took a leisurely look at his coterie. "I don't think anyone here would object to the loss of a few mud huts."

Heads shook very slightly. Megan seemed to stiffen, as though wishing she was invisible.

"And the Manor House – Duffy?" ⚡

One of the tame academics immediately coughed and turned red. "We already know the construction sequence of the Manor, it's all contained in the deeds and the estate maps."

"So we forget the Manor too?" Flint said between his teeth.

"No, not entirely, but one could be circumspect," the robot continued in his pre-programmed objection.

"You are going to have to redraft this report slightly," Grimston said. "Before we let any clothheads read it."

"Meaning English Heritage, or the Inspectorate, or the local authority . . ."

"Anyone outside this room. Let me have your revised project plan in seven days, with costs. Keep 'em low, Jeff, I don't want to muck around obtaining quotes. Better the devil you know."

The lord had spoken and the lady gave the besieged Flint just a little twist of a supporting smile. Grimston announced he was buying lunch and named the local hotel. Flint tagged along with the crowd, just to find out if there was truthfully any such thing as a free lunch.

Something was wrong with the green van, which had gone to be "looked at" by a garage recommended by Carl. Flint travelled to the meal in Megan's car, with Tyrone's Spitfire overtaking them after the first bend.

"I can't believe we're doing this," he said.

"Believe it. The rat race is over and the rats have won."

"We should just refuse to have anything else to do with the whole crazy scheme."

"And lose your job? This money is worth one-and-a-half posts to the department. Guess who the whole post is?"

"Me?"

"Some bright spark has waved his magic wand and turned our poor, neglected polytechnic into a university. It's the same buildings, the same staff, the same students and the same funding. I'm under orders to cram in as many students as I can just to make money – have you seen the size of your class lists yet?"

"Yes and I groaned long and loud."

"You can always go back to your ivory tower in London."

"No, they were glad to get shot of me. Professor Grant decided he didn't like me about three years ago."

"I heard he didn't like your extra-curricular activities."

"Yes, I suppose I lost him a few friends in Greece last summer. It means I'm here to stay."

"Good, we need you. All is not lost at Shadesmoor, they are amenable to suggestions, we can make an impact."

"The only impact I can think of is a palaeolithic hand-axe thunking into Tom Aitken's skull."

"Oh you're not still on about that!"

"Megan, he's dead, he was your lover after all."

"Ex-lover, and it was never official."

"What is your angle on this Megan? You used to be such a radical."

"So did Betty, and she fell for it. So did you, and you're falling for it."

"You don't have a hidden agenda, by any chance?"

"Whatever do you mean?"

"I'm hoping you're some kind of communist mole burrowing deep into the project only to expose it to the world."

"You sound like Tom now."

"Aitken said that?"

"No," she said quickly.

"Was that his plan? Was that why he sold out?"

"No – I don't know, and I wouldn't ask."

"Why?"

Megan jammed her foot hard on the brake pedal and the grey hatchback screeched to a halt. Someone hooted and swerved past them. From her handbag Megan took an envelope.

"I received this today."

He pulled out a folded sheet of A4 typing paper, reading the simple, cryptic message:

THERE ARE MANY GHOSTS AT
SHADESMOOR CASTLE

As far as he could remember, the typing was reminiscent of the "FLINT KNOWS" letter Bob Grimston had shown him in June. It was identical to the typeface of another letter which had been troubling him since the weekend. Flint reached into his jacket pocket and proffered a slip of paper.

"I've had this three days. The postmark is York, so we're down to a suspect list 100,000 strong."

Megan took the slip of paper which read:

TIN TAX TIN TAX
POP POP POP
DROP DEAD DROP DEAD
DROP DROP DROP

"Tin tax?"

"An in-joke on site, but I wouldn't ask Joss to explain it."

"It's Ruth Hauxley sending these letters," she declared.

"Poor Ruth."

"Poor us. She's a menace. Jeff! A murdering menace who's determined to wreck everything. These are death threats, if you hadn't noticed."

And they had been posted just a day or two after Ruth's resurrection had been made official. "Don't show them to anyone, will you?" Flint said.

"What?"

"Not Bob, not the police, not yet."

"Why the hell not?"

"Because that's what we're supposed to do. Ruth wants us to play her game, but from now on I'm making up my own rules."

Megan swallowed. "You keep the letters then. I hope you're right about the game."

She re-started her stalled engine and said nothing more until they reached the restaurant. Ruth the mystery vandal had been too expensive to hunt down, but Ruth the murderess warranted a huge expenditure of resources. The police had declared that she would soon be caught, but at least one lecturer in archaeology did not share their confidence. He'd borrow a pile of Barney's forensic science books as bedtime reading, then begin the detective work in earnest.

Chapter Twenty

His first seminar had been met with a mixture of shock and delight. A varied assortment of second and third years had been confronted with an equally varied assortment of philosophies on the significance of the past. Flint had thrown around names like Barthes, Marx, Foucault, Derrida and various other (mainly dead) philosophers, then left the class to chase ideas around the table.

"It's all crap," one student asserted.

"Define crap," the departmental smart alec responded.

"What do we mean by crap?" offered another.

"Doctor Flint! There's an urgent call," Debs stuck her blonde perm around the door of room E47.

He excused himself and left the class de-constructing the word "crap". Who said UNY students had no intellectual depth?

In the adjoining office, a phone was held up for his attention. A familiar, if quavering voice spoke to him. "Doctor Flint?"

"Is this who I think it is?" He dare not speak the name Ruth. Covering the receiver, he whispered that he needed privacy. Debs took the hint and closed the door on him.

"I need to talk to you," said the voice. "On your own."

"Fine, so where are you?"

"Y7." She hung up the telephone.

He closed his eyes tightly then re-opened them, rubbing hard. Ruth must have cracked up. Flint knew how hard living on the run could be. Without friends, it soon became impossible. The seminar group could wait. He jogged along the corridor and into the UNY-DIG office. Joss was sitting closest to the door and Flint handed him a pile of change.

"Buy us three coffees, Joss."

Another hint was taken well and Joss departed with a mock salute. Tyrone raised his eyebrows.

"Ruth has made contact. Does Y7 mean anything to you?"

Tyrone slowly shook his head, making an effort to frown.

"It's what Ruth said when I asked where she was; I guess she imagines I'm bugged. You've been through Ruth's history and the FAS archives, Y7 must have some significance."

A brightness came to Tyrone's clouded features. "Ah, Y-7. That's the FAS site coding system isn't it? Form Farm was A-9, because it was one of the A1 road widening sites: each was designated A something. Likewise, R is for Ripon, H is for Harrogate, so Y must be one of their York projects."

In moments, Flint was on the phone to Clive, the chap employed on a short contract to work through the FAS material. Only two minutes later he learned that Y-7 had been the last evaluation project undertaken by FAS in York.

Fixing the carburettor on the green van had cost more than the estimate. Flint paid, cursed Carl silently, then drove directly to York. He approved heartily of traffic calming and pedestrianisation of city centres. Unfortunately, when one is in a hurry and one has to park half a mile from the city centre, green ideals tend to be submerged in red frustration. Map in hand, he found himself in a sidestreet running off Stonegate, the old *via Praetoria* of the Roman fortress. Its gambrel roofs overhung the street, deserted of shoppers, not yet thronged by youths hunting half-timbered pubs. He walked around and about, finding a "snickleway" devoid of people. The alley broadened to reveal a trio of derelict shops and the back of a red brick warehouse. Like so many towns, York seemed to burst with new retail schemes, yet dozens of older shops always stood empty. The Bob Grimstons of the world had much to answer for.

It was late evening, virtually dark. The Ghost Walk Tour would be abroad, spreading legends of haunted snickleways. For just a moment, Flint paused, remembering Ruth's bizarre behaviour at Shadesmoor Castle. There was a very real chance she was a murderess and a very real chance she was completely mad.

He gingerly tried the front door of the second house, but it was locked. At floor level was a grating, which he tapped vigorously with his keys, hissing Ruth's name. The door opened a crack.

"Hello," he said, then proffered a bag of doughnuts. "I imagine you're hungry."

Ruth's face was unwashed, yet pale beneath a greasy, matted mess of dyed, clipped hair. She quickly closed the door behind him and led down into the basement, closing two more doors.

The room was quite amazing. Cold, dank, cobweb-filled, it was lit by a single candle. A mountain bike stood in the corner. Windows looked out onto blackness and a door led beneath the street. Ruth pushed this door open to reveal an old basement well, covered over when the street above was moved to accommodate the warehouse.

"We surveyed this house," she said. "They were going to knock it down to build a new shopping complex, but the recession killed it off. Good old recession."

"How are you?"

Ruth sniffled and dabbed her nose with a dark grey tissue.

"I can't hide any more. I've no more money, I've got a cold and I don't know what to do."

"Have a doughnut."

She took one and bit it almost in half. "'scuse manners."

"Thought of giving yourself up?"

Ruth lolled back on the heap of cardboard boxes and carpet remnants that served as a bed. She finished the doughnut before answering. "Can't. Not until I've got them."

"Who?" Flint remained standing.

"Grimston, and Eleanor Balleron." Her words were edged with venom.

"What are you going to do? Assassinate them in turn?"

"No! Don't you see? You're all falling into Grimston's trap. He framed that burglar, but you saw through the plot, so he framed me instead."

"Grimston had nothing to do with it: it was the police who had you down as the suspect."

"And you helped them. That's why I ran away from The Old Rectory: the whole world seemed to be working for Shadesmoor. I knew if I was arrested, it would take the police another six months, or longer, to find me innocent. By that time, Grimston would be safe."

Flint had himself once followed the same train of logic. "So the purpose of the pantomime at the castle was simply to delay the project long enough for the police to discover new facts?"

"Not the police – you. You're right in the middle, you're inside, you're close to them all. You can find out what is really going on."

He did not share her confidence, or her line of argument. "Give me one good reason why Grimston should have killed Tom Aitken. Grimston bought him, he told me himself, he bought Aitken over to his side, so why have him killed?"

"Because Tom was only pretending to go along with the project."

"Why?"

Another faint shake of the head. "Because of that woman. She finally broke us up. I tolerated the others . . ."

"Including Megan Preece?"

Ruth groaned. "He was so indiscriminate."

It was Flint's turn to feel pain. "So why was this new woman the final straw?"

"She was different, she effected him, she effected his work and she wrecked all the effort we'd put in to smash the Shadesmoor project."

"Eleanor Balleron?"

"How did you know?"

"I guessed."

"Has she been after you too?"

"Me?" He was immediately fearful that the answer might be yes. "No, she's too old and too upper class."

That was part of her appeal, so Tom said." She dabbed her nose again and sniffled.

"Did he ever say anything about Grimston's reaction to this relationship?"

"Grimston likes to own things, own people. I threatened to tell him what was going on, then Tom threw me out of The Rectory."

"And did you tell?"

"No. They all deserved each other."

Still, Flint thought, the liaison would have given Bob Grimston sleepless nights. Jealousy and paranoia could be a lethal mixture.

"So Tom treated you like a doormat, threw you out and ruined your save Shadesmoor campaign. You had a pretty good motive for slugging him with that hand-axe."

"He wasn't worth it."

"Do you truthfully believe that?"

She gave a deep, well practised sign which terminated in a cough. Ruth's tone mellowed. "He wasn't as awful as I make him sound. He was too good, and he knew it. That was his problem. I don't believe he loved that woman, and I don't believe he sold out. I think he was just protecting me until he discovered the truth."

"About what? What is all this about?"

"I don't know!" Ruth moaned. "I'm trying to find out."

Could he believe her? Ruth was more rational than he had expected. "What was the point of the silly letters?"

"What letters? I never sent any letters."

Flint couldn't see a typewriter in the room, but thought it likely Ruth was not telling the whole truth. He'd set aside the question of the letters until he had a means of distinguishing whether she was lying. He offered Ruth another doughnut.

"Just for my own sanity, you ought to tell me how you got away from the moor. That was very clever, using those bones to fake your death. We were all fooled."

For the first time, Ruth showed a spark of warmth. "Good, wasn't it? When I was trying to get away from that maniac in the sports car, the idea just came to me. If I'd stuck to the road, I'd never have got away."

"So you fooled us. Then what?"

"When I got away from the fire, I hitchhiked back to our office: I had two sets of keys, I left Tom's in the car. Anyway, when I got to the office, I took out all our small finds and sold them in the antique market round the corner."

Sin piled on sin.

"They were only a few coins and buckles, oh, and a bellarmine jar. I kept my mountain bike at the office: there wasn't room in my friends' flat. So, I made myself a nest here and waited. Then, I'd ride out to the moor and camp out in an old shed I know, in the woods where Grimston is going to build his wild west train set."

"And you'd hit and run?"

"I'd see a chance to do some mischief, then I'd come back here and hide for a few days. No-one notices me here: the Government has thrown so many kids onto the streets, I'm just another beggar sitting in a doorway."

"So what do you do next?"

"Die of pneumonia."

Flint fished in his back pocket and found he had twenty-three pounds. He gave Ruth the twenty and the rest of the doughnuts.

"Promise me you're innocent."

"I haven't killed you."

"You nearly did at the castle."

"Did I? Sorry, I was pretty wound up that night, I nearly fell down the keep getting up there."

"And you escaped down the *garde-robe*?"

"I knew Grimston had hired security men, but I had to get into the keep to show him he doesn't own the place. That's our heritage he's destroying, and you're helping him."

"And you're wasting police time. They won't start looking for the real killer until you hand yourself in and we can convince them you're innocent."

"I can't give myself up – I hit that daft copper."

"Simon Thorne's a reasonable guy, for a copper. I might be able to point you in the direction of a good lawyer."

"I'll think about it."

"You do that, but promise me, no more midnight malarkey? If you decide to stay here, I'll post you fifty pounds each Monday. Look upstairs for a white letter addressed to The Occupier."

She hugged him. Unwashed and unloved, Ruth hugged Flint, then kissed his bearded cheek.

"You're a saint," she said.

Flint was barely comforted. Just around the block was a shrine to Margaret Clitheroe, another of York's saints. Caught aiding fugitives in the Middle Ages, she had been crushed to death as punishment. He hoped D.I. Thorne might be a little more sympathetic.

Chapter Twenty-One

Rain drenched Shadesmoor, drumming on the roof of the Portakabin. Flint had no lectures scheduled on Thursdays and had gone to the site to assist with redrafting the project plan for Phase II. As raindrops exploded on the wire mesh protecting the hut windows, Tyrone watched with gloomy disinterest.

"At least it's not snowing yet," Flint said.

"Brilliant." Tyrone was wearing a thick, white, submarine commander pullover. The comment did nothing to lift his mood.

"This is the hard reality of British field archaeology, son. Mud and rain and peanuts in your pay packet."

"I never thought Yorkshire was like this," Tyrone said, unusually distracted, unusually fatigued.

"You mean not a satanic mill in sight?"

"No. I mean the people," he said. "I didn't expect to be dealing with people like Eleanor and Bob."

"Ah, you were expecting to be surrounded by flat-capped northern stereotypes, labour voters to a man and proud of it. Well, up here you're in solid Tory territory, all green wellies and wax jackets. You should be settling in nicely."

"Oh I am. I like it. I like the space, if you don't mind me sounding like a greenie."

"There's going to be a little less space when the big yellow machines move in. Have you had thoughts on the mitigation study on the DMV?"

Tyrone made an attempt at raising his enthusiasm output. "I think we can sell it to Bob next week. We dig five percent of the site, we lose another five percent to the bulldozers and the rest should be sealed when they level up the site."

"Not level-down?" Flint asked, concerned that Tyrone might have sunk too deeply into the Shadesmoor slime.

"No, the engineer is worried about flooding. The lower meadow is a swamp as soon as it starts raining. Do we have the manpower to start Phase II digging in November?"

"We will: you may have to excuse my presence on site, at least in the mornings. I'll try to keep afternoons clear as best I can." Flint tried to see what Tyrone had been doing with the computer. "Have you got anywhere on Aitken?"

"I've hardly had time . . ."

"Come on, Tyrone. I keep telling people how tirelessly efficient you are, don't let me down now."

"I don't have enough data."

Flint sat on the table beside the laptop. "What about all those speculative scenarios you were going to draw up?"

"Ruth did it," he said. "Whatever motive you choose, crime of passion, anti-Shadesmoor conspiracy, theft of artifacts, Ruth could have been behind it." Tyrone finished with a yawn.

"Have you tried turning the conspiracy around and making Bob Grimston the villain?"

"No, there's nothing to go on."

"Okay, try this. Megan hinted that Aitken was

playing a deep game in order to smash the system from within. Perhaps Bob got wind of what he planned."

"No," said Tyrone firmly. "I double-checked with Megan. She said you misunderstood her."

Flint began to be exasperated. He was unused to such negative responses from Tyrone. "Bob could have other reasons for disliking Aitken."

"Such as?"

"Eleanor."

"No. Ruth did it." Tyrone said with tiredness. "Whatever sob story she sold you, she's just trying to paint this project black. Why don't we just shop her so we can get on with our proper work?"

Yes, the tentacle had reached Tyrone. Flint wanted to believe Ruth's story, he wanted the conspiracy theory to lay at the root of the plot, and he began to want to see the project sunk by the weight of its own guilt.

"I'd like to see any new data on Bob . . ." Flint began, but was interrupted.

"Bob still thinks you're on his side," Tyrone added. "We'll lose the contract if you make the wrong line of enquiry."

He was making strong use of the word "you", not "we". Tyrone was no longer a reliable ally.

"Bob can't be guilty. It would be stupid to upset him just because you don't like developers."

Stupid, yes. Flint had no intention of becoming a fallen rebel, noble but unemployed. Like Q. Fabius Maximus, he would avoid any battles he was unsure of winning. If he wanted to pin the blame on Bob Grimston, he was going to need firmer evidence. Perhaps he needed a little legal advice.

*   *   *

A happier, yet still introverted, Sue Carrick was persuaded to take dinner with Flint that evening. When given a choice of restaurants the solicitor had been politic, choosing a mercifully cheap Italian place off the Headrow in Leeds. Sue was in the brick-red suit she often wore at the office and she began the evening by showing Flint a photograph of her husband, and her daughter, as if to lay ground rules from the start.

"I did investigate your background," she added, once the waiter had left the cubicle with an order for Chianti.

"How?"

"I asked your former friend when we lunched together."

"Vikki?"

Sue nodded, mouth too full of bread to answer.

He grimaced. "How are you on libel?"

"It would be slander," she corrected, "and it would have to be untrue."

"How is Wayne?"

"Back inside. Wayne is one of society's losers. I can't imagine this will be the last time I will defend him."

Chianti arrived to order. Sue tasted it, pronounced it acceptable, then gave her order in Italian. Just to make the point, Flint did the same. Sue smiled quietly, as if a tie had been declared. For a while they made small talk, with Flint mainly talking, Sue mainly listening.

"You want something," she suddenly said.

"Do I? I suppose I do." Had he become that transparent? "Okay, I confess, I want to beg a favour."

"If by that, you mean you would like to engage my services, I can provide you with our fees sheet."

209

"Sadly, I'm not one of the privileged few who can afford to buy justice."

"Vikki told me you were anti-establishment."

"My salary is a third of what you get paid."

"By choice – you probably have a third of my workload. So tell me what I have to do."

"I need to know about the legal side of the Shadesmoor Castle caper. Who owns what, what hoops were jumped through to get the project approved, what legal loopholes were exploited . . ."

Sue literally chewed over the idea. "That would cost you, ooh, fifty thousand pounds."

He flinched.

"Plus VAT."

"Aw, come on; the action group have piles of papers, they did all the legal legwork . . . I've read it, but I can't see the wood for the gobbledegook."

"I don't understand why you would want to know."

"I need to square my data. I seem to be the only person left in the known universe who thinks the Shadesmoor project is dodgy."

"If by 'dodgy' you mean 'illegal' then I think you're wrong. You will find that the project is watertight. If you mean it is unethical, that is another matter. Ethics and the law are not always compatible."

"Okay. A man was killed, why? What circumstance was so desperate that the only solution was to have Tom Aitken killed? More important, what possible threats to the project were closed once he was eliminated?"

"Why don't you ask the police? There are fifteen detectives working on the murder, they will ask the questions you're asking, but they will pay their own legal bills."

"Please?" Flint adopted a pleading expression. "Give me a pointer at least. If I start to trawl the paperwork, what sort of thing do I look for?"

"It won't be in the paperwork, or the action group's solicitors would have spotted it." Sue took revenge on another piece of French bread, ripping it deftly in half. "Oh, perhaps I'm being unfair to your argument. Forget the available paperwork. All the required legal processes will have been followed, all the necessary authorities will be satisfied with every facet of the project. However . . ."

Two portions of tuna and pasta bake arrived to interrupt her (more tuna had died for the sake of the project). Sue would say nothing more until they were alone, making a preliminary foray into the food.

"Perhaps I can construct a line of argument that there is additional information which has not been made public. They will have prepared their own mountain of paper for the planning enquiry, perhaps aspects of their submissions were fraudulent. Perhaps they have broken the letter of their signed undertakings. Perhaps their finances are not in order. There will be a whole host of legal documents pertaining to the operation of the company, its ownership, and so on, which could contain deeply hidden flaws."

Flint nodded in agreement.

"I could speculate forever and you could hunt forever and find nothing, so is there anything in particular that causes you concern? In all the films I've seen, you private investigators operate off lucky hunches. What's your hunch?"

"Okay, for a start Eleanor may be landed gentry, but I get the feeling she's broke."

"Most of them are, on paper."

"Her father only left her fifteen thousand pounds

211

in his will; but the house alone must be worth half a million, then there's the land, the cottages, the family silver and so on. That sounds like a pretty big fiddle to me."

"It's no fiddle, the estate will be held in trust, possibly somewhere offshore. A family trust is a very common device for avoiding death duties and other capital taxes."

He narrowed his eyes, thinking the word "fiddle" had been completely apt. "So Eleanor doesn't actually own the estate?"

"Probably not, in the strict technical sense. There will be a clause in the trust deed giving her certain rights to income, or to residence in the house for example, but the estate need not legally be hers."

"So if Eleanor wanted to throw up a theme park on the estate, could she?"

"It would depend on the wording of the trust document and the goodwill of the trustees."

"Who would be?"

She gave a shrug. "A lawyer, a bank, family friends."

"Can you get hold of a copy of the relevant document for me? I imagine they must be at the public records office."

"No, trust deeds are not public documents. They don't have to be registered like wills or land deeds. Likewise, the identity of the trustees is not necessarily known."

Flint was shocked. He had always suspected such legal chicanery existed but assumed that tight official monitoring limited its extent.

"How do we find out?"

"We?"

"This is part of the Wayne Drabble case: you'll

only clear him by pinning the crime on someone else."

"No, no, that's an illusion promoted by American
court room dramas: it never happens in real life. Most
people who escape prosecution for murder do so on
technicalities, or because the police are unable to
build a watertight case. The murder charge against
Wayne has been dropped because the police cannot
find any evidence to *prove* he committed the murder
beyond all reasonable doubt."

"But he's still charged with burglary?"

"Yes. The case is held over, pending the murder investigation being completed because, as you
very well know, there are allegations of a criminal
conspiracy."

"So my evidence would help him." Flint fished for
a little aid. "If I dig too openly into the Shadesmoor
books, my contract will be terminated and writs will
come flying in my direction. One wrong move and
their lawyer sues me."

"Who is he?"

"Thurlscote – he operates out of Harrogate."

"Oh yes. I've met him."

Each profession moved in its own tight little
world: lawyers were probably as incestuous as
archaeologists.

"Dig?" he asked, making motions towards the tuna
with his fork.

"Digging's your business."

"We usually hire a sub-contractor to loosen the
topsoil."

"Vikki said you were irrepressible."

"In so many words?" Could Vikki Corbett spell
irrepressible?

"I never reveal confidences."

"Good. Now to the real reason I asked you out for dinner tonight."

Sue raised an eyebrow over her glass.

"I have another client for you."

Chapter Twenty-Two

It was time Ruth came in from the cold. She had been persuaded to leave her hideout and spend the weekend at Flint's house, using the bath, savouring the soft sheets and the international cuisine. Flint tried to make amends for his part in framing her: he went into Harrogate and bought her a pullover and jeans, he found her a couple of shirts which had shrunk away from his size and a nightie which Vikki usually left "just in case". Such a long shot could easily be discounted now. A real fire, the early nights and the willing provision of hot water bottles and lemon-scented drinks attacked her cold and restored her morale. Without the pressure of suspicion, Ruth told him a little more about Tom Aitken, a softer, deeper Tom Aitken than had ever been revealed before. Flint regretted that he'd never cornered the man in the conference bar and bought him a pint.

Over the weekend, Ruth reserved her energy for destroying what remained of Flint's trust in Bob Grimston. Subtly indoctrinated by her passionate argument, Flint the anarchist became ever more convinced he was finally on the right trail. The scalp of a capitalist was a prize he would dearly love to win.

He cancelled his Monday morning lecture and drove to Leeds, delivering Ruth to Sue Carrick and then moving on to the BBC local radio station. Flint wanted to give an interview straight away, on air, where the facts could not be distorted as strongly as in print. Close companionship with Vikki had taught him a thing or two about the media.

As Flint drove back towards college, he listened to the replay of his interview over the car radio.

"But why do you think she telephoned you?" The radio journalist asked.

He'd squirmed at that question. "I . . . I . . . guess she knew I could be trusted," he had blurted.

"Trusted not to go to the police?"

"Yes . . . I knew she was innocent, so as soon as she is cleared the police can try to find the real culprits. We know there was a woman involved . . ."

"I don't think we can go into the facts of the case now, can we?" The reporter had looked out through a glass screen to where his producer was desperately waving a clipboard.

"Doctor Jeremy Flint, thank you.

"Fool!" Flint growled, as he drove through the red-brick pillars at the entrance to the university.

Full of enthusiasm for the chase, he bounded into the Mandela building and up the stairs. Tryone was on site, so he took a seat in the deserted UNY–DIG office and switched on the PC. For the rest of the day, he hunted around files, adding information, printing lists, sketching charts. Ruth was still the prime suspect, there was nothing to prove her innocence, but that was not the way the law operated. Flint needed to shift the blame and the suspicion, if his own gut feelings about Ruth were correct. Time and again he came back to Grimston.

*　　*　　*

Robert Lancelot Grimston, aged forty-eight, born in Leeds, left school at sixteen. Just made it into the list of Britain's Top 500 richest people in the *Sunday Times*, his fortune being a paltry thirty million, but difficult to quantify with any precision. Bob had begun life as a bricklayer, quickly moved on to form his own building firm, then into property deals. A holiday park at Bridlington had been his most ambitious project before Shadesmoor Castle reared out of the moorland mist. Flint reflected on the hundreds of clench-fisted bargains driven by Grimston on his road to the top: men sacked, tenants evicted, landowners short-changed, local authorities brow-beaten, financial institutions sweet-talked and donatives scattered liberally to those who smoothed the path for his plans. The man's history would be loaded with graft and petty corruption, yet he was the cleanest person on the file. No psychiatry for Bob Grimston, no criminal convictions, no hints of broken romances or broken dreams. The hard edge of his character cut through where the Ruths, Waynes, Megans and even the Tom Aitkens had failed.

So where did Eleanor fit in the conspiracy? His finger had run the mouse of the computer to the point where the files linked Eleanor and Bob. Bob was very protective of Eleanor, but she appeared to resent, even fear him. It was to Flint (a stranger) she had turned in her moments of crisis. And she had called him Tom. Flint yawned, but the yawn turned into a smile of satisfaction. Back in 1478, the lord of the castle had murdered his wife for being unfaithful, and had proved himself to be above the law. Now Bob was lord of the castle, and his lady had been unfaithful. History has a habit of repeating itself.

* * *

217

Barney was lounging in the staff Common Room when Flint walked in, slightly jaded. He dropped into a low chair beside Barney, waiting for the coffee queue to shrink before he joined it.

"So, Jeffrey old bean, how has the first fortnight at our humble seat of learning struck you? How are your comprehensive school dropouts bearing up?"

Flint found computers drained his energy and he was too exhausted to rise to the bait.

"Do you know, four of my lot have technically failed their A-levels. Our minimum entrance requirement is that our students fail in three subjects. It's laughable – pile 'em deep and sell 'em cheap."

"Blame the government, they keep chopping our per capita grant."

"Someone was saying you've caught the mad murderess." He leaned in close. "Good show. Any rewards going?"

"No, sadly. Ruth ain't our moorland murderess."

"Oh?"

"No, she's chalked up a few petty felonies, like swatting a policeman with the *Newstead Report*, but she's no murderess. I've fixed her up with a lawyer who seems confident she'll walk free."

Barney was genuinely surprised. "So the hunt goes on? If you need to borrow any more of my books, please do, I don't need them."

"Thanks. I'm pretty clueless and so are the police. I'm hoping they can make something out of the freaky letters – Ruth says she wasn't the one who sent them."

"Who were the proud recipients?" Barney asked.

"Myself, Bob Grimston and Megan."

"Megan? That would make her feel important. She would enjoy the thrill of it: a secret letter, a threat.

Ruth and she were deadly rivals you know, fighting for the hand of Tom Aitken."

"Literally?"

"Who's to know? I can't see why he was special to her, she's not normally very choosy."

Flint felt mildly insulted.

"I saw her this morning, you know, about to pounce on that new Nigerian postgrad," Barney continued.

"How do you mean 'pounce'?"

"Grab, ensnare, drag back to her boudoir and devour. You escaped just in time my lad. It was nauseating to see her hang over him like that, I mean, she's a good fifteen years older than him and . . ."

". . . he's black," Flint added dryly, "the ultimate sin." He had begun to notice an unsettling reactionary tone to Barney's comments. Tyrone he could tolerate, at least he had a consistent (if misguided) philosophy.

"Oh it doesn't bother her, black, brown, male, female . . ."

"Female?"

"If pushed. Any port in a storm for old Megan."

Flint's heart sank further. He hated to hear a colleague being denigrated, still more hated to think of himself as an object of somebody else's dalliance. Barney had certainly stacked up an arsenal of grudges against Megan.

"Have you heard about the A1 Club?" Barney continued. "It has a large and not very select membership. Ask around in the Union bar."

Was this fact or fantasy? "A1?"

"Everyone's been up the A1."

Within thirty seconds, Flint was at the door of the

room, forgetting coffee, wanting to forget Barney. Thumping colleagues was probably a disciplinary offence, as was gross sexism. How did Betty tolerate it? He'd ask her.

Professor Vine was at her desk, still labouring through a month of accumulated correspondence.

"Jeff, not gone home yet? Sit down, I hear you missed a lecture this morning. How are things at the coal face?"

"Tough. Your department is wound up in a cat's cradle of corruption, jealousy, bigotry and, let's face it, murder."

The professor gave a smile, not the shocked reaction one would expect to such an outburst. "Why do you think I appointed you? You don't surprise me, I know what's going on. I could see all this unfolding before me last year, and so my solution was to ask Tom Aitken to form a University Unit. It was not my most successful idea. In fact, it only made things worse, tragically worse."

"You blame yourself for Aitken's death?"

"I'm not confessing to the crime, but my actions were, perhaps, as the wing beats of the Brazilian butterfly that causes hurricanes to strike Dorset."

"Chaos theory?"

"It applies very well to archaeology, I can let you have the references."

"Please do," Flint had been thrown off the scent. "I've noticed there's bad blood between Barney and Megan."

"Yes, my children do bicker. Do me a very large favour and keep your head well clear."

The next part was delicate. "I've heard a number of unkind rumours about Megan. Mainly from Barney, but not exclusively. I go to the bar, people talk, students gossip. Are people being unfair, or is she the official departmental man eater?" He dare not mention the A1 Club (if it existed), but Betty knew precisely what he meant.

"Let us be kind and say that Megan has acquired a certain reputation, but then so have you. You have been described as 'a compulsive womaniser'."

"Compulsive is stretching a point."

"That wasn't my choice of words, I'm sorry if the quotation causes you offence. You're not the first college lecturer to be cast in this mould. Megan is another, but because she's female, she arouses ridicule. She has what I might describe as a male attitude to sex and seduction. People raise their eyebrows, but I can't condemn her, without also condemning you and a score of other academics in the Arts Faculty. To accuse her of nymphomania is simply not fair."

"Everyone needs a hobby," Flint mused.

The professor simply smiled and shook her head.

"Have she and Barney . . .?"

"I wouldn't pry, but we can suppose, he was new once. Now what about your students, what do you think of them?"

Flint puffed out his cheeks. "They have potential," seemed a constructive comment.

"Good. I hope you grow to enjoy it here. Mr Grimston seemed very impressed by your work at Shadesmoor."

Impressed by the balance sheet thought Flint, rising to leave. "You've never mentioned my history to Grimston have you?"

"By that you mean your novel application of forensic archaeology? No, we must keep some cards

221

in our hands. He might however learn something from your appearance on the radio."

"That was the point of performing on air; I had to get my story straight from day one, rather than the press grabbing the wrong end of the stick and putting me on Ruth's side of the argument."

"If that happens, we will lose Shadesmoor. Can you step aside from this now and leave the police to do their job?"

Betty was being so nice, but Flint began to be suspicious about the way the conversation was turning. Grimston had an impressive array of techniques for winning people over to his point of view.

"I can't leave this to the police. Our murderer is extremely clever and ten steps ahead of them all the way. All the evidence seems to have been faked or twisted around so that it only serves to confuse. We're all being toyed with."

"But what can you do?"

"I'm trying to imitate that butterfly of yours; fluttering my little wings in the hope it's sufficient to make a difference."

"Leave it alone."

"I can't. Consider this: as we don't know why Aitken was killed, we don't know whether the murderer will strike again."

The professor's face fell and she glanced across at her pile of letters as if to anchor herself to reality. "This is all too frightening. I can almost see it happening again. I asked Tom to join the department and he died: you will be careful, Jeff? Be very, very careful."

Tyrone was not expected until the morning, bringing in the Phase II proposals to be checked before they could be faxed to Bob Grimston. Two over-keen students waited outside Flint's new office: he asked them to go away and come back on Tuesday afternoon. Once alone, he rolled around in his chair, staring at the ceiling, thinking he really ought to drive home, but dreaded mixing with the rush hour traffic. He'd stay a while, perhaps attack another chapter of Tyrone's thesis.

Down came the blue volume and Flint was soon embroiled in the argument for Sub-Roman pottery production in the South-East. He was only onto his third page when the phone rang. Someone knew little about university lecturers if they expected them still to be at their desks after five-thirty.

"Is that Doctor Flynn?" asked the female voice, well spoken with a hint of a Yorkshire accent.

"Doctor Flint," he corrected.

"You were on the radio, today. You found that girl and you said you were going to get her off."

"Who is this?"

"You said you could be trusted. You said she rang you and you could be trusted."

"Yes, yes, who is this?"

"Call me Janet," she said, after some hesitation. "Can you really get that girl off?"

Flint could afford to be more certain than he truthfully felt. "Of course, I've got cast-iron evidence. The police will clear Ruth in a day or two, then re-open the case."

"Is it worth anything?"

"Is what?"

"Catching the one that did it?"

"I imagine so."

"How much?"

"Why – can you help?"

"'ow much?" the accent was stronger now, her voice had obviously been disguised.

"Look, can I have your number?"

"Tell the police and there's no deal."

"I need your number . . ."

The phone went dead, but Flint's brain sprang into life.

"'Posh' woman," he breathed.

Chapter Twenty-Three

The butterfly had flapped its wings, a far-off echo had been heard but the storm had yet to break. The phonecall had given Flint the opportunity to make the breakthrough which had eluded the police. Janet had spoken to him and only him. He needed to keep her confidence, attract her interest and draw her gently in.

Driving to Leeds, he carried two separate plans in his head and Grimston had to swallow both. Grimston's company headquarters was located in a newly revamped multi-suite office complex overlooking the Leeds Transport Interchange. Tyrone had been left at home; the last thing Flint wanted was amateur attempts at the hard sell.

Grimston was in a crisp (possibly new) suit and he took the revised Phase II specification with hardly a word, turning straight to the costings.

"Better," he said.

"The labour costs are up because we can't use students in term time."

"I understand." Grimston closed the report and laid it on the green leather surface of the desk, which had the huge, flat-topped proportions of an aircraft carrier. Around him, a 1969 office had been given an interior suited to 1869. The dark red walls were hung with portraits of Victorian businessmen, mill owners and railwaymen. Bob Grimston was perfectly at home in their company.

"I hear you've become a radio star," he said.

"Look, to keep a long story short, what I did was ease Ruth into the hands of the police. It got her off the streets and off our backs."

"Good," Grimston said, without sincerity. "Well done," he added a little irony. "Remember that I warned you not to nose around?"

"Do you want the killer caught?" Flint counter-attacked. "Or do you want this to keep over-shadowing the project until the day the park opens?"

"I wanted her caught, now she is."

"But she's not the killer. Ruth's done some pretty wild things these last few months, but she's no killer."

"You're a sentimental so-and-so, Flint. We all know Ruth did it."

"Three months ago, we all knew Wayne Drabble did it."

"Leave it to the police. They can sort this out without your help."

"Why not put up a reward?" Flint suggested. This was the bait he would dangle before Janet.

"What?"

"Ten grand, by anonymous businessman. Ten grand for information leading to a conviction."

"Ten grand?" Grimston screwed up his eyes. "What's ten grand?"

"Half your salary after tax."

"But what's it to you? What does ten thousand pounds buy? One advert for the park in a national paper? Ten seconds on local television? It's probably a tax-deductible expense."

Bushy eyebrows formed a conspiratorial huddle on Grimston's brow. "You know something?"

226

Flint nodded ever so slightly and Grimston began to make guesses. "Ruth Hauxley told you something? No, someone else did – who was it?"

"I can't say."

"No, of course you can't. You're the man everyone can trust, I heard it on the radio."

Flint felt warm below his own beard as Grimston's nail-hard stare tried to read his mind.

"It might be worth a poke. Let's try five grand: but I want to know what you hear? Understand?"

He understood, but Flint had not the slightest intention of complying. "Yes," he said. "I've got the name of the radio reporter here, that seems the best way to advertise the reward. Perhaps it would be best if it came from you."

"No," said Grimston, his eyes wary, his lean cheeks emphasising the menace in his voice. "You tell him. He'll believe you."

Five thousand pounds, for information leading to a conviction. The radio carried the story that day, the newspapers picked it up the following lunchtime. Ruth's sudden reappearance and protestations of innocence had sent both police and local media into a frenzy of activity. Odd snatches of evidence began to emerge which supported Ruth's alibi and threw the police on the defensive. D.I. Thorne and his colleagues were juggling with a potato which was microwave hot and the pressure was on from all sides.

Flint stayed late in his office for the rest of that week, making a final effort to finish Tyrone's thesis, but with his ears awaiting the sound of his telephone trilling for an external call. Janet had found his direct line number from somewhere. The date for Tyrone's

227

oral examination had been fixed for November the 8th, and the glowing comments made by Flint's two co-examiners implied that Tyrone was going to pass.

At a quarter past six, the telephone rang once and Flint grabbed at the handset before it had chance to ring a second time.

"Janet?"

"Five thousand isn't enough," she said.

"It's all that's going."

"It isn't enough, I need more."

"Can we quibble afterwards? I mean, if you were involved in the set up . . ."

"I never said that!"

Carefully, Jeff, carefully. "Can we meet up sometime? Pick somewhere you feel safe."

"No, no meeting, you'll bring the pigs."

"Look Janet, I need to know . . . at least tell me when you're going to ring again."

"I need more. I want twenty thousand pounds."

Out of the corner of his eye, Flint could see a pile of brochures from banks offering personal loans. For a house, yes, but to bribe an informant?

"Hello? I'll try to get more, but I can't promise anything."

She put down the phone when the pips sounded: she'd used a public call-box. Flint banged the table in frustration. He was so close, only a mere fifteen thousand pounds lay between him and the truth. For a moment he considered ringing D.I. Thorne, but knew that would frighten Janet away. Then he thought of fraudulently enhancing the reward, but Janet sounded a sassy girl; she would want her handbag stuffed with used fivers before the truth tripped from her lips. He reached for the phone and dialled the first five digits for police headquarters, then killed the call with his index finger. It was all up to Janet, he decided, the next move would be hers.

He'd never been more wrong.

The weekend was tense: Janet couldn't know his home number, or lacked the will to try to find it. Flint unpacked a few boxes to distract his mind, but all his thoughts came back to his tantalising lead. The urge to unburden himself on Thorne was intense, but he knew this could destroy what fragile trust existed between himself and the mysterious woman.

Flint found himself back at the university on Monday morning, selecting slides, checking notes and begging a few more overhead projector sheets from Debs. At 11am, the second year undergraduates should have received his thoughts on the impact of the Claudian invasion. Instead they would celebrate a cancelled lecture with an extra plastic cup of coffee, for by that time, Flint was sitting beside a police constable, being driven north on the A1.

A section of the nearside carriageway had been coned off – nothing unusual there. What was unusual were the eight police vehicles sheltering behind the cones and the mob of uniforms swarming over the verge.

D.I. Thorne met him as he got out of the police car.

"Doctor Flint – expert witness," he explained to a constable who was taking names of all present at the scene.

"Sorry to drag you away – we've been here since six."

Thorne led the bearded academic in the RAF greatcoat towards a line of blue and white tapes which sealed off a lay-by. Flint had seen this scene on so many news bulletins, he knew what to expect. But who did he expect? He was tense with foreboding as people parted to reveal a pair of bare feet sticking out from below a winter hedge.

"We've, erm, found a woman."

So who? Flint's mind fell on Ruth, then on Eleanor. It stayed on Eleanor.

"Can you stand this?" Thorne asked.

"If I must."

"Bodies is your business, right? I bet you've dug up hundreds."

"Not fresh ones."

"No, well, I'm sorry to ask you. Know her?"

Someone had struggled to stuff the body into the hedgerow and an arm still stood semi-erect, snagged by a cardigan sleeve to a broken branch. Grotesquely staring at them was the face of death, oddly pink. Flint absorbed the details: the bulging eyes, the receding chin, the mean, upward curling nose, the pouting lips, still blood red with lipstick. Her hair had been short and mousy, concealed by an improbable wig of bleached blonde which now dangled from the hedge. Something about her disarrayed clothes betrayed her profession.

Flint turned away as fast as he could. A juggernaut hurtled past the lay-by, heading north.

"Have you met her?" Thorne asked.

"No."

"She's called Sharon Turpin, she worked out of Chapeltown in Leeds."

"So what's she doing here?"

"Last ride."

"And what am I doing here?"

The policeman made a tight, lemon-sucking face.

230

"This has kind of become your patch. I thought you could tell me something."

"Look, I'm pretty hot on anything that happened between 55 BC and AD 410. I'm mugging up on the high Middle Ages, but anything later than that, forget it."

He glanced back at the body again, seeing now that a nylon stocking was twisted around her neck. Was this Janet? If she tried to claim the reward for giving evidence, might she also have tried to extract a reward for her silence? Whatever the truth, she was certainly silent now.

"It looks like she was strangled from behind," Thorne said. "The Doc guessed she was killed late last night. A trucker nearly tiddled on her this morning."

Flint shivered at the indignity of death and looked around at the crowd of fussing specialists. Sharon Turpin had surely never attracted this level of attention whilst alive. "I see you're spending your full budget on this one."

"Have to, the press will be all over us by dinner time."

Yes, thought Flint. Vikki would have loved it.

"Come for a ride."

On the evening news, Chapeltown would be referred to as "The Red Light Area" of Leeds, unfairly if one asked the residents.

Amongst the rows of rented terraced houses and council estates are found arcades of shops. Each has its newsagent, its video shop and its late night store, inevitably owned by members of the Indo-Pakistani community.

"The knocking shop's over the betting shop,"

231

Thorne quipped as they ducked under another police cordon. He spent a couple of minutes talking to a constable guarding the tape, then to a plain-clothes detective who had hurried out of the doorway. Thorne was from the North Yorkshire force, but as Leeds was in West Yorkshire, protocol had to be followed.

Thorne was given the go-ahead to enter the flat. "Sharon had been on the game since leaving school. The local uniformed boys picked her up every now and again."

Unfortunate turn of phrase, thought Flint, but possibly appropriate. His elbows scraped the wall as he followed Thorne up the narrow staircase.

A tall grey-haired detective met them at the top of the stair. "Hello, Simon. You can touch things now, forensic have done their stuff."

Thorne introduced Flint then the pair were shown around the flat. As a bordello, it was a disappointment: no lurid pictures on the walls, no mirrored ceilings, no whips or chains. It was clean and well ordered, if cheaply furnished. Ornaments mainly consisted of holiday souvenirs; a plate from the Algarve, a plaque from Majorca, a resin lighthouse from Jersey. Sharon Turpin could easily have been a waitress, hairdreser or bank clerk. Her mum probably assumed she was.

"We're taking away the kinky gear," the grey-haired detective said. "Undies, split-crotch panties and a gross of condoms, you know the kind of stuff."

"I don't actually," Flint said.

Piles of items sat on the patent leather settee, each wrapped in plastic. Thorne put on a pair of surgical gloves and took out a file of documents. "Do you recognise this?" he asked.

He proffered a photocopy of an article from the Yorkshire Post. The picture was of the Form Farm torc. "It's that torc thing."

Flint tried to look nonplussed, but behind the facade he was trying to draw links between Tom Aitken, Wayne Drabble and a Leeds streetwalker.

"We don't understand it either. That's why we dragged you out on the scene this morning."

"What did she do?" Flint asked the grey-haired detective.

"Anything you paid her to do."

"No, no, specifically. Was it bondage, or school-girls, or what?"

"In there," the detective showed Thorne which wallet to choose. Thorne ferreted deep inside and took out a pile of business cards, neatly held together by a rubber band. Sharon would presumably use them to decorate local telephone boxes.

LADY LUST
Call me for a class act

Down one side of the card was a pen sketch of a pouting woman in hat, jodhpurs and boots, riding crop in hand.

"Did you find the horsy gear?"

"We did." The grey-haired detective dipped into another bag, pulled out a riding crop and passed it to Thorne.

Thorne gave the air a smart swoosh with the crop. "I just can't see the fun in it, can you?"

"No, but I wonder what she sounded like."

Thorne was no flatfoot, Flint had decided this long ago. This was one case where the police were ahead of the game. The crop twitched in his direction. "You mean this is the 'posh' woman?"

"It's unlikely she was preparing a thesis on the late pre-Roman Iron Age," Flint said.

"Do you want to hear my thesis, Doctor Flint? Try me on marks out of ten. I think someone hired our Sharon to play the 'posh' woman and act as go-between with Wayne Drabble. He used to live less than a mile from here; she might have known he was coming out of the nick and needed the cash."

Yes, Thorne was right on the ball. Flint made a stab at claiming some of the intellectual credit. "You realise that this means Wayne was telling the truth about the 'posh' woman and the torc? It also confirms there was some sort of conspiracy to have Tom Aitken killed. This has to clear Ruth Hauxley: unless she squeezed out of your cells last night."

"No, we still have Ruth under lock and key. I don't forgive her for belting me, but I'm starting to believe her story. The regulars at the Green Man say they saw a Land Rover driving past at chucking out time on the night of the murder and her flatmate says she was home by midnight. We didn't believe the flatmate at first."

"So why is this girl dead?"

"Villains fall out. Maybe Sharon got greedy and wanted a bigger cut Maybe she threatened to go for that five thousand quid. When she took on the job, she won't have known Tom Aitken was going to be killed."

It was possible, no, probable that Flint had caused her death by his ploy of raising the reward. How much had he given away to Grimston? How much had the millionaire's cunning mind been able to extract from his crude attempts at deception? Should he now

234

confess to having spoken to "Janet"? Was his hunch even correct that Sharon was "Janet"? Flint was confused and deeply troubled by his conscience.

The two detectives seemed not to notice the change in Flint's demeanour. The grey-haired one proffered the plastic bags, and Thorne popped the evidence back inside with jaunty satisfaction. "We're almost at the bottom of this, you know? If someone wants that reward, they better hurry. The forensic boys will have bags full of evidence from the scene, so all we have to do is call in our suspects one-by-one and the case is closed. It's sad being a villain these days."

Chapter Twenty-Four

Returning home to a cold, dark, lonely cottage on the edge of Shadesmoor, Flint proceeded to lose a night's sleep. A rouge-tinted face gazed his way each time he closed his eyes. It would end soon, he knew. Evidence would cling to the corpse long after the soul had departed for its sins to be judged so, oddly, the death made him feel safe, as it brought a conclusion so much closer. When all this was over, he vowed, he'd see no more real corpses, nothing with flesh on, nothing less than five hundred years old.

On Tuesday, with his mind sleepy, Flint simply let two dozen holiday snaps pass before the eyes of the Art & Architecture class, then sleepwalked to find caffeine. Megan was in the Common Room, reading the early edition of the *Yorkshire Evening Press*. Barney was leaning over her shoulder.

"Oh yucky yucky," Barney said.

Megan turned to him with disdain. "Find your own paper."

Flint walked past, stirring his coffee thoughtfully. Barney seemed to want to draw him into the conversation. "Was our sleuth at the scene?"

"Yes, and it was truly awful. I'll let you have those books back, Barney. I've been put off forensic science for life."

"They have to get this man," Megan stated.

"Who says it was a man?" Barney chided. "Women can be psychotic too."

"Women don't . . . don't do what was done to that . . ."

"Tart. Sorry, must be politically correct here, prostitute. Or whore, streetwalker, hooker, call-girl . . ."

"Crawl back under your stone!" Megan hissed.

"Go molest an undergraduate."

The newspaper was violently crumpled. "This has gone far enough!" Megan whirled to her feet. "Jeff, you heard what he said?"

Flint nodded, without enthusiasm. For a moment, Megan glared at Barney, panting deeply. She was bigger than he was, and Barney seemed to shrink before her. When Megan rushed for the door, Flint bounced over the back of the seat and chased after her. Shoulders pumping, she marched rapidly towards Betty's office. Flint slid around her left side.

"You better not have told that insect anything about me," she threatened.

"Look Megan . . ."

"I've had enough of men for today."

"What now?"

"It's him or me, sexist, fascist, racist, misogynist chauvinist insect."

"He was baiting you."

"Well I've bitten the bloody bait, I've had enough, it's him or me." Her Welsh accent was strong when she was roused. She gave a peremptory rap on the professor's door, then took two steps inside.

"Wait here!" Megan commanded, "I need a witness."

Like a naughty schoolboy, Flint waited outside the head's door, yawning heavily. After a minute or two, in which he caught snatches of muffled anger from within the office, he put his head around the secretary's door and passed a few words with Deborah.

"How many years have you been here, Debs?"

"Six?", she guessed, taking the end of a pencil from her mouth.

"You know, in my old college, we used to say the place was run by the secretaries. Nothing happened without their say-so, or their knowledge."

She cocked her head to one side and gave a slight giggle of admission. He jabbed his thumb at the office next door.

"The crunch has come, Barney versus Megan, two falls or a submission. He caught her at a bad moment."

"Oh."

This was not unexpected, it was clear.

"Delve deeply into your mine of ancient gossip, could you, and tell me about that pair. Did they ever have a relationship?"

"You mean?" She twirled the pencil around in a tight circle.

"I do."

She shook her head.

"Okay, let me pose a pair of scenarios." Flint said. "Number one is that when Barney was the new boy in the department, Megan spent much time and effort trying to seduce him – she does have that reputation. The seduction having failed, she now hates him with all her heart."

Debs looked a little less secure now, perhaps weighing up how much of her treasured information she should disclose.

"Scenario two, the situation is reversed."

Debs had made her decision. "Seduction isn't Barney, is it? He's not a ladies' man."

"But would he like to be?"

"Wouldn't all men; wouldn't you?"

Flint had always thought he was. Perhaps Debs hadn't noticed, or perhaps he was slipping.

"He used to hang round her," Debs said, "when he first came. You know how he hangs onto people when they'll talk to him."

"Betty wants to see you." Megan put a red-flushed face around the door.

Flint raised a swift finger to his lips and Debs caught the message. He grimaced at Megan, then tried to squeeze past her into the professor's office. She stopped him by grasping his arm, digging her fingernails into his wrist. "Remember what we've done. Remember how close we've been. Comrades stick together. Remember that."

Betty's voice could be heard from within the office. Megan released her grip and allowed Flint to enter the room. He closed the door behind him.

As Betty talked and Flint responded, he thought about Megan and Barney. Men who attempt to seduce women fail on most occasions. They become used to failure, accepting it as part of the sexual game, seldom holding grudges. Women who attempt to seduce men mostly succeed, the man being flattered by the novelty or simply lunging at the opportunity.

How would Barney have reacted to Megan's hyperactive libido? If she had thrown herself at him, rejection would have humiliated her and set their professional relationship on a disaster course.

"Candidly, he was not one of my wiser appointments," Betty continued. "We needed someone who could handle the early medieval period and Old Norse." Betty was obviously a veteran at repairing departmental cracks.

If the situation were reversed, how would Barney have reacted if he had tried to seduce Megan and failed? Failure seemed to be his trademark. Given that she reputedly distributed her favours widely, to be actually refused entry to the A1 Club could be galling.

"He's majoring in bigotry," Flint responded, deciding which side to take in the conflict. "From what I've seen, he's lazy, and a classic underachiever. He speaks well, his learning is deep enough to bluff his way through lectures, but he's a passenger. Tyrone would say he's dead wood and you should chop him."

"Thankfully, Master Drake is not yet running this department, though daresay he'd like to. Now Megan is going to press for a formal hearing, she has quoted all the relevant sections of the college disciplinary code, I must read them again myself. The problem I have, Jeff, is that she's not virgin pure, is she? I've protected her all these years, but if there's a hearing Barney will bring out all the dark tales and insist they are recorded. This could destroy both of them. Will you speak to her? Take her out for dinner, try to explain things."

He nodded. He wanted things explained too.

"Be nice to her, but not too nice. We don't want any more complications do we?"

Too late, thought Flint. "No," he replied.

Flint left college soon after four, drove to the cottage in Urethorpe, and flopped onto the dog-eared rented couch. He surveyed the mess in the room and the mess in his life. He had still not unpacked. The green van seemed to be driving oddly. His mother kept telephoning him, asking him why he never came over to Leeds and why he never mentioned that nice girl Lisa (by which she meant Vikki). Megan and Barney had thrown the department into civil war, Tyrone had become moody and distracted, Ruth was still in custody and yellow earth-moving machines had started to congregate at Shadesmoor Castle. That a young woman from Leeds had been brutally strangled not ten miles from where he lay added another frightening dimension to his crisis. Only one course of action lay open to him: stick a pizza into the oven, open a bottle of Sam Smith's and slip a video of *The Big Sleep* into the machine. His mind was full, the real world could wait.

The pizza gave him indigestion and the beer only made it worse. He'd seen the film so many times before, he scarcely took notice. After an hour he turned off Bogart and Bacall, dumped greasy dishes into the sink beside yesterday's greasy dishes and took up the phone. Tyrone was not at his digs.

Each problem needed to be eliminated in turn, so that his life could return to normality. His eyes rested on three bills pinned to his cork board, his mind mentally adding the three totals. Money, money, money, Megan. Dial M for Megan. He dialled, and she was home, barely giving him the time of day. Two minutes later he was in the green van, daring it to fail him. In a quarter of an hour he pulled up beside a neater, cuter cottage settling into darkness.

"Jeff, I don't want to see anyone," Megan looked pale and strained, but he eased his way into her hallway.

"I'm busy. I'm writing my submission for the hearing."

"You were going to let me have a look at your essay on the death of Margaret de Balleron." The excuse came quickly to his lips.

She said nothing and went into her lounge, which also served as a study. It smelled heavily of smoke.

"Why not ease off?" he suggested.

The file she wanted was soon found and she passed him a folder of typed notes, sat at her typewriter and groped around for a cigarette packet.

"Smoking is bad for you," he said.

"And so is drinking, and sleeping around and chasing murder suspects across burning moors . . ."

"Point taken, but don't destroy yourself. We should talk."

Megan turned her back on him and began to attack the typewriter with her forefingers. Several pages lay by her elbow, beside the empty Martini Rosso bottle.

"No word processor yet?"

"I know what I want to say and I don't intend changing a word."

The battering of keys continued.

"Did you have an affair with Barney?"

"I would rather mate with a slug."

"But did you?"

She turned around and glared. "Did he tell you we did?"

"No."

"He probably has fantasies about me."

"Violent ones, presumably."

Another line of vitriol went onto the paper, then the doorbell rang. Megan shot from her seat and out of the room in seconds. Flint casually wandered over to the typewriter and winced at what she had written.

The door closed, then a car drove away noisily. She returned to the room a different woman, flushed, flustered, taking a minute or so to recover full blown militant aggression.

"Who was that?"

"You're a nosy blighter Jeffrey Flint."

"I want to help. And you put a double 's' in 'disaster'."

She let out an unfeminine curse. "Who cares?"

He tried a new track of trivia, hoping to break through the aggression. "You do need that word processor, they're very cheap now. Tyrone talked me into getting one and I can't live without it now."

She rang her knuckles against the outdated machine. "College was turfing these out a couple of years ago, so it cost me next to nothing. It was worth every penny. I'm not spending a thousand quid just to type letters." Megan shook her head, then let out another, even cruder, oath. "Go home, Jeff, all this is getting too much. The murder, bloody Shadesmoor toy town Castle, then Barney, it's the limit."

Megan was angry and anger always looks ugly. Flint was trying hard to like her, but losing the battle. "Have you ever thought of settling down, and smiling at the world a little?"

"You mean find Mister Right? I was married for eight years, no more thank you. Men are good for one thing, two if you count fixing the guttering. I don't want one cluttering up my house."

"So you don't find life lonely?"

Yin (the black one) chose this moment to slink his way across to his mistress. She picked him up and cuddled him close to her cheek. "You're never lonely with a cat around."

*   *   *

243

Problem one solved. Megan wanted to fight her own battle with Barney, unhindered by men, even well-meaning "new men". Flint drove into the night, determined now to let the Barney-Megan feud run its natural course; neither party would win his help.

The green van coughed a little on its way to Acomb, west of York: Tyrone had a friend at university there and was sharing his digs. In rows of tightly packed back-to-back houses, Flint found the parked Spitfire then hunted for a space to squeeze the grumbling van against the kerb.

Tyrone was surprised, even alarmed to find his boss on the doorstep of the terraced house. From the lounge came the sound of something violent – a video of *Terminator XIV* or its ilk.

"Sorry it's late, but have you got our laptop here?"

"It's upstairs."

In moments, Flint was squatting on Tyrone's unmade bed, gratified that someone lived in a greater degree of chaos than he did. The blue-white screen flashed before them.

"What's wrong?" Tyrone asked.

"Everything. We've made a right mess of this problem and I don't believe it is as complex as it appears."

Tyrone finally seemed to switch on his own brain. "So?"

"I want you to link everything together."

"I've done that. I did it this afternoon."

"So who is our suspect?"

"Ruth."

"No, wrong!" Flint said.

"Right!" Tyrone sat on the corner of the bed and

raised a fist full of fingers, imitating one of Flint's modes of expression. "First, a woman was involved, the 'posh' woman. Second, that footstool was found by the desk which made her the right height to slug Aitken. Third, there's the sex dimension, there is so much tension that sex must have played a part in the motive. Fourth, whoever killed Tom Aitken was anti-Shadesmoor."

". . . not necessarily."

"Yes, necessarily, because it has caused so much damage to the reputation of Bob Grimston and it draws attention to the negative aspects of the project."

"Carry on."

"The person must be associated with archaeology, hence the use of the Form Farm torc as a red herring."

Tyrone had run out of fingers. "And the person had to know Tom Aitken, because there's no evidence for two break ins at The Rectory and the alarm was turned off. Aitken was knowingly with the person who killed him."

"Money," said Flint, "add money to the equation. It seeps into every layer of our problems."

"Okay, Ruth got nothing when Aitken dumped her."

"So you're sticking with Ruth?"

"No one else fits."

"Add another factor – let's call it the X factor. Suppose there was something wrong with the Shadesmoor project, let's say it isn't kosher. We can turn most of your suppositions inside out and we still have a motive."

Tyrone was unconvinced.

"This acquaintance of Tom Aitken could be an

enemy meeting him under duress. Money could be the motive and sex only the background. It may have been Tom who was anti-Shadesmoor and the killer therefore in the other camp. The prostitute could have been the 'posh' woman, so we don't need a woman suspect. The position of the footstool could be coincidental and the Torc is a red herring through and through."

"I can't do this any more," Tyrone stated. "It's useless, let's leave it to the cops, they'll make Ruth confess and it will all be over."

"Letters; why the cranky letters and why to me?"

"To encourage you."

The thought hit Flint like a house brick. After he had recoiled from the impact, he realised something in his own analysis was flawed. "Brilliant."

"Don't be sarcastic, I mean what I said. Our suspect knows you like this sort of thing and wants to entertain you."

"And to confuse me?"

"To draw you onto false conclusions about Shadesmoor. To make you think this is a big conspiracy and that there is some hidden secret you have to find."

"As I said, the case is less complex than it looks."

"Yes. Ruth complicated it in the hope the police would listen to your mad ideas and waste time harassing Bob Grimston."

"Bob has really got to you hasn't he?"

"He's a decent bloke, he's not Adolf Hitler. You're so taken up by Eleanor that you hardly give Bob the time of day."

"Me?"

"All the lads on site noticed. Whenever she visited the site, you treated her like the Queen Mum. I

246

thought you hated the upper-class, I thought you were a socialist."

"I don't fancy Eleanor, right?"

"Aw, come on. She's gorgeous, and she's your age."

"She's ten years older."

"She's single."

"Divorced twice."

"She's got her own castle."

"Which she's pawned to a shark." Flint saw how Tyrone took attacks on Grimston's plans as personal insults.

"You're defending her," Tyrone said, with a sly look of devilment in his face. "She isn't your type Doc, admit it."

"And what would you know about 'my type'?"

"Well, you claim to like intelligent women."

"Eleanor is very sophisticated."

"By sophisticated, you mean she can shop in three languages?"

"I know she's got this veneer, but underneath . . ."

". . . you'll find another veneer. She's a vacuous air-head, like my mother's friends on the cocktail circuit. I know the type. She's a two-dimensional cut-out you can stick in the corner of a party to look pretty."

Flint drew breath. Without care, this project could cost him all his friends. "I'd better get home."

With the smug assurance of having scored a victory, Tyrone closed his files, then watched the screen fade as he turned off the computer. "You need to come on site tomorrow, the contractor is ignoring me. His machinery is all over the DMV and not just on the surveyed areas."

"And you still think Bob plays with a straight bat?"

"Bob hasn't been there."

"Convenient, huh? The boss goes out for lunch and, oops, when he gets back he finds the JCB driver has accidentally scooped up half the site. It's standard practice, you've got a lot to learn about this game, kid. I'll see you tomorrow."

Chapter Twenty-Five

Like so many wasps, the contractor's vehicles swarmed over the lower meadow. Phase II was hardly begun and the volunteers slipped around on the greasy grass, boldly marking the ground for the machines to gouge, then watching helplessly as their guidelines were ignored. In his green protective hat, matching wellies and sky grey RAF greatcoat, Flint hopped in and out of the ruts, speaking to digger drivers, labourers, charge hands and foremen, but each simply passed the buck to someone else.

Archaeology had been receding as one of his priority areas, but now Flint was back with mud on his coat-tails, on the porch of the manor, demanding to see Eleanor. Why did his heart lift a little when she emerged, elegant if not wholly composed? Why had he been so relieved it was not her lying in a hedge beside the A1?

"We need to talk," he said.

He flicked his head towards the site. "We've got problems."

They walked to the top of the hill, keeping off the subject of the site. She asked him about college and he replied "don't ask". He asked her about her sick horse, and she passed a few minutes talking heavily of vets shuttling to and fro, before telling him the beast was on the mend. At the back of the castle ramparts, where the whole shallow valley could be seen, Flint could explain his problem and point out the areas causing concern.

"We didn't expect the heavy machinery to move in so quickly. I've only had a week to recruit staff and we're still twenty short."

"You'll have to talk to Bob when he comes back from Germany," she said.

"Can't wait. By the time he's back, who knows how much of the nation's heritage will have been scooped into the back of his trucks? Forget Bob, as far as I'm concerned, this is your estate and you're in charge."

"No, I . . ."

"You're the partner and I need you to issue orders to those hard-hats down there. They won't listen to Tyrone and they won't listen to me. Joss can match them curse for curse, but they ignore him too. Now, we've marked some of the areas where they can start work, but they're gaining on us. We need three days to finish the pegging out. Meanwhile, no one must disturb the ground beyond our tapes."

"I don't see why . . ."

"It's the law, Eleanor. Your planning consent contains binding obligations to deal sensitively with the archaeology, and to follow *bona fide* archaeological advice. If those monkeys wreck the DMV, or the manor, or the castle, you're breaking your planning consent and there will be inspectors and God knows who else hopping around your site. Am I being unreasonable?"

Flint had tried to speak with authority, but he knew he was on shaky ground. Developers commonly rode roughshod over their planning requirements, leaving consultant archaeologists scrabbling in the mud for what evidence could be saved from the maw of the bulldozer. The law was weak, proof of infringement was difficult and penalties were dwarfed by the rewards of uninterrupted progress. Eleanor knew nothing of this and the way she nodded her head in rhythm to his words showed she was totally convinced by his hollow bluster.

"I'll talk to them. Outside the tapes you say?"

"Please. And they're to listen to my people."

"They seem so young . . ."

"But they know what they're doing. They are saving your estate, your heritage. The Ballerons of the future need something of their past preserving."

She gave a little twisted smile. "Tom again."

"You must tell me about Tom one day, before it gets too late."

"Too late?" she echoed.

"This project is becoming a tragedy in three acts. Did you read about the woman killed on the A1? She was connected to Tom Aitken somehow. That's two people dead and I don't see any reason it should stop at two. Do you?"

She shivered in the tweed jacket, although the sun was now warming the Yorkshire hills from between shifting cloud. Gently, Flint began to probe for information.

"You'd do us all a big favour if you told me about your affair."

Eleanor began to shake her head.

He reached out and touched the arm of her jacket. "Eleanor, you're rich, you're beautiful . . ."

"I'm not rich," she retorted, looking down at the backs of her hands.

Flint noticed that even the most careful manicure could not retard the aging process.

Her glance shot back to meet his eyes. "Do the police know about Tom and me?"

"Ruth must have told them, even if only in her own defence. She isn't our murderer, by the way."

"You're helping her."

"Yes. I owe it to her."

"But she must have been the one . . ." Eleanor looked down as she spoke, all the conviction being leached out of her words.

"No, I know she's innocent, and so do you. All Ruth has done is throw a hunk of metal through your window, pop a tyre and run us around for a few nights. She's going to be out in a few days. If you ask the police nicely, they'll drop the charges against her for all the things she did on your estate. It would be a nice gesture, Ruth's a decent girl, she only wanted to draw attention to Tom's death."

The lady of the manor was easily swayed. She had the resistance of a leafy sapling against the north wind. "Charges? Yes, of course, I'm not going into court."

"You could help her more, with all you know about Tom. You must hold secrets in your head, little confidences perhaps? Did he ever say anything about Ruth, for instance?"

When Eleanor chose to speak again, she spoke obliquely, skirting the hard truth that Flint wanted to hear. "Tom liked Ruth, he said she was just a friend, but I knew he thought her special, even after she left him. He and Ruth went together well; I'm not sure Tom and I . . ." She broke off, apologised, then continued. "I need to tell someone," she said, eyes wet against the breeze. "But I'm afraid . . . I told Tom and look what happened."

"What sort of hold does Bob have over you?"

"He owns me!" She shrieked, clenching her fists and darting away towards the castle. He darted after her and Eleanor turned around.

"You're broke. You're totally broke and Bob pays all the bills?"

Eleanor nodded, smearing her mascara with a hand.

"Death duties?"

"No, Daddy was too clever to pay death duties, or his lawyer was too clever."

"Thurlscote?"

"All the money is in the family trust: I can only get it by applying to the Trustees."

"Who consist of Thurlscote and your uncle Bernard?"

"Yes."

"And Thurlscote is in Bob Grimston's pocket, so what handle does Grimston have on your uncle?"

"Uncle Bernie drinks, he gambles and he's broke too."

"He sounds like a bad choice of Trustee."

"He was sober until Aunt Catherine died."

"You could take legal advice, you know."

Eleanor shook her head. "Tom promised he'd find a way out of this. He only said he'd join the project because of me. We were going to work together, in secret. He looked at hiring a solicitor, but the cost . . . we would both have been ruined before it ever came to court. I couldn't turn to anyone else, because Bob knows everyone and everyone wants to be Bob's friend."

"So did Bob find out what you were up to with Tom?"

Now she bit into her finger, hard.

"Has he ever said anything?"

"He'll get his own way, he always does."

253

"So how far did Tom's plan get?"

"He asked me to show him everything; all the papers I signed, all the documents and letters."

The sweeping westerly wind blew the answer into Flint's mind before Eleanor had a chance to articulate the words. "So you gave them to him?"

"Yes. Tom and I made notes on everything we thought we could use against Bob. He had me tape phone calls and we copied all the letters before they were destroyed. I gave him the returns from our Jersey accounts."

"Did Tom find anything he could use?"

"It's all legal." Her answer came all too quickly.

"It doesn't sound legal."

"He showed what we had to a friend who knew the law, but Jeff, if Bob's done anything illegal, then so have I. I've signed those papers, I'm a partner, I own half of this, even if it seems I don't."

"Do you think Tom tried to work some deal with Bob behind the scenes? That way, the police could be kept out of things."

"We talked about that, I think Tom planned to do something like that."

"But he was killed, there was no deal, and everything disappeared?"

"Yes – if you tell anyone, I . . ." She looked again at her inheritance, kept out of her grasp by a legal artifice.

"Mum's the word, but I expect Bob already knows all about the papers."

"I'm so frightened," she said.

"Go to the police."

"The police thought I was a suspect."

"They thought you were the 'posh' woman?"

"Yes. I told them it was probably Ruth, or that Welsh college lecturer, pretending to be me."

"Megan? Did Tom say much about Megan?"

"No."

Ever-cautious was Tom Aitken, thought Flint. Possibly he had been too polite to mention an old flame, or too embarrassed to admit being enrolled in the A1 Club.

"So did the police ask you about your relationship with Tom?"

"Yes, and I lied. I didn't want the newspapers making up lies about me, they do that."

"I know."

"I told the police that we were just business associates and he was teaching me about history."

"You didn't tell them about your secret plan?"

"No, how could I, what could I prove? And, I was too frightened."

"You mean you might be next?"

Flint reached into a pocket and took out a folded piece of paper. He showed the typed capitals to Eleanor:

FORGET THE PAST BEWARE THE FUTURE

"Ever had any letters like this one?"

"No," she said, allowing her eyes to re-read the words.

"This is my second little *bon mot*. Megan's had one, Bob's had one, I thought perhaps that you, too . . .?"

"Is that all?" she said hurriedly. "People might suspect something, I ought to go."

He let her walk away from the castle, experiencing a battle of emotions. She appeared so vulnerable, but

255

how much was an act? Tyrone had sneered about Eleanor's veneer, and Flint saw his point. There was a class of dilettante with little to do and less to say who would carry a set of personae around with them; one for the hunt meeting, one for the cocktail party, one for the chaise longue. Each time he saw Eleanor, she deployed her maiden-in-peril face and shrank behind him for protection. Tom Aitken had fallen for the same act.

A confession, no, a partial confession was what Flint had been aching to hear. Eleanor had seemed to recognise the style of the cranky letter, but had denied it. Why? Perhaps Eleanor was the "posh" woman after all, feigning conflict with Grimston in order to disperse the idea of a conspiracy. Grimston had the money to pay a killer, but Flint realised something which disturbed him more: Grimston would also have the resources to construct a multi-layered bluff in order to conceal the guilt of someone he wished to protect. Flint too felt protective, watching the figure of Eleanor shrink ever smaller against the dominating landscape. He would have to suppress his feelings for Eleanor and clear his head if this affair was going to end happily.

Leaning against a stump of fallen castle wall, he thought over the Anarchist theory on how to immobilise the aristocracy: blackmail them by revealing their "dirty secrets". Eleanor clearly had many of those, but he still could not conceive that it was her hands that guided the conspiracy, let alone wield the hand-axe. Application of the Anarchist theory required a shrewd, intelligent, middle-class suspect to be behind the plot. Bob Grimston was a Johnny-come-lately who had cut across class barriers to buy the allegiance of lawyers, landed gentry and digger drivers alike. It was time to employ another dictum: Julius Caesar's Divide and Rule. A wedge needed to be placed between Bob and Eleanor, then driven home, hard.

Chapter Twenty-Six

Sue Carrick was fussing over a heap of mail when Flint was shown into the solicitor's office the next morning.

"Start the meter running," he quipped.

"You've already exhausted your credit."

He was undaunted. "How is Ruth faring?"

"Very well, and the press is now on her side. The police originally dismissed the submission of her flat-mate that Ruth was in by midnight on the night of the murder, but they're now taking it a little more seriously. I'm finding other fragments of evidence to dilute the crown case; half the population of Urethorpe seem to want the reward."

"What about the minor offences? Are they being dropped?"

"Miss Balleron has said she won't press charges for the window being smashed – I presume you won't want Ruth prosecuted for damaging your equipment?"

"Of course not."

"You'll have to talk to your insurance company in that case; it will mean you have to bear the whole cost yourselves."

"Fine." Flint knew that Tyrone would protest, but who was boss?

"I'm hoping to have Ruth out on bail at the next

hearing; her family are willing to use their house as surety."

"Super news, so what have you discovered about Shadesmoor?"

"I've hardly had time, but I've found out that there is a family trust, and the Trustees are a Harrogate lawyer named Thurlscote and Bernard Balleron, the uncle of Eleanor Balleron. I came across a court case, dating back a couple of years: it was an eviction. Both of them appeared as Trustees."

"I've never met uncle Bernard, but Thurlscote is one of Bob Grimston's creatures. Are the Trustees supposed to be independent?"

"Yes, which is why one of them is a lawyer."

"Ah, but this lawyer is also Bob Grimston's chief legal advisor: that's rather close for comfort, is it not?"

"Possibly, it depends on his integrity."

"Integrity and lawyers don't mix – present company excepted."

"You have a terribly low opinion of the professions, Doctor Flint, you're very naive."

"Cynical perhaps, but I'd argue about naive."

Her face slipped into a smile. "We solicitors may be as popular as traffic wardens, but we do have our uses, otherwise why would you be here?"

"Sorry about the jibes, I do need your expertise, honest. Correct me if I'm wrong, but if Bob has the Trustees under his thumb, and they control the trust funds, Bob therefore controls Eleanor Balleron."

"That would be broadly correct."

"Is that illegal?"

"Oh, Doctor Flint, how many hours do you have to spare?" She selected a trio of books from the shelf behind her. Each was well over an inch thick.

"Here's your bedtime reading, it will give you a basic grounding in Trust Law."

He shook his head, feeling as impotent as when faced by the dead engine of the green van.

Sue seemed satisfied with her demonstration and re-shelved the books. "See, we overpaid lawyers are necessary. Breach of trust is not like a speeding offence that can be settled in a ten minute hearing. When such cases occur, they can be very complex and the outcome depends on detailed legal argument rather than a simple question of right or wrong."

"What about fraud?"

"Legally there's no such offence; you have a case if you can prove theft or deception, but what the press calls 'fraud' can be the most difficult and expensive offence to prove."

"So if Eleanor Balleron wanted to break Bob Grimston's grip?"

"The likeliest option would be for Miss Balleron to bring a civil action under the Trustee Act."

Flint had a vision of a case which kept a pair of legal firms in profitable work for years to come. A case where Grimston's liquid capital would beat Eleanor's captive assets. Tom Aitken had clearly reached the same conclusion and chosen a different route.

"Would you like to come for a drive with me one day?"

"No." Sue gave this less than a second's thought.

"I want to hunt out Bernard Balleron; he's the only member of the circus I haven't met yet."

"Why would you need me?"

"To pick his brains, to find out if he is a model of integrity. You never know, he might spill the beans if we get him drunk enough. We could combine the trip with your lunch hour. You do have lunch hours?"

"Yes, yes I do, and I normally spend them working. Take a piece of advice, Doctor Flint. Confrontation is for the public gallery, it rarely elicits facts. Bernard Balleron may be completely honest, in which case you would learn nothing. Or, he might be less than honest, in which case he would conceal what he knows."

"Or?" Flint suspected he had a third option.

"He could be a fool – it happens. I've come across several cases of family members appointed as Trustees or Executors who prove less than able to carry the job out correctly."

"Incompetent rather than dishonest? Easily misled?"

"You can make up any assumption you like, but I doubt if you could discover his motives over lunch, let alone find any admissible evidence. Now, I'm sorry but I have a client due."

"Ching!" Flint made a till-ringing noise.

Sue rebuked him. "There's more to life than money."

Flint rose to leave. "Yes, there's sex."

"Meaning what?"

"The motive; sex and money, money and sex. Money and/or sex. Take your pick."

"I think I'd rather see my client."

The green van laboured its way across the hills to Shadesmoor Castle, its accelerator reluctant to be pushed, the engine resisting the urge to increase its revs on command. Spectral garage bills floated before Flint's eyes as he jolted over the cattle grid and drove up to the Portakabin. This was now the first in a row of five grey huts, identical except that the other four were for the contractor's staff. After a few words with

261

Joss, Flint jogged downhill to the manor. Blue plastic sheeting now shrouded scaffolding across the whole front of the building.

He'd telephoned ahead and Eleanor was waiting for him. As she bounded down the steps in a green wax jacket, a head bobbed into view in the adjacent window. It was the man called Hurst, who may have been Eleanor's groundsman, or may have been a minder planted by Grimston. Whatever his role and his motive, Hurst took interest in the meeting and Flint immediately wanted to escape from his eyeline.

"Where would you like to go?" she asked.

Huge, yellow and noisy, an earthmover rumbled past.

"The river, we can't be seen from the house."

The pair walked back over the cattle grid, then turned south to follow the banks of the narrow stream. On the far bank were the back gardens of the estate houses in Burton-by-Shadesmoor. The air carried a sharp chill, the sky was clear, but the weather gods had moved south for the winter.

Along the riverside path, the vegetation was dying back; brown, limp grass stalks flipped globules of water as they brushed past.

"I love this land," Eleanor said with a deep sigh, hands thrust into her jacket pockets.

Flint recalled a dark night when she had professed to hate it.

"I was born in the manor, if you believe that."

"To the manor born?"

"Absolutely."

Why was he jealous? He was a proletarian socialist and yet he envied Eleanor; not for her land, but for her sense of place. She belonged at Shadesmoor, he belonged nowhere.

"I used to ride Shammy along here, he was my first pony. We'd ride along as far as those trees, then up the valley to the castle, then down over the meadow, where they're going to build . . ."

The nostalgia halted in mid-hoofbeat, as if Eleanor had remembered her age and her station. She swiftly shifted the subject: "Have you, ah, found anything new at the castle?"

"Up at the castle? To be honest, there is so much else going on in my life, I've hardly been paying attention. There are more pressing things in life than green-glazed pottery and plans of bakehouses. My latest topic of research has been your predicament. I took legal advice."

"You can't!" For the first time that little-girl-lost veneer slipped and Eleanor's face narrowed. "Say anything and I'll be in the tabloids – you're a friend of that awful reporter."

Vikki, presumably, Flint surmised. She seemed to leave an indelible mark of distrust wherever she walked. "Vikki Corbett and I had a big falling-out; our friendship is ancient history."

He glanced around, hoping the histrionics had not been noticed, half expecting to see the figure of Hurst plodding along behind them. It was quite likely he was skulking at the back of the bird garden, turning a pair of binoculars away from the birds and onto the pair by the riverbank. Flint started driving in that wedge.

"You remember you mentioned you had passed a heap of documents to Tom?"

"I shouldn't have told you."

This was a different Eleanor, the short-tempered,

selfish star of many gossip column cuttings in Tyrone's files.

"You also said that Tom took legal advice; who from?"

"A friend; I don't know who. Tom knew lots of people, real people who did things." She gave a huff of indignation. "That's the trouble with my life. I never meet real people, only false ones. You have to smile, all the time," she spread those perfect teeth, "even at people you detest."

Yes, he understood her better by the day, Flint reflected. She had too much money and too little to do. Tom Aitken had opened a door onto another world and Eleanor had run into his arms. "Tom didn't hand over the documents to his legal friend, by any chance?"

"No, he'd never do that."

"So where did he keep them? At his office?"

He thought of Ruth and an empty safe.

"They were at The Rectory."

"Did you ever go there?"

"Yes, but it wasn't like that," she said quickly. "We were friends, he was helping me. You mustn't get the wrong idea."

Wrong ideas were in surplus within Flint's head. "But you went to The Rectory? Into his study?"

"Yes."

"Where did he keep the documents?"

"He hid them with all his archaeology papers; they were just in two of those green file thingies."

"Box files? Can you remember what was written on the spines?"

She frowned. "One said 'pottery' and the other said 'bones'."

Flint's mind verged on the photographic and he

mentally reviewed the bookshelves in the study. He remembered seeing a large bank of the ugly box files down at ankle level behind the sofa, but hadn't taken notice of their titles.

"Have you tried to get them back?"

"They're not there, of course. When the police interviewed me, I made an excuse for them to take me to The Rectory. The files had gone, I could see two little spaces where they should have been."

"So either the killer has them, or Bob has them, which may be the same thing."

"Bob hasn't got them," she said, closing her jaw into a firm line.

"How do you know? Has he told you?"

"He asked me about them, soon after we heard Tom was dead. He was very angry; I could see he was worried. I enjoyed seeing him in that state, it made a change."

An evil glitter was in her eye. "Bob and I had dinner together in London. Bob was . . . Bob is just such a fucking philistine; he's mean, he's a bully, he plays at being everyone's friend when he's really out to screw them. He knew the whole story and he threatened me. Don't you see, if the police find those papers, it's not only Bob who's in trouble."

When a woman of breeding used the "F" word, Flint gained the impression she spoke with sincerity. Eleanor reached into her pocket and withdrew a pair of folded sheets of paper. Each carried a cryptic typed message, in a style which had become so familiar. The first one read:

I HAVE THE FILES

The second:

265

Only yesterday she had denied having received one of the letters. Flint wondered how much more Eleanor was hiding, or concocting.

"I'm being blackmailed."

Yes, blackmail had to fit in somewhere.

"I think Bob's getting the same kind of messages, that's why he became so frightened."

"But that was always part of the plot, wasn't it? You and Tom would blackmail Bob into running the project the way you wanted it running?"

"I just wanted him off my land, I just wanted my home back."

"Ah well, the stakes have changed." Flint was tempted to guess that Bob was being blackmailed by his own assassin. "Do you think he'll pay up?"

"He'll pay the money if he's got no alternative. Knowing him he'll haggle and try to make a deal, so he thinks he's won. It will be my money, of course, he'll tell me he's buying my protection."

"I thought you were broke."

"My father left seven million pounds in Jersey, or somewhere, but I can't have it. Thurlscote controls it."

"You mean Bob controls it?"

The tendons in her neck tensed. "I've got nobody to turn to Jeff, nobody. Even my staff are watching me."

"That man Hurst?"

She reached out a hand and laid it on the sleeve of his greatcoat. Her hard expression melted and was replaced by designer pathos. "Help me. What am I going to do? Do I pay?"

His pulse was running and the stakes grew higher

with every moment that passed. One wrong decision may have cost Sharon Turpin's life, now another life may rest in his sweating palms.

"No," Flint said with unreasonable certainty. "Don't pay. Our murderer is becoming desperate: he or she killed the prostitute, who was obviously an accomplice. These letters are a mistake: at first I didn't understand them, but if blackmail is at the back of all this, they make perfect sense. When did yours begin?"

"Early summer – then I had none, until two weeks ago."

"Such a long time between demands?"

"Bob and I have been partners for seven years: we all have to be patient."

"Can I see the letters again?" He took them from her, aware for the first time of facts coalescing at a point. "How are you supposed to pay? Is there a rendezvous?"

"One letter said I had to go to a place on the moor with the money. I wouldn't do that, not on my own."

"But no new instructions since then? Weird."

Was the blackmailer serious, or was this another false trail? "Can I keep these? There's something I want to try."

"Yes of course, but don't show them to anyone, not to anyone!"

She touched his sleeve again as she appealed to his honour and just for a moment he wanted to throw his arms around her, hold her tight and tell her the princess would live happily ever after. Instead, he just smiled and told her to trust him.

Leaving Eleanor to walk back to the manor alone, Flint headed across the pasture, taking a twenty minute round about route to the far side of the castle, where it reared sharply over a grassy coomb. The detour gave him time to think and time to clear his head. Pristine and perfumed, Eleanor simply pumped out allure, which he had to resist.

Sheep scattered at his approach and a pair of crows rose lazily into the air with a mocking "caw, caw" of complaint. He used his hands in the final stages of his sneak assault on the rear of the bailey. Here the masonry still stood to wall-walk level, with machicolations wobbling uncertainly above the ditch. He found a fallen rock and sat to survey the valley, unravelling the notes Eleanor had given him.

Bob was being blackmailed.

Eleanor was being blackmailed.

Flint was being taunted.

So why was Megan receiving the letters too?

He looked hard at the typing – always in capitals: why? He looked again at the letters, one by one, stopping at the word BURN. At that moment, some deeply buried piece of information fell out of the filing cabinet at the back of his mind. All the problems were about to be solved.

Chapter Twenty-Seven

Flint left his perch beside the castle and walked down to the UNY-DIG Portakabin. One of the new diggers said, "Hi" as she walked past in derri-boots and hard white helmet. Tyrone's Spitfire was parked close by, splashed with mud and grey grime. Some wag had written "wash me" on the door, then written "A1" on the bonnet.

It was as if someone had just slapped Flint in the face with a wet fish. How much more foolish could he become?

"Howdy, partner," he said, pushing the Portakabin door open, then halting, allowing himself to be silhouetted against a brilliant sky. It was ten minutes to high noon and time for a showdown.

"Oh, hi Doc," Tyrone seemed tired and listless again.

"I think, sunny Jim, it's time we had a little chat, supervisor to student."

"Have you marked my thesis then?"

"All done and dusted, and I found it a magnificent, magisterial work. It's your other activities that I want to talk about. Are you, or have you ever been, a member of the A1 Club?"

Tyrone turned pale, then a light pink. "That's not funny."

"It's written on your car, so I assume the whole

digging team think it's hilarious. It wouldn't by any chance have been your car I heard screeching away from Megan's house last night?"

"Okay, so what if it was?"

"Does this explain where you've been all the nights I couldn't find you? Does this explain the slightly less-than-candid excuses?"

"You don't own me, we're not married! Okay, I'm sorry I screwed your woman, but she started it!"

"She's not my woman – or anyone's woman, as far as I can see. No reproaches, Tyrone, I'm not judgmental, it's a free world, you can do what you like and so can she." Flint sucked in his cheeks, swallowing pride, planning his tactics. "Was it Megan that told you we had something going?"

"No. I heard rumours back at the poly."

"It's not a poly. Christ Tyrone, she's fifteen, twenty years older than you!"

"So? You keep telling me not to be racist or sexist or ageist. I'll try a one-legged, black lesbian next, if that's okay."

Flint disregarded the jibe. "What worries me is this, Tyrone. I've been relying on you to watch my back, but you're just floating. Joss is hammering the site, earning his keep, but you're too busy sucking up to Bob Grimston and adding yourself to Megan's little black book."

"I didn't know she was like that – not at first."

"Turn your infernal computer on."

"It's on."

"Database on Megan."

Aged 41, born in Gwent, educated at Cardiff University, four years as a teacher, married to Peter Bott (another teacher) for eight years. Dropped out of teaching to become a postgrad. at Southampton. Thesis on women in medieval Wales, several books followed. Took up post at the Polytechnic of North Yorkshire, promoted to Reader two years ago. Militant on women's rights. Former girlfriend of Tom Aitken from c. last Easter to c. last Xmas.

Flint opened his briefcase and took out the script Megan had given him on the death of Margaret de Balleron in 1478.

"I've lived with this woman," he said. "And I've grown to know her – in the biblical sense. You too?"

Tyrone nodded.

"Do you like her?"

"Yes," he responded, then qualified his feelings. "Well, she's okay."

"You mean she's easy? Would you like to move in with the cats and spend each tea time discussing the inherent sexism of the university system?"

"No, that's not exactly my scene."

"Nor is it anyone else's, especially not Tom Aitken's." Flint was flicking through the script, pausing at the beginning of each sentence. "I don't quite know whether Megan twigged that, or whether she deluded herself into seeing more in the relationship."

"He was two-timing Ruth."

"Exactly – if you were Tom Aitken, which one would you pick?"

"Neither."

"Okay, add Eleanor to the list; now you have a choice of three. No contest, is there?"

Tyrone reluctantly shook his head.

"So you see where I'm leading? Now I've read

almost everything Megan's written – get to know your colleagues, that's my motto. I tried the same on old Barney, and it took at least two hours to read all his output; Megan is the one with the depth."

He spread Eleanor's letters out on the table, then took out his own pair of curious notes, the ones Tyrone said were sent to entice.

"Megan likes to entice," Flint said. "Why would a murderer taunt us with these notes? Where could she get the idea from?"

"This isn't the first time we've been sent death threats and weird letters," Tyrone reminded him. "Everyone back at Central College will know that, and so would anyone who cared to look back at our previous investigations."

"Exactly: everyone at college knows they would attract us and if properly played, they would lead us to the wrong conclusions." Flint prodded a familiar note. "What do you make of this?"

FORGET THE PAST BEWARE THE FUTURE

"It's a real Tom Aitken-ism," Tyrone observed.

"Look at the letter R, see how it's damaged?"

The upper left of the letter was always missing, giving it the appearance of a squashed K. Flint passed across the typescript on the medieval murder.

"Snap."

Tyrone compared letter with manuscript, his head nodding slightly. "Megan uses a typewriter," he said slowly, "but I don't believe she could kill anyone."

"Megan had found someone to love, at last: Tom Aitken. Now Tom was shacked up with Ruth, so had an excuse to string Megan along. Then Ruth walked out and who walked in? Not Megan, but Eleanor. So

272

Megan contrived the plot to kill him and heap the blame on the "posh" woman: Eleanor. Megan is too Welsh on the phone, she could never have managed that act on her own."

"But where did she befriend a prostitute?"

"Barney says she likes girls too."

"But she's not kinky in bed, is she?", Tyrone protested. "You wouldn't call her adventurous, she's just ordinary, just cuddly."

"If you say so." Flint agreed, but was never going to admit it.

"But Doc, a prostitute?"

"Who knows how they met, or if they met? Perhaps they went to the same self-awareness class or women's self-defence group."

"You sound like me."

"And you sound like me, defending the indefensible. We've got to get back to college right now, ring Thorne, then talk to Megan."

Tyrone seemed totally dejected, as if it were his mother being accused of double murder. Perhaps Megan was not the only lonely one. He lethargically picked up the mobile phone. "We don't have to go to college, we can shop her from here."

"No, I've talked some sense out of Eleanor at last. If you're back on the team, I'll tell you why we've got to reach Megan before the police."

Flint allowed Tyrone to drive him back to the university. The open top and the speed blew away the guilt of what he was about to do; rushing air obliterated anything he and Tyrone might say to each other. The Spitfire was driven straight to the staff car park and slid into a visitor's slot next to the big blue Rover.

The pair entered the department at a run, Flint pausing to check the lecture board. Megan was teaching Medieval Art and Symbolism until three pm.

"Doctor Flint!" Debs shouted from the far end of the long, polished corridor. "There's a policeman in your room, I tried to ring you on site."

"They're recruiting bloody clairvoyants now," Flint muttered, pushing open his office door.

D.I. Thorne was sitting in the guest chair. He'd thrown off his overcoat and was engrossed in "*Popular Archaeology*".

"Ah, at last!"

Tyrone looked at Flint.

"I've brought some news," Thorne said.

"Good news?"

"That depends who you are. We've been going through that Sharon Turpin's book of telephone numbers. Guess what? She had the number of this department."

Flint frowned, it was time for a quick confession. "Ah, yes. I was going to tell you about that. I had a couple of calls from a woman calling herself Janet. She asked me not to tell the police."

"And you were true to your word," Thorne stated, a steely edge to his voice.

"It seemed the best thing to do." Flint continued to rapidly summarise his brief conversations with "Janet".

Thorne made odd sucking noises as he became increasingly restless. "Your extension number is what?"

"2047 – we're on direct dial, just add the digits."

"The number in Sharon's book was 2044. She might have rung you, but it looks like she rang someone else too."

274

"And that someone killed her?"

"It looks like it. I am right in saying that Dr Preece is on extension 2044? We've interviewed her before, of course, but this time, things may be different. D.S. Patel came up with a new way of looking at the evidence at the case meeting this morning."

"Did you find lots of forensic evidence from the scene of the second murder?"

"You name it, we found it."

"Have a look at this," Flint said, passing over the incriminating typescripts. "Megan owns an old Imperial typewriter: you should check it out. Could you get a warrant?"

"I don't need a warrant to arrest her for murder. At this stage, I'd rather she came along to assist us, as we say in the trade. Could we have a little look in her office whilst we wait?"

"It's two along the corridor."

Thorne was on his feet and Flint led the way. Megan's office was locked, but Flint obtained a pass key from Debs, and in moments the three men were inside. Thorne made straight for a black address book beside the telephone and began to search through its pages. A pile of business cards fell from a flap in the rear.

Flint fished the prostitute's calling card from the pile of detritus. "I don't believe it."

As if on cue, the door opened and Megan's voice challenged him. "Jeff, what's going on?"

It was all happening too quickly, Flint needed to talk to Megan about Eleanor's missing files, but all this was being overwhelmed in the rush. Another man, tall, and of Indian complexion, appeared behind Megan. She glanced anxiously at him and he set his

275

mouth in a satisfied smile. Thorne raised himself to full height. "Dr Megan Preece, where were you on the night of 15th April?"

"You already asked me that question," she said, her face turning into solid stone.

"I'm asking you again."

"I was on a blind date," she snapped, looking angrily at Flint. "I was sent a bunch of flowers and a card, with a date and time for a meeting in a York pub."

"Did your date appear?"

"I was stood up."

"That was a bit convenient. Dr Preece, I think I am going to have to ask you to accompany me . . ."

He launched into the jargon of the legal caution, whilst Megan turned a grey shade, losing all her fluffy pink appeal. Flint half expected her to run, anticipating another wild chase, but Megan remained stock still in the doorway, with D.S. Patel hovering behind her. Tyrone was looking out of the window, hands in pockets. Flint felt utterly sick.

Chapter Twenty-Eight

The telephone line crackled, but the policeman's voice was unnecessarily cheery. "The forensic matches, Jeff, we've got her!"

"What matches?"

"Can't tell you all the details, mate, but we can match Megan Preece to Sharon Turpin's flat and to the scene of her murder. I think you can call this a closed case, nice work. Thanks for all your help. We got the right one in the end."

Thanks for the help. Thanks for sinking a colleague. Thanks for betraying a bedmate. Amateur detection had led Flint nowhere except to a bitter end. He had so wanted to pin the crime on Bob Grimston and had taken deep pleasure in imagining the collapse of his property empire. Glittering fantasy had been replaced by grim reality. Outside the window of the UNY-DIG office, a heavy fog blotted out the view and emphasised the air of gloom.

"What now?" Tyrone asked.

"We go back to doing what we're paid to do. We're just whores with trowels, Tyrone. He who pays the piper and all that."

"It wasn't us who found the evidence, it was the police. Even if we'd done nothing, Thorne would have got her in the end."

"I don't care any more, I don't care about Tom Aitken, the daft git. Look at the women he chose, for goodness sake: one fresh off the psychiatrist's couch, one trainee terrorist and one murderous nymphomaniac."

"Megan could have been framed," Tyrone offered.

"She fits all the criteria, everything fits: motive, opportunity and hard evidence. There's no shadow of a doubt, as Sue Carrick would put it. The best we can do is salvage something from the wreckage."

Neither spoke for some time, only the whirr of Tyrone's PC and the hum of the striplight disturbed a disturbed calm.

"I had a final look through your thesis over the weekend."

"Oh," said Tyrone.

"I think the viva is a formality," Flint added. He hoped to elicit a typically arrogant Tyrone answer, perhaps "I know", or "What did you expect". Instead, Tyrone said "Oh," again.

"We need to be on site by noon," Tyrone said. "Bob wants a meeting, he sent us a fax this morning."

"Did it say 'Well done for nailing the bitch?'"

"No."

"I wanted it to be him."

"Yes."

"Will you drive me up? The van needs its fuel pump looking at, or something equally expensive."

"I'd prefer it if we drove up separately. I've things to do."

"Okay, fine. I'm lecturing in ten minutes, so I'll see you up there about lunchtime. We could stop at that pub on the way."

"No," Tyrone said.

"What's wrong? Don't feel like eating?"
"No."

The clocks had gone back, the day had been trimmed at the latter end. Flint's fuel pump continued to play up. He avoided the A1 (traffic bulletins warning of delays) and snaked through a misty landscape of small villages. He hated driving, why on earth had he decided to rent a house in the country? Why had he fallen for the lure of a campus university? Why had he ever fooled himself that the Shadesmoor project had any merits?

A billboard twenty feet high by thirty feet long had been placed at the entrance to the estate, broadcasting the names of all the companies who would hang, draw and quarter Shadesmoor before dangling its entrails for the public to oggle.

Grimston's Jaguar was already parked by the row of Portakabins. Tyrone's Spitfire, still unwashed, sat alongside.

"You're late," Grimston snarled as Flint stretched himself out of the van. "Mind you, what's fifteen minutes to the average archaeologist? The castle's been here for five hundred years, why not wait another five hundred before you pull your fingers out?"

"Sorry."

Tyrone appeared at the door of the UNY-DIG Portakabin, hands in the pockets of his leather bomber jacket. He leaned on the door frame, seeming reluctant to join them.

"So," Flint said. "You wanted to see us?"

Bob's face was full of amused satisfaction. "For the last time. You're fired."

"What?"

"Pack up your goods and clear the site. You've got two days."

"What about our contract, we've got a contract."

"Clause twenty-four. Read it. I've had people look into you Flint. You're a regular little Sherlock Holmes and you've been sniffing about. When I want to hire private detectives, there's a firm I know, and they're good and they don't crap in their own nest. That's what you've done, Flint. I've given you this job on a plate and what have you done? Crapped in your own nest."

Flint was recovering from his shock now, thinking that Grimston was playing a bluff in order to gain some advantage over him. "Your planning permission requires you to have archaeologists on site at all time. If we go, your project halts. Don't tell me you're going to lay off all these men until a new unit has put up a tender?"

"One has – and I've accepted it." Grimston turned to Tyrone. "What's your outfit called? Diggers Unlimited?"

Flint glared at Tyrone, whilst his erstwhile ally shifted weight from one foot to another.

"You're washed out Flint, but Tyrone knows where he's coming from."

"Does he now?"

Without the fog, without the Yorkshire accents and the coats, the shifting of eyes from man to man was pure Sergio Leone. Flint checked Tyrone, Tyrone looked to Grimston, Grimston nodded to the man he had just purchased, then his eyes laughed at Flint. If only there were a trumpet braying and a six-gun handy, Clint Eastwood would know what to do.

Tyrone broke the stalemate. "Actually," he looked from one employer to another. "Diggers Unlimited is kind of shelved for the future."

It was Grimston's turn to be dumbfounded. "What?"

"It stinks, Bob, the whole project stinks. Money doesn't buy everything. It doesn't buy me."

Flint laughed aloud, beaming, wanting to rush across and hug his student. Grimston swore. "Right, you'd both better clear off. Twenty-four hours, then anything left will go in a skip."

Tyrone turned up the lapel of his bomber jacket, and Grimston walked to his car, shaking his head and swearing.

"You can rat, but you can also re-rat, it seems," Flint said, walking towards Tyrone. "If you want, you can still run after him; it beats being unemployed."

"Three million people can't be wrong."

"Why the big sacrifice?"

"I guess I owe it to you, after Megan."

"You thought I might just burn your thesis?"

"No. I do listen to you sometimes, when you go on about human values and equality and all that. It's not all hogwash. I only disagree to wind you up."

"Well you certainly had me fully wound just now."

"Sorry, Doc. We'd better tell the squad. They're going to riot, especially the ones who've only just got here. I mean, who's going to employ diggers in November?"

"No, I'll do the dirty; I'll think up a good rabble-rousing speech about how we've been betrayed by the filthy, capitalist running dogs. After that, we're going to have to move the equipment sharpish if the van can cope. Maybe we can ship it all as far as my place, then sort it out later. The team can squat on my floor and we'll have the mother of all booze-ups if we get it all done by tonight."

"Are you going to make a stink with the Inspectorate?"

"And the local authority, and anyone else who has the slightest interest in this mess. Bob's climbing a greasy pole and he thinks his money can keep him up there. All along, I've been damned sure he had something to do with that murder, or knows more than he's telling the police. Do you believe me now?"

"I always did."

The mother of all booze-ups left the mother of all hangovers. Worse, it was a shared, group hangover. The site had not been cleared until long after dark and the Portakabin and Portaloo still had to be collected by the hire company. Ten or so of the Phase II crew lived locally and had managed to drive home, the remaining two dozen, plus their baggage and equipment, had piled into the minute two-bedroomed cottage Flint shared with his packing cases. Drinking and talking continued to dawn and beyond.

Set an example to youth, Flint thought, having chased the milkman down Church Hill and carried back six extra pints. Get fired, get drunk, get laid, get radical. Who cared for suburban norms, other than his neighbours? He met one on his unusually slimy doorstep, offered some kind of hazy apology, then stumbled into the commune. Fresh, damp, morning air was replaced by the stench of state tobacco, spilt beer, close-knit bodies, and worse.

Tyrone was on the settee, one arm around a rather weighty, sleeping lady digger, the other cuddling a quarter bottle of Bell's.

"Who moves the Portakabin?" Flint muttered, stepping over the bodies on the rug.

"They do. I'll ring when their office opens. I'm trying to make plans here, I'm just a bit tired. Anna's got the right idea." He nodded towards the sleeping girl.

"That one's Harriet."

Tyrone extracted his arm and shook life into it. "She kept calling me Richard, so all's fair."

The cottage was too crowded for serious hanky-panky. The depth of relationship which had sprung up between Tyrone and Anna extended to a long argument about nuclear weapons, after which she'd fallen asleep. Tyrone followed Flint, picking their way to the kitchen.

"Black or white?" Flint flicked the switch on the kettle.

"Blackest black fits the mood. Grimston has fouled everything up. He's fouled up our unit, fouled up the estate and fouled up lots of peoples lives."

"I'd use a stronger word than 'fouled'."

"I mean, poor old Ruth. She's going to be let out now, but what's she got? All her friends were in that Civil War Regiment. They'll be up at the castle next week, having their battle and she'll be where? Think about Marston Moor and how happy she was. Remember how good her costume was? And her musket was really authentic."

"The way to a man's heart; show him your musket."

"When I was talking to Grimston about the arrest, he said that as soon as Ruth was free he'd put an injunction on her not to go near the castle." Tyrone no longer referred to Grimston as "Bob". "He's scared she'll load her musket for real and give him one up the backside."

"Couldn't happen to a nicer guy. What do you think of capitalism now, Tyrone?"

He took a swig from the whisky bottle, then raised it in clench-fisted salute. "Up the revolution!"

Hungover, and in some cases still intoxicated, the team completed the removal of equipment. Shadesmoor Castle had resisted another siege, its lord victorious over his enemies. Flint telephoned Debs at the college and cancelled his Art and Architecture lecture, plus all his tutorials. Students were the last thing he could face that morning.

By early afternoon, his house was free of its last refugee so Flint drove to college to delve into the paperwork. He re-read the Phase II contract to discover whether the UNY-DIG bills would still be paid by Grimston. By rights, he should see a solicitor, but knew the cost would cripple the shaky finances of the unit. Perhaps he could beg one final favour from Sue Carrick, or at least pick Barney's brains. He thought better of both ideas: Sue would be obstructive, Barney had actually failed Law so was of questionable competence. No option remained but to prostrate himself before Betty and confess to having failed utterly. Had he been a Carthaginian general, he would expect crucifixion for returning in defeat.

With a thick head induced by tension (and other causes), he prowled around the corridor, pretending to read the notice board, still not anxious to break the latest bad news. Debs breezed past as if oblivious to the series of disasters which had struck the department.

"Afternoon, Jeff, feeling better?"

"Debs!" He wanted distraction.

284

"Hmm?" She paused and turned, hugging the pile of photocopies to her breast.

"Do you remember those old Imperial typewriters you used to use?"

"Yes, they were awful. We sold them off about three years ago." She paused and lowered her tone. "Megan bought one, as you know."

"How many did we have?"

"Three."

He questioned her further. A fact was hammering at his reluctant brain, much as a battering ram against a crumbling castle gate, then a curious thought sallied into his head and would not be dislodged. Debs knocked on Betty's door and Flint shrank away. Confession could wait. He turned about and left the Mandela building for the adjacent block where the Student's Union were based.

"MORE GRANT NOW!" demanded the poster by the door. He'd seen variations on the same slogan plastered on Union walls for the past twenty years, and would for twenty more without witnessing the slightest change in Government thinking (if Government thinking wasn't a contradiction).

The office walls, floor and table space were completely cluttered with paper. The wiry Union Vice President was earnestly writing at her desk, and smiled an acknowledgement. In the corner, on another desk was an Imperial typewriter of the same model as Megan's.

"Can I play with this for a minute?" Flint asked.

"Be our guest."

He dropped a sheet of recycled paper into the machine, set it up and hurriedly typed:

ROUND THE RUGGED ROK THE RAGGED RASCAL RAN

He'd never been very good at typing before the microchip had come to his rescue. Rolling the paper from the machine he examined the faint typeface. There was no damage to the R, but the A was slightly cocked. It had been worth a try. Still, he observed, if he could repair that A and if he took a nail file to the R he could make a fairly good imitation of the typeface used in the cranky letters and in Megan's scripts. He could then fake another death threat letter, post it to Thorne and Megan would be in the clear. Yes, if he could find a motive, he could cook up a little more phoney evidence and try to pin the crimes on an unsuspecting student. The fantastic idea had a macabre appeal.

"Thanks," he said, slipping the paper into his jacket pocket. "Could I use this machine again one day?"

"Anytime."

Flint looked at his watch, thinking he just had time to drive across to his mother's house in Leeds for tea: the diggers had ravaged the contents of his kitchen more thoroughly than a band of marauding Huns.

As he worked his way towards Leeds, Flint drove on autopilot, whilst most of his brain wandered. Shadesmoor Castle had high and very thick walls, but no fortress was impenetrable. Walls and moats delayed attacks but seldom defeated a determined assault. Cars flashed past in the growing gloom of afternoon, but Flint was lost amongst the books of medieval siegewarfare he had read whilst at Megan's cottage. The ways to capture a castle could be summarised thus:

Escalade (over the walls)
Battery (through the walls or gates)
Mining (under the walls)
Starvation (sitting outside the walls)
Stratagem

He'd been over the top in his enthusiasm to capture Ruth. He'd battered his head against the problem without overcoming any resistance from Grimston and his cronies. Undermining the project had begun with his conversations with Eleanor, but how far would she go and how much of her tale could he believe? He could hardly afford to sit and await events or Grimston's juggernaut would simply roll him over with its own impetus. Stratagem? He thought of *El Cid*: overlong and wooden as epics went. In one siege scene, the King was lured to a postern gate, then killed in a treacherous double-cross.

As usual, his mother tried to spoil him. He'd told her a dozen times that he avoided red meat, but she simply served his steak well done. Flint smiled and chewed, his mind passing on to the English Civil War when castles had still been formidable obstacles. Royalist Shadesmoor had been battered by cannon and surrendered when its walls were tumbling into the ditch: the victorious Roundheads then blew up the gatehouse, but lacked the powder to do a proper job on the keep.

Stratagem, Civil War, Ruth, missing files and a veteran typewriter. He chewed and he chewed and gradually things became clearer.

His mother seemed to be speaking. ". . . he's gazing again, Stan, just like when he was little."

"You all right, lad?" his father asked from the far end of the formica-topped kitchen table.

Flint rejoined the real world, cleared his mouth and grinned at both parents. "I will be."

Chapter Twenty-Nine

D.I. Thorne looked incredulous. He was sitting in Flint's office, being asked to participate in what he'd called a charade.

"I can't play games, I have a job to do."

"Play, please, humour me."

"I tried your idea at The Old Rectory, and look where it got us. I can't risk corrupting the evidence we've assembled against Megan Preece."

"No chance of that."

Tyrone sat quietly in a corner, sifting a large pile of notes.

"Did your people build up a psychological profile of the killer?" Flint asked.

"Yes – Ruth fitted it well, and so does Megan Preece as a matter of fact. They both had motives, and the opportunity. We can sometimes tell if a crime is committed by a man; in this case, the position of the footstool at the scene of the crime makes it look like a woman killed Aitken. Both Ruth and Megan are stronger than the average woman, they're both clever enough to have hatched the plot and they both know enough about archaeology to dream up that cover story."

"What about the hand-axe, has anyone explained why that was used? It's not the traditional blunt instrument is it?"

"No, but that rock lays the crime firmly at the feet of one of your people."

"It's a bit of colour added to make the crime look bizarre?"

"Yes, I couldn't have put it better myself. If Wayne had done the killing, he'd have used his crowbar. If we'd found this contract killer Ruth went on about, he'd have used something a bit more professional."

"You said that if you had the right person in a cell you could break the case?"

"I said that, and I'm right. Dr Preece has no defence except a terrible alibi."

"For the first crime: but what about Sharon Turpin?"

"You weren't with Megan Preece that weekend?" Thorne asked over his shoulder.

"No," said Tyrone. "But women don't strangle."

"They can and some do."

Flint changed tack to focus on the complex plan ahead. "We had a brainstorming session last night, Tyrone and I. We came back to the office with plenty of coffee and a box of Family Assorted and we went through every piece of evidence we have."

Tyrone lifted his pile of documents.

"Very nice, but we have a hundred times as much as that."

"True and your case against Megan progresses from fact A to conclusion B, it's all perfectly logical. So Tyrone and I tried being illogical and threw around all the silliest theories we could think of. Then, when we'd reached a consensus on the most far-fetched idea of all, we had to compose a suitably silly way of proving it."

Flint held up two pieces of paper. Both had writing

on the front, but Thorne could only see the blank side. One had a silky, vellum quality, the other was standard A4 typing paper.

"Two letters, okay?"

Thorne nodded very reluctantly.

"For my next trick, follow me." Flint stood up and led the way out of the office, down the corridor to where the much abused departmental photocopier stood.

Flint asked Thorne to stand back, then fed the two letters into the machine. He laid the output face down and asked Thorne to sign the backs of the two photocopies.

"Why? What am I confessing to?"

"Nothing I can't explain. This is an experiment and it probably won't work. I don't know much about the law, but you boys are supposed to play with a straight bat: no entrapment."

"We have the murderer in custody."

"Oh, the murderer is trapped." Flint said. "No escape, no worthwhile alibi plenty of evidence; circumstantial, forensic, psychological. And the murderer knows it."

"As I said, we've got her. There's no need for entrapment, or this paper chase."

"There is; bear with me. There is a twist which still needs untwisting. Think of yourself as a latter-day knight, thwarting the wicked to save the maiden. It is a noble deed we do."

"Noble?"

"Noble."

"And it won't screw up my case?"

"Quite the reverse."

"Tell us what it's about."

"Can't. I'd be letting someone down."

Thorne took out a pen and initialled both sheets. "I'm going to regret this."

Flint dropped the two signed copies into a single, plain brown, A4 envelope. He then folded the originals and placed these into suitably contrasting envelopes, sealing them and putting both face-down on the photocopier. He pressed the key and took a copy of the addressed side.

"I sign this too?" Thorne was warming to the game. He signed the reverse without further protest.

Flint put the copy with the others in the A4 envelope and sealed it. Thorne signed the envelope, then Debs was asked to bind up the seal with parcel tape.

"This is our control envelope. If we open it in a few days time, you can read the letters we are about to send. Now comes the farce," Flint said. "First, we ask the Registrar to pop this into his safe. Then, we have to drive to Harrogate to post the 'posh' envelope, then down to York to post the other. I want you to do the posting too."

"And I can't even read the addresses?"

"It would spoil the validity of the experiment. What are you doing on Saturday?"

"I'm off duty – I'm going down Elland Road to see Leeds beat Everton."

"You don't fancy a trip to the seaside do you?"

Low, overcast skies threatened rain to spoil the battle. With drums beating and pious colours waving, Marwood's Regiment of Foot marched steadily up the slope towards Shadesmoor Castle. Scudding cloud and diffuse light gave the ruin a bleak, unloved aspect. The crowd was large for a November display, the numbers swelled by the curious events, and lurid reporting which had surrounded the Shadesmoor project. Later that evening, a bonfire and firework display would celebrate another piece of popular history.

On the castle mound, a cannon fired and muskets offered a desultory volley. The sixty men and women advancing in period dress responded to the command of one of their members. White-coated musketeers rushed out to flank the pike block, then by numbers returned fire on the castle.

It was all a little pathetic. Hats blew off in the breeze as the tiny force tried to represent a whole besieging army. The dozen or so defenders of the castle ramparts made an equally feeble show.

Flint stood by the roadside, on the left flank of the musketeers. According to the script they had to assault the castle, then fall back in disorder. This they were now doing. He laid eyes on Ruth, holding grimly onto her hat, and at her side, Joss and Tyrone, the Regiment's newest recruits.

Ropes and a handful of marshalls kept the crowds off the excavations and away from the modern armour of the contractor's army. JCBs, trucks and bulldozers were parked wheel-to-wheel, their presence visibly threatening the whole display. Next year, the battle would have to move to the less scenic southern flank of the hill whilst the theme park took shape in the meadow.

Flint donned a floppy hat and cartridge belt, fitting in with the mob now rushing towards him in mock panic. Members of the public applauded, but this was not the show he'd come to see.

Unmistakable even at a distance, Eleanor Balleron emerged from the back of the crowd, walking off towards the river. Flint lifted his field glasses to watch her go. Everything was proceeding to order: Eleanor carried a shopping bag in her right hand and moved with self-conscious glances to left and right. He swung the glasses around to check the temporary car park beside the bridge. He recognised several of the vehicles. One was a brown Volvo, Sue Carrick was here: all the pieces should now be on the board. It was time to play.

The routing Regiment re-formed itself to make a second assault up the slopes. Flint jogged out to join the rear ranks, feeling only slightly silly. With its rag stunts and carnival floats, college life had knocked the edge off his fear of being ridiculous in public.

Ruth was a little short for a musketeer, shorter indeed than her musket, which she loaded with difficulty. Bang-ba-bam-bang! The rolling volley went off just as Flint slithered into place on the left flank. At a command, the Parliamentarian line charged. The castle gun fired and Flint flinched: the muzzle was aimed at *him*. Thank God he had not been born in the seventeenth century, or a big iron ball would now be chasing his head towards the river.

He broke into a run, almost left behind in the rush. Up streamed the Roundheads, over the ditch (mind the excavations!), up the mound, over the feebly defended breech in the curtain wall. History lessons were never like this when Flint was a lad.

As mock deaths were enacted in the mock mêlée, Flint slipped to one side and raised the field glasses. A lonely figure was walking north up the river, towards the woods.

"Is it time?" Joss came up beside Flint. "I feel a right pillock in this hat."

Ruth joined them, rubbing a smear of black powder across her cheek.

"Ruth, this is Joss. Joss, Ruth."

Joss slapped her on the shoulder. "Don't worry about the tyre, love, the tread was illegal anyway. It were good to screw a new one out of Tyrone."

"New what?" Tyrone arrived breathless, clearly enjoying the period romp. "Anything happening?"

"I've just seen Sue Carrick, she's in the car park. Eleanor seems to be waiting by the river." Flint lifted the field glasses again. A second figure had left the car park, following Eleanor up the path. Flint knew that figure had received a letter, which Eleanor had handwritten on her personal stationary. It had read:

I know who you are. Meet me at 1.45pm on November 5th, during the mock battle at the castle. I will be on the path next to the river, north of the bridge. I will give you £10,000 for the files, and we will say no more about it. If you fail to come, I will give your name to the police.

E.S.D. Balleron

An essential part of the plan was that Bob Grimston was kept well out of the way. Bob had received the second letter: if he'd acted on its instructions, he should at that moment be many miles away.

Flint glanced around. Ten faces looked back at him from beneath wide-brimmed, black felt hats: bank clerks, school teachers, postmen and metal-pressers who found something rather more exciting to do on a damp November Saturday.

"Shoulder!" Ruth shouted.

The white-coated musketeers formed in ranks of two and began to march briskly downhill, applauded by the crowd. Once on the level meadow, they were screened from the river. Ruth was the first to duck under the rope and forced a passage through the three ranks of onlookers. Her musketeers followed, now only fifty yards from the river. Two figures could be seen in conversation some distance off. One carried a bag, the other held something bulky under each arm.

Flint was at the back of the group, as were his two assistants, hiding their scratch uniforms. Ruth led the tiny band, a broad, fanatical smile on her face worthy of a Roundhead Captain. The unholy were about to meet justice.

Eleanor was trying to conduct her conversation, but the shorter figure in the blue-black raincoat had now been distracted by the approaching musketeers. The figure turned, as if to wait for the procession to pass. Except, it did not pass. With a rush, the musketeers engulfed the pair, giving no time for the little man to run, or to fight, even if he were blessed with the physique. Eleanor stepped back, mesmerised by the scene. A sharp sound of flesh on flesh came from the centre of the brawl and Ruth withdrew, shaking her stinging knuckles, face red with anger.

The dupe was holding his jaw as the crowd parted. He turned to face Flint.

"Hello, Barney."

Chapter Thirty

Barney said nothing, his mouth opening and closing in breathless protest. Flint looked at the man through new eyes, trying to believe he had been responsible for so much mayhem.

"So this is how you obtain your research grants?"

A state of shock induced by the ambush, or possibly by Ruth's whole-hearted punch, had stunned the lecturer. "Assault," Barney mumbled. "I know my rights, I studied Law you know, Jeffrey Flint."

"And you failed."

"Story of his life," Tyrone added the insult.

Eleanor darted into the group and recovered two box files which had fallen to the ground. She hugged them close to her chest, then stepped away, to distance herself from Barney. For six months, Barney had been in complete control, manipulating all their strings by clever deceit. Now, he was powerless.

"Let him loose chaps, he's not going to run off, are you Barney? You were only safe whilst no one thought you could have killed Aitken, but now we all know."

"I was in Carlisle . . ." he began, "at the pot conference."

"Yeah, but who remembers seeing you? Who talked to you in the bar that night?"

"Nobody would bother," sneered Tyrone.

297

"I'm on the attendance list."

"I rang the organiser: he compiled the list a week before the conference began, he always does. Come off it, Barney, you always thought you were smarter than you really are. The footstool was a dead giveaway, you should have spotted that."

Barney looked down at the ground. He pushed his hands deep into the pockets of his blue-black raincoat and a series of short, low gasps came from his lips. As he fell, Joss and one of the musketeers grabbed his arms and pulled him upright.

Flint took out a scribbled note and passed it to Ruth. "Get him to the manor, then ring this number. Ask for Detective Sergeant Patel."

Ruth had been quivering with a mixture of rage and exhilaration. She took the card, then without a word, led the company back towards the manor, with Barney stumbling along in the midst of Tom Aitken's friends. Tyrone gave a whoop of victory, spinning the fancy hat into the air, then catching it. "Got him: too fat to run, too dumb to hide."

"Poor sod," Flint watched the figure shrink into the distance and shrink from his life. "I always tried to like him."

"That's your problem, Doc. You try to like the wrong kind of people."

True, thought Flint, turning back to Eleanor. The lady of the manor was trembling, clutching the box files, ignoring the shopping bag which she had dropped on the ground.

"Who is he?" She watched the pathetic figure walking towards retribution.

"A nobody," Tyrone said.

". . . who wanted to be a somebody," Flint added. "You did brilliantly, Eleanor, but I'll have to explain everything later – we're due in Scarborough in just over half an hour."

Tyrone picked up the fallen bag, checking that it contained a telephone directory, not £10,000. They began to move towards the car park with Eleanor still ridden by angst. "Must you?" she asked.

"It's the only way. Trust me."

Quickly they made for the brown Volvo.

"The two musketeers," Sue Carrick observed after her window had whirred open.

"That's an old one. We've got the files."

"How many civil liberties did you infringe in getting them? Let me guess; Assault? GBH? Wrongful imprisonment?"

Eleanor was hesitant when asked to pass the box files through the window, but her willpower had never been great. Sue accepted the files, then Flint offered her the use of his mobile phone.

"I have my own. I hope you know this evidence is probably tainted by what you've just done."

"Good – the prosecution don't need it. All they need is to find where Barney hides his typewriter."

"Is it the same as Dr Preece's machine?"

"Yes, the department sold three off. Megan bought one, the Union bought one and the third went to one of Barney's final year students. It took me a day or two to track her down, but she confirmed that Barney offered to buy her typewriter when she graduated. I think he customised the keys to copy the damaged R on Megan's machine."

"Clever."

"Oh, he's got a shelf full of forensic science books: the police will find he carefully faked every piece of

299

evidence against Megan. Now we have to rush, can Eleanor sit in with you? You two need to do some business. She might be able to answer a few questions on the files, save you time."

"Climb in dear – I'm one of the sane ones around here."

Raindrops began to fall and Eleanor shuffled into the protection of the car.

"We'd better go," Tyrone said.

Flint exchanged mobile phone numbers with Sue then began to back away from the car. "You've got half an hour."

"As much as that?"

"You're an angel."

"I'm a fool. Now scram before I regret what I'm doing."

Barney had received the first letter, which Eleanor had written on her own notepaper and which D.I. Thorne had reluctantly dropped into a Harrogate postbox. The second letter was on plain A4 paper, of a common brand available in the college stationers. Flint had typed it on the Imperial in the Union office, after the capital R had been re-shaped with a nail file. The postmark on the envelope was York, the message read:

MEET ME SCARBOROUGH HARBOUR OP-
POSITE LIGHTHOUSE. SATURDAY 3.00PM.
£10,000 AND THE FILES ARE YOURS DONT
COME AND THEY GO TO THE POLICE THIS
IS THE LAST LETTER NO TRICKS

Scarborough seafront in late November has all the charm of a seaside town in late November.

Nobody plays the Winter Gardens, the arcades are closed, the gypsies have foreseen the weather and gone elsewhere. Flint had always loved it.

Rain came from the land, thin and wet, whilst a high tide pounded Marine Drive and gnawed at the roots of the castle mount. Tyrone parked in the town and as they walked down to South Bay, he sheltered his tutor with a corporate umbrella given by a friend in the City.

"Will I pass the viva?"

"Wait and see."

"If I get shot today, do I get my Ph.D posthumously?"

"We could ask a medium to sit in on the viva; there's one old girl who used to work a booth over there, by the rock shop."

The pair crossed the almost empty seafront road then turned north along the promenade, towards the lifeboat shed, the closed whelk stalls and the harbour. High up before them, another sad, red castle continued to defy the elements. Fishing boats shifted on their moorings and seagulls made distress calls as they side-slipped against the wind. The mobile phone beeped for attention.

"Mobiles are such a horrid idea, but they have their uses," Flint said. "Hello?"

It was Sue Carrick.

"Have you found something?"

"Eleanor has been guiding me through the papers. At first reading of the Trust Deed, it looks like pretty standard stuff, with a whole host of clauses stating what can and can't be done with the estate."

"What about building a theme park?"

"Probably not allowed, but I need to read more."

"So what sins has Grimston committed?"

301

"It appears – and I stress the word, appears, that he's over-ridden clauses in the Trust Deed."

"Which means he's bribed the Trustees?"

"I wouldn't be prepared to make that statement before witnesses."

"Ever cautious?"

"I always am. You should try it."

"Yes, well, we're going fishing now. Keep reading. I'll be in touch."

Flint had just seen a blue Rover cruise past. The rain lashed harder for a few moments, then eased as they reached the landward end of the harbour arm, with the closed pleasure beach beyond. It was a Grimstonesque place to meet: castle, commerce and kiss-me-quick all converged at that corner of the bay.

The old harbour closes to a jaw-like entrance, where stands the lighthouse shelled by the battle-cruiser *Von der Tann* in 1914. All around, Flint saw heritage under threat and one of the greatest threats leaned on the railings contemplating the grey sea and the gunmetal sky from beneath a black umbrella. A briefcase was beside his ankle.

"Hi, Bob."

Grimston turned to face the pair. His face registered shock, and alarm. "You two?"

"It was our letter," Flint said.

The millionaire was not his usual, abrasive self. "Your letter?"

"Scarborough harbour, ten grand?"

"You scheming bastards," Grimston's eyes glowed with a curious respect. "So I give you ten grand, you give me the files and that's the end is it? Where did you get them from? The Welsh bird?"

"Oh no, Megan had nothing to do with it, she's

been well and truly framed. It took some organising, I tell you."

"You don't mean . . . not you two? You didn't kill him, you wouldn't have the nerve. And what about that tart?" Grimston guffawed and looked away. "I'll be damned." He turned back. "So what happened to needing £200,000 then? Lose your nerve? Police getting too close?"

So Grimston had been blackmailed by Barney, and the asking price had been t200,000. Barney had clearly not received anything like this sum, but his trip to Denmark had been remarkably unexpected. Flint continued to gamble. "The advance payment was well used."

"I should bloody well hope so; now where are these fucking files?"

"You came here to meet the man who killed Tom Aitken."

"And?"

Flint pointed a finger at a distant blue Rover. "In that car is Detective Inspector Simon Thorne. We've brought him here on a sort of magical mystery tour, he's not sure why he's here. He's going to ask you some very embarrassing questions about that letter."

Grimston took the letter from his pocket. "This letter?" He screwed it into a ball and in moments it vanished into the grey-green water. "What letter?"

"Does the briefcase go next?" Flint asked.

Grimston looked down at his briefcase, and for a moment seemed to consider throwing £10,000 in used fivers into the North Sea.

"Thorne is going to want to know how much you've already paid to the killer – and why."

"Look, take the money and give me the files."

Flint took the briefcase, weighing it in his hand. "I

303

don't want your money, just abandon the project. Leave the castle alone, and leave Eleanor alone."

"That crazy woman! Have you been shafting her too?"

"Don't be crude, just use your brain. My lawyer has read the Trust Deeds, she's working through the letters and the tapes. We know what tricks you've pulled, so the project is dead. The question is whether you pull out before legal action, or afterwards."

"And the police?"

"They've got their man."

"Who?"

"Keith Barnes."

"Who?"

"He had a nice jolly in Denmark on the first case load of money you sent him. How much was it? Five? Ten?"

Grimston shook his head, admitting nothing. He was a poker player who had beaten harder men than Flint in face-to-face combat.

"Barnes killed Tom Aitken, for a whole host of reasons which I won't go into. This left him in control of the files. He was the one sending you the blackmail letters, he was the one you paid off."

"You're just guessing."

"Now we might surmise that you asked Barnes to get those files off Aitken, and that he only blackmailed you in retrospect . . ."

"You can't prove that."

"Then why are you here, bearing a suitcase full of cash? If the fortune-teller over there was open, she'd predict very nasty charges of conspiracy to murder. Then we can add theft, deception and all the fun of a fraud trial. As a finale, we have the civil action for breach of Trust. It's costly, it's hassle; win or lose, it'll kill your business prospects."

Grimston looked glum rather than angry. He was not used to impotence.

"Now, we could imagine a different future. Let's say that you leave Eleanor alone, and that she keeps the files to herself. We play down the blackmail, despite whatever Barnes says at the trial. The police are going to give you some stick, but they've got their killer and it was thanks to your help. You did put up the reward, after all."

He was a businessman. In former times Grimston would have been a knighted lord, skilled in battle and intrigue, surviving only if he knew when a position was untenable. "And what happens to the files?"

"They're in Eleanor's hands, it's up to her. When the air is clear, she may just burn them."

"You win," he said, sharply, holding out a hand.

Flint was nonplussed, but shook it.

"I was never here, I never got that letter, understand? And I never paid anything to anyone?" Grimston looked hopefully at the briefcase.

"We'll keep this for a week or so," Flint said. "Evidence of good faith."

"And fingerprints," Tyrone added.

"I'll speak to Eleanor, see she does alright," Grimston said.

"That's very noble of you."

"Oh, and there's this." Tyrone suddenly produced an envelope from his pocket and passed it to Grimston.

"What is it?"

"Our invoice."

Chapter Thirty-One

The fuel pump on the green van had finally given up the struggle, so Professor Betty Vine had offered to drive Flint to York station for the fast train to London.

"I'm a professor without a department," she said as they took a diversion onto a wet and terrifying A19. "I fear you hit us rather like an avenging gunslinger in one of those dreadful westerns. I collected Megan from the police station yesterday, welcoming her back into the fold, but she insists she's resigning. I've told her the post will remain open until the New Year, I hope she'll change her mind."

Poor Megan. Flint would try his best to mend fences, but the fences had been demolished, chopped up, carted away for firewood, burned and the ashes scattered. He'd sent a huge bunch of flowers to the police station with Betty, but Betty had brought them back, with the message card unread.

"Promise me you will come back from London? You won't desert us? I can't dangle any carrots in front of you, but if Megan feels she must resign . . ."

Promotion, again! More money, more power, but he had little appetite for either. Outside the car, rain-washed and mist-shrouded fields swished by.

"Did you ever suspect Barney of the killings?" Flint asked.

"No, not in the slightest, I completely misread him."

"But didn't we all? In fact, the only reason he got away with it for so long is because we wrote him off as ineffectual. He failed at Law, he had his Ph.D commuted to an M.Phil, he couldn't manage a proper job, couldn't cut his way in field archaeology . . . it was as if lecturing was all he could do."

"And the only job he could get was mine, in my deeply unpopular, unfashionable polytechnic."

"He did apply for other jobs, I imagine?"

"He was always applying; I stretched the truth enormously in his references, but he interviews so badly."

"So Barney watched the rest of us forging ahead in our careers, watched everyone else having fun and felt cheated because he was never part of whatever was going on."

"We all knew he was a loner," Betty said, never taking her eyes off the road. "He never fitted into college life, but I couldn't bring myself to ask what was wrong. When a lecturer doesn't sleep with his students, or drink too much sherry at the end-of-term party, one doesn't call him into the office and demand to know why."

The idea was almost amusing, were it not so pathetic. "In retrospect, it's easy to see why he built up a grudge against all of us. He was rejected by Megan, reputedly the most promiscuous woman in college, and ended up cruising around Leeds picking up prostitutes. When Shadesmoor came along, he was the only member of staff excluded from the project and he was passed over for promotion, first by Tom Aitken, then by me."

The road was long and straight, but Betty drove sedately through the rain. Other heedless drivers tore past, taunting the devil. Betty sighed heavily, peering ahead into the early morning murk. "I feel responsible, I should have known. I caused so much harm by trying to broker peace between Tom Aitken and the Shadesmoor people."

"You did what you thought right. Tom Aitken was everything that Barney was not. Tall dark and handsome, surrounded by women and, worst of all, a real red-blooded, mud-on-yer-boots, archaeologist."

"So it was jealousy which pushed him over the edge of reason?"

"He saw a chance to get even. He killed Tom, wrecked your department, framed Megan and sank Shadesmoor. Barney nearly proved he was sharper than us all. His house is full of detective novels and true crime books, can you imagine the fun he had putting this all together? Doctoring his typewriter so that it looked like Megan's, collecting her hairs and fibres from her clothing to plant at the scene of the second crime, concocting those cryptic messages to keep me entertained."

"They were for you?"

"They were intended to steer me towards Megan and to cause havoc with Bob Grimston. It was pure devilment."

Flint had decided not to publicise the blackmail element of the plot. Betty need not be told of the source of Barney's research grants.

Betty gave a sigh. "I should be grateful it wasn't me he decided to kill as part of his game."

Yes, Flint thought. Had Barney got away with one psychotic plot, he might have been tempted to contrive another.

"Would I not have made a better victim?" Betty asked.

"No, Tom Aitken set himself up for the fall. He knew Barney had the legal grounding and all those law books which he needed in order to work out an escape route for Eleanor. You know how Barney tended to latch onto anyone who would talk to him. Tom must have thought Barney was safe to befriend simply because he was so short of friends. He knew Barney would love a conspiracy, and how right he was! If Tom had kept those files to himself, he might still be alive, and so would Sharon Turpin."

"The prostitute? Poor girl."

"Barney must have been a regular client who talked her into playing the 'posh' woman: that was to confuse the police by pointing a finger at Eleanor Balleron. It was only bad luck, and bad science, that led us to the wrong conclusions about Ruth."

"What a sad and twisted man. If only we could have helped him, if only I'd seen his torment."

"I've read that mental illness can easily be masked by intelligence. The line between a genius and a madman is very thinly drawn. You mustn't blame yourself."

All the same, Flint felt deep down that society had been a conspirator in the plot. Lonely people surrounded him, he met and worked with them every day. All had their histories and their dreams, all had their regrets and their dark side. Any one of them could be the next to crack under the strain of living.

Train travel became ever faster, sleeker, cozier, if more expensive, with York and London now separated by less than two hours of gliding comfort.

Tyrone Drake was sitting his viva – the oral examination of his thesis – and it proved the formality that Flint had expected. *De-Romanisation in fourth and fifth century Britain* had been a brilliant work, the lad would go far if he kept his head and took care in his choice of friends.

At the end of that long day, Flint walked down the Kings Road alone, away from the party in the Italian restaurant where Tyrone had celebrated his success. Tyrone was now Doctor Drake.

"Bye, Jeff," Tyrone had said when Flint left the table. Not "Doc" but "Jeff". It would all take some getting used to.

He walked a quarter of a mile, brolly in hand, deep in thought. His feet chose the route, all his eyes had to do were watch for speeding Mercedes at junctions. He might return to Yorkshire, he might not; a big world waited out there. Eleanor had been overwhelmingly grateful to the white knight who had delivered her from the tentacles of Bob Grimston's organisation, but what currency was there in gratitude? She had the castle, the manor, the breeding and the contents of the unfrozen Trust Fund, so what could a penniless anarchist offer her? It was time to stop dreaming.

Without planning it, he arrived at South Kensington Tube station and found himself testing for a working telephone. He inserted his phonecard and chose a number. A few moments later, he could hear Vikki Corbett's distinctive voice.

"Corbett," she said.

"Hello, old girl, it's me, the bearded layabout. Would you like a story?"

310